Going Deep

Roz Lee

DEDICATION

For Terrell, whose love keeps me going..

ACKNOWLEDGMENTS

First, and foremost, I have to thank my family for putting up with my crazy ideas. What began as a whim, and perhaps a mid-life crisis, has blossomed into a full-time job that I absolutely love. Through it all, my daughters have been wonderfully supportive and surprisingly, are not embarrassed to tell people what I do. However, my greatest support comes from my husband, who not only encourages my fantasies (the ones about one day becoming a well-known author), but puts up with all my others! I couldn't write these stories without the love and encouragement of the people closest to me.

I have to thank Sharon Buchbinder and her wonderful husband, Dr. Dale Buchbinder. When I wrote myself into a corner, Dr. Dale was there with a scalpel to open a new door while Sharon slapped an oxygen mask on my plot and breathed new life into it. Jason's story would have been D.O.A. without their skilled emergency response.

Chapter One

The gray concrete-block basement walls matched Jason's mood and amplified the soft whir of the automatic pitching machine. *Fuck*. Someone else was using the batting cage. Showing up on the team's day off was tantamount to admitting your hitting sucked, and he had hoped to find the place empty. He briefly considered turning around and leaving before whoever it was saw him. But hell, who was he kidding? His batting average sucked lemons and everyone on the team knew it. If word got out he was taking extra swings, then at least his teammates would know he was trying to fix the problem.

Jason rounded the corner to see the Mustangs third baseman swing at a perfect pitch and miss.

"Morning, Todd," he said with a wave.

"Hey, Jason, I'll be through in a few."

"No hurry." Jason sat on the bench where he could watch.

Todd took another swing. "Maybe you can help me. Take a look and tell me what you see." He fouled the next ball off. "Man, I'm getting too old for this shit." Todd tightened his grip on the bat and glared at the pitching machine.

"You're only what, thirty-five? You still have a few

1

good years in you."

Todd grunted and connected with another pitch. The ball fouled. "Damn it. What the hell am I doing wrong?"

"You're dropping your shoulder, getting under the ball too much."

"Thanks, man." He took a few more swings, connecting better on each one. "Now see, that's what I'm talking about. I've been struggling for weeks, and no one said a damned thing. Not even Tuley. What's a batting coach for if he doesn't coach?"

Jason shrugged. "I don't know. He hasn't done a damned thing for me either. I've never hit this bad in my life."

Todd continued to swing at the oncoming balls. "I hear you. Sometimes there's no explanation. It just is what it is."

"What it is, is crap," Jason said, shaking his head. "I led the league in home runs last year. This year, I can't get a base hit to save my life." It seemed everything in his life was out of control these days, and he didn't have a clue how to change any of it. All he knew was he had to do something—and fast. "I gotta fix whatever's wrong before I end up on the bench."

Todd laughed. His bat connected with the last ball from the automatic pitching machine. "The Mustangs aren't going to bench you. You're the best catcher in the league." He grabbed his towel hanging from the fence and wiped his face. "They might put a Designated Hitter in to bat for you, but take you out of the game? Ain't gonna happen."

"Yeah, well, that's not a chance I want to take."

They switched places, Todd collapsing on the bench with a water bottle and Jason taking his place inside the batting cage.

"Why don't you see if you can figure out what *I'm* doing wrong?"

"Sure. I've got time," Todd said.

Jason fouled off the first two pitches and completely missed the next four. "Fuck." Totally unacceptable.

"There's nothing wrong with your swing. You aren't

concentrating. You just gotta focus."

Jason hit the stop button, leaned against the far side of the cage, and studied his shoes. Swinging at meatballs any high school kid should be able to hit wasn't going to fix anything. "I don't know what's the matter with me. I can't get my head in the game."

"Troubles at home?"

"Not anymore." Apparently there had been trouble, but he hadn't seen it, probably because he had his head up his ass.

Todd raised an eyebrow. "What happened?"

"My girlfriend dumped me." Jason was careful to keep his face neutral as he inwardly winced. Christ, the wound to his ego was still raw. Stacey wasn't coming back so he might as well get over it and move on.

"The cute physical therapist who was working with Jeff?"

Jason nodded. He'd met her when she took on his twin brother Jeff as one of her clients following surgery on his elbow. She'd bullied his brother through twelve months of physical therapy and he was back in the Mustangs bullpen where he belonged. Jason pushed away from the fence and, after racking his bat and helmet, joined Todd on the bench. "Yeah, that one. She booted me to the curb."

"When did this happen? I thought you two were firm."

"Me too. It's been a couple of weeks, I guess." Two weeks of hell wondering if he was as warped as she'd accused him of being. Two weeks of wondering what he was going to do now.

"About the time you quit hitting?"

"Yeah. I know. It's stupid, but I thought we had something going on, and then…"

"Then…what?" Todd asked.

Jason grabbed a water bottle from his duffel. "Surely you have better things to do with your day off than listen to my sad story about the one that got away."

Todd sat back, stretched his legs out in front, and crossed his arms over his chest. "Nope. Not until tonight.

Spill. Maybe if you tell somebody, you can get your head back in the game."

Well, shit. Now he'd gone and done it. He rummaged in his bag for a towel while he tried to figure out a way to get out the hole he'd dug for himself. He wiped his brow and took a long pull on the water bottle. He should have kept his mouth shut, but he hadn't, and now he was going to have to tell Todd something — unless he could get him to back off on his own. Yeah, that might work.

"What are you, some kind of shrink?"

"No, but I do want to win. And the Mustangs need you to start hitting. If I have to listen to your sad tale, then I'll take it for the team."

"Okay, but if you tell another soul I'll use your head for batting practice and smile while I do it."

Todd raised both hands in surrender. "I don't doubt that for a minute. My lips are sealed, *compadre*. Now, tell me what happened."

Jason glanced around the cavernous basement below the stadium to make sure none of the other team members were around. Assured they were alone, Jason began, "You know that book, the one everyone's talking about? The one all the women are reading and saying it's making them horny?"

"Yeah. What about it?"

"Well, Stacey bought a copy. We'd had some awesome morning sex, and I didn't have to be at the field for a few hours, so we were just chillin', you know?"

"Uh huh."

"Well, after breakfast, she picked the book up again — man, she couldn't put it down. I swear, every time I saw her for days she had that book in her hands."

Todd nodded, and Jason continued. "I asked her what was so interesting about it, and she started reading me some of the sexy parts. We laughed about a couple of them, and then she read this one where the guy handcuffed the woman and did some kinky stuff to her. It was hot, I'm telling you. Anyway, I said I wouldn't mind doing some of those things to her."

"And?"

"She looked at me like I'd turned into some kind of monster. She couldn't believe I'd even think of doing those things to a woman, much less *her*."

"What did you do?"

"I told her I wasn't going to do anything she didn't want to do, and she should have known that." Jason shook his head. Stacey's behavior still didn't make any sense to him. "Anyway, the next thing I know, I get a Dear Jason text. A *text*. We were in Atlanta and went from there to Cincinnati."

"I remember that trip," Todd said. "I didn't have a single hit against the Braves."

"Yeah, well, I wasn't much better," Jason said with a sneer. "By the time I got home, she'd cleared out of our place."

"Had you ever asked her to try any of the things in the book, or done any of them without her permission?"

"No! I'd never force a woman to do anything she didn't want to do. And honestly, I've never had to."

"Your charisma aside, was there anything else she said?"

"Just that I was too demanding. That it's always my way in bed, never her way. Shit! I asked her all the time to tell me what she liked." He raked his fingers through his hair. Now that he'd started talking, he couldn't stop. His frustration poured out faster than fans scurrying from the stadium when the home team was losing by a dozen runs.

"She said she didn't like the way I tried to take care of her, as though she couldn't take care of herself. It sounded like a bunch of women's lib shit to me. You know. She said she could pump her own gas, and she didn't want me ordering for her at restaurants. I'd call to check on her when I was out of town, just to make sure she was okay. I thought I was being considerate, but she said I was smothering her. And then the kinky sex thing…she said that scared her."

When he finally wound down, it was as though the concrete walls had absorbed all the sound. The silence was deafening. Aware that Todd hadn't said anything, Jason dared to look at his confessor. He didn't like the way his

5

friend eyed him.

"What?" Jason asked.

"Do you want to do those things to a woman? *Really*, want to do those things, or was it just some fantasy?"

Jason nodded. "Yeah, I think I'd like that. You know, calling all the shots, having a woman at my mercy. Willingly. I'd only do it if they wanted it, too. Stacey had to know that."

Todd stood. "You have plans tonight?"

The abrupt change of subject caught him off guard. "No. Just gonna watch some TV, maybe have a few beers. Why?"

"I want to show you something." He pulled a team notebook out of the bag he'd crammed underneath the bench. He scribbled something, tore out the page, and folded it in half before handing it to Jason. "Meet me at that address around nine. Dress casual."

Damn, he didn't feel like going out. "Thanks."

"Sure." Todd grabbed his duffel and left.

He hoped Todd wasn't going to try to fix him up with some bimbo. The last thing he needed right now was a woman messing with his head — it was plenty messed up already.

≈≫

The giant standing sentinel in front of the red lacquered door in Dallas' industrial district didn't look friendly. Jason checked the address again. Right place. He scanned the brick façade for a sign and found none. What kind of place was this, and where was Todd?

He'd heard of exclusive bars, the kind requiring an invitation to get inside. Maybe this was one of them, but he couldn't imagine the place was doing well in this neighborhood whose better days were long behind it.

"Um…." He had no clue what to say to gain entrance.

"Are you a member?" the guard asked.

Member? You have to have a membership to get in this place? Seriously? "No, but I'm supposed to meet someone here."

"Name?"

"Mine or the person I'm meeting?"

"Yours. I'll see if you're on the list and if you are, I'll notify your party that you're here."

"Oh, okay. Jason Holder." He relaxed a little when the guy didn't react. This didn't look like the kind of place he'd want his name linked to in tomorrow's gossip column.

"Wait here, Mr. Holder. I'll check the list." The guy disappeared behind the door so fast Jason didn't get a glimpse inside. Shoving his hands in his pockets, he paced a few steps then returned to his spot in front of the door. He'd completed the circuit several times by the time the guard came back. He held the door open, indicating with the sweep of his arm for Jason to go inside. "Enjoy your evening."

Jason turned to thank him only to find the door shut. He stood in a small, dark vestibule, big enough for maybe four people, if they stood close together. *Now what?* It took a moment for his eyes to adjust to the dim lighting then he noticed a sign on the door in front of him.

Non-members must be accompanied by a member beyond this point.

Okay. He guessed that meant he'd have to wait for Todd to show. But he had no idea whether Todd was already inside, or if he had yet to arrive. Jason checked his watch. Five after nine. He listened for music, anything to indicate what kind of club lay on the other side, but not a sound penetrated his little cocoon. He was just about to leave when the inside door swung open, and loud, pulsing music filled the room. Todd stepped inside, closing the door behind him, sealing them both inside the quiet vestibule.

Man, that's some excellent soundproofing. Jason eyed Todd's outfit and smirked. "Leather?"

Todd smiled. "Yeah. It's not my favorite, but my sub likes it, so I wear it to please her."

"Your sub?"

"Brooke," he confirmed. "I'll introduce you later. First, I hope you were serious this morning about wanting

7

to do kinky things to a willing woman."

"Uh, yeah, I was. I think." A bad feeling churned in his gut. What the hell had Todd gotten him into?

"Good, then let me be the first to welcome you to The Dungeon. If you really want to try the things you've been thinking about, this is the place you need to be."

His gut twisted tighter. "Dungeon?"

"Yep. You've never been to one before?"

"No. I kind of knew they existed, but this is my first." *And hopefully, my last.* He should thank him for the invitation then get the hell out, but as much as the idea of going into the dungeon scared him, it excited him, too. Maybe he'd just look around, see what it was all about. How bad could it be? Todd was here, and he was a normal sort of guy.

"A dungeon virgin." Todd smiled. "Nothing to worry about. After our talk, I thought you might be interested. I've been a member here for about ten years. Everyone inside is into the BDSM scene to one degree or another. I'll warn you, there are things in here that will make that book of Stacey's sound like a kid's bedtime story. If anything bothers you, you're free to leave at any time. We just ask you keep what you see here to yourself."

Just thinking about the kind of things behind the door made his cock hard. He wasn't going to leave. He wanted this, wanted to see what he'd only dreamed of. He wished he'd worn trousers instead of jeans, that left no doubt about his state of arousal.

"People don't know who you are?" he asked before his big brain shut down completely.

"Hell, yes, they know, but we don't discuss our outside life. In here, I'm Master or Sir. If you join, you have to sign a confidentiality agreement. It probably wouldn't stand up in court, but most people don't want the rest of the world to know about this side of their personality, so they won't talk. You'll probably see other people you know. Maybe not tonight, but eventually. Just keep it to yourself."

"I can do that." *Good Lord, wouldn't the media be in a frenzy if they found out.*

"Okay. Let's go, then. It gets loud sometimes, so save your questions. I'll answer them when we're done with the tour."

Jason followed Todd's leather-clad ass into the club. The walls of the reception area were deep red and adorned with canvases he figured might have been painted by zoo inhabitants but could have been famous pieces for all he knew about art. A grouping of comfortable looking leather furniture occupied the center of the room, and a raised black granite desk blocked a darkened portal that presumably led to the club. The place was clean and neat and, despite being unconventional, had an unexpected aura of wealth and good taste. Not at all what he'd expected. Hard rock music blasted somewhere in the back of the establishment, but out here was bearable.

Todd spoke to the Goth girl seated at the desk. "He's with me, Janette."

Janette waved them on with a smile on her pierced black lips. Jason glanced around Todd's tall frame at the long hallway lined with open doorways. A few were covered with heavy velvet curtains matching the black and red paint scheme on the walls.

"These rooms are available on a first-come, first-served basis," Todd said. "If the door is open, you're free to watch what's going on. No touching, no interfering, no commenting on the scene. If the curtain is closed, respect the privacy of the people inside."

They stopped in front of the first un-curtained room. Todd stepped to the side, and Jason peered inside. A woman lay naked, strapped spread-eagle to a medieval looking table in the center of the room. A man dressed in leather and chains held a lighted candle above her, allowing the hot wax to drip and run in streaks over her breasts. She moaned when it touched her skin. *Damn. She's aroused by the pain.* His cock stirred.

Todd tugged on his sleeve, yanking him out of his thoughts and down the hallway to the next open doorway. Jason cringed at the man shackled to giant wooden X, while a woman in black leather called him names and slapped his junk with a riding crop. Jason shuddered. Todd laughed, and as they walked away, he leaned in to be heard over the music. "Not my style either. But hey, whatever gets your rocks off, you know?"

Jason wasn't sure he agreed, but he wanted to see more. By the time they reached the social area, Jason's dick was in serious pain. He'd seen things he couldn't imagine anyone doing to another person, and plenty of things that sent his imagination into overdrive.

Todd led him to a table in the back where a beautiful blonde sat alone. Her shoulder length hair framed her face in soft waves. She stood when they approached, but instead of a traditional greeting, she dropped her chin to her chest. Jason sucked in a breath at the sight of her slim body clad in nothing more than a few scraps of black lace and a pair of fuck-me-now shoes.

"Master," she said.

"This is the man I told you about. You may speak to him."

She turned devastating blue eyes on him. Her crimson lips curved into a smile. "I'm pleased to meet you. Any friend of my Master's is a friend of mine."

"Thank you," Jason said.

Brooke returned her chin to her chest.

"Sit down, subbie." He waved her back to her seat and took the one next to her. "Let's just talk."

Jason took the only other chair at the table. Todd's arm snaked beneath the table, and it didn't take a genius to figure out where his hand was.

Chapter Two

"So, what do you think?" Todd asked.

Brooke's eyes closed, and a soft moan spilled from her parted lips.

"Do you want to see more?" Todd continued as though he didn't have his hand in a woman's panties in a public place.

Hell yes! He swallowed. "Yeah. I think I do." "How do I, you know, find a woman to…?"

Todd chuckled. "How do you find a woman who'll let you do whatever you want to her?" He glanced at Brooke, who squirmed in her chair, her head back, her eyes closed, her mouth open. "Come for me. Come for Jason, subbie."

An orgasm ripped through her. She gripped the edge of the table to steady herself as her body jerked and spasmed in ecstasy. Jason almost came in his pants.

"That's my girl," Todd said when her body quieted. He pulled his hand from beneath the table, bringing his fingers to her lips. "Clean my hand, baby."

She obediently licked her juices off while they continued the conversation. He did his best to listen, but his cock was threatening to burst out of his jeans, and he couldn't take his eyes off her pink tongue lapping Todd's fingers.

"Don't worry. There are plenty of unattached women who come here looking for someone to take care of them. If you're interested."

There was something here that called to a dark place inside him. If all these people had thoughts and urges like his, maybe he wasn't such a sick bastard after all. "I'm interested."

"I thought you would be," Todd said. "You'll need to learn a few things first. There are some good books on the subject of Domination/submission. I'll recommend a few, but the best way to learn is to participate. I'll show you what you need to know, mentor you, if you want."

"Sure, that sounds fine," Jason said.

Brooke finished cleaning Todd's hand, and he thanked her with a kiss that had Jason reaching for his fly.

"Good," Todd said. He stood, helping his sub to her feet. "Come on," he said to Jason. "Let's get started."

They led him through several public rooms dotted with all manner of exotic and erotic furniture, from spanking benches to elaborate metal riggings that Todd explained were for suspension play.

"It's a weeknight, so the place isn't that crowded. Come back on the weekend, and all these will be in use."

They stopped in one room to observe a woman receiving a public spanking. Her Master whipped her with a sinister looking leather strap.

"She's broken one of her Master's rules. For whatever reason, he's chosen to punish her in public," Todd explained.

Jason couldn't take his eyes off the girl's reddened ass, marveling at how gentle her Master was with her, stroking and kissing the red welts, speaking with her in a low, sensual tone while he administered her punishment. Between her legs, her pussy glistened with evidence of her arousal.

Jason followed his guides down yet another hallway. Darkened windows, evenly spaced between closed and numbered doors, lined the red walls. Halfway down, they stopped in front of one with a brass number nine on it.

"These rooms are reserved in advance," Todd said.

He opened the door and ushered his sub in first. Jason followed then Todd closed the door behind them. Brooke moved to the center of the room and dropped to her knees, her chin tucked to her chest, her legs splayed, and her hands, palms upward, on her thighs. Todd ignored her. Jason couldn't take his eyes off her.

"There aren't any locks on the doors. A safety measure, just in case emergency services are needed," Todd explained. "No one will enter unless invited, so no worries. The window is a two-way mirror." He pulled back the curtain Jason hadn't noticed to reveal a mirror. "If you want to invite people to watch, just open the curtain. Keep it closed for privacy."

Jason nodded. He didn't know if he liked the idea of an audience, but maybe...someday...with the right woman.

"As you can see," Todd continued, "The room is equipped for just about anything you could want."

Jason looked around, swallowing hard. Various apparatus he'd seen in the public rooms filled the space. The lighting was subtle, bathing the dark walls and a large platform bed in cool tones. His heart pounded against his ribs, and his hands were clammy, but despite it all, a calm settled over him. This was where he belonged. These were his people. This was what he wanted with Stacey, and she'd seen just enough of his desires to be scared away.

For weeks, he'd harbored thoughts that scared him, too. Maybe he was too kinky, wanted to do things a sane, healthy man shouldn't. But now, he realized he wasn't...

"You aren't a perv if you want to do some of the things you've seen here tonight," Todd said, as if he'd read Jason's mind. "This is normal for a lot of folks. Most of society doesn't see it that way, so we try to keep it to ourselves. But once you walk inside the door here, you're considered normal."

"How did you know?"

"About you?"

Jason nodded.

"Because when I was your age, I was in exactly the same place you are. A friend showed me the way, and I've been happy ever since. I've had plenty of subs, but Brooke has been with me now for over a year. We're thinking of taking our relationship outside the club, becoming a couple in public. Maybe even making this a permanent arrangement."

"People do that?" He hadn't considered the possibility that a real relationship could develop from a place like this.

Todd shrugged. "A few. We wouldn't be the first."

"You're exclusive? You don't mess around?"

"If you're asking if I do this in every city we go to, the answer is no, I don't. There are clubs everywhere, and I've been to a few, but I've always played here. If you're asking if we take on other partners, the answer is sometimes. We've discussed our limitations, and abide by them."

"I see." No, he didn't see. Not at all. They were exclusive, but they took on other partners? Limitations? Not that he wasn't versed in multiple partners – he'd shared enough women with his brother to know what fun that could be. But in this setting? He and Jeff had never discussed limitations with the women they shared. Clearly, Stacey had limitations, and the idea of breaching them had sent her running.

"Want to give it a try?" Todd asked, jolting him out of his thoughts.

"With who?" He almost choked on the question.

"With Brooke."

"But…she's…"

"She's my sub. She does what I tell her to do." Todd looked at the woman on the floor. "Don't you, subbie?"

"Yes, Master. My body is yours to command."

"See?" Todd turned to Jason. "She'll do what I tell her to. What would you like her to do? You want her to suck your dick? You want to spank her? Clamp her tits? Make her come? I don't mind watching tonight, but if we're going to do this again, we're going to have to find you your own woman."

"You're serious?" Jason asked.

"I'm serious," he said.

Todd slid a finger beneath her chin, tilting her face

up. Her eyes sparkled with anticipation. Everything about her posture and facial expression spoke of the trust she placed in her Master's hands, yet there was something else there…. Love?

Jason's gut clenched. What would it feel like to have a woman look at him that way? He wanted that more than he wanted his next breath.

"Be careful with him, subbie. Give him what he wants, and show him what he needs."

"Yes, Master. Whatever you wish."

He bent and placed a gentle kiss on her lips. "I wish to see you submit to my friend." He walked to the far corner of the room and relaxed into a plush leather chair there. "Tell her what you want, Jason. Be precise in your commands, she doesn't read minds."

Holy shit. He glanced at the woman on the floor, her head bent in submission to him. *Him.* What the hell had he gotten himself into?

"She's all yours. Remember the things you said you wanted to do to Stacey? Well, here's your chance to live out the fantasy. I have only one rule, no penetration of her vagina or ass. You can do anything you want with the mouth. She gives good head."

"And you're going to watch?" Did his voice sound squeaky? He couldn't tell with his blood draining from his head, rushing past his ears and causing all that racket.

"You have a problem with that?"

Jason shook his head. "No. No." He wasn't shy about his dick, but sharing a woman with his brother was one thing. This was different. This was commanding another man's sub. He'd have to be blind to miss how Todd felt about her. "Todd, man. I can't…she's…."

"She's my sub. She does what I tell her to do, for my pleasure and hers. She has a safe word, Soccer." He winced at the word. "If she says it, stop immediately. Otherwise, you can assume she's enjoying what you're doing, or she thinks I am. That's how this works. She submits to me because it brings both of us pleasure. I need her submission. I need to be in charge. I need to do things to her. And in order to achieve the utmost sexual pleasure possible, she needs me to push her to her limits and beyond. In return for her complete trust and submission, I see to her pleasure, which of course, pleases me to no end.

"She trusts me to care for her in every way. She knows I would never let you or anyone else harm her. Inflicting pain in order to achieve sexual fulfillment is one thing, causing physical harm is another. I know my sub well, and she knows how much I like to see her with other men. She'll do anything to please me, or suffer punishment for her insubordination.

"So, give her pleasure. I know you want to. When she receives pleasure, so do I. In fact, I'm not happy if she's not happy. That's her power in the relationship."

Jason nodded. It made sense — sort of. "And your power is?"

"She gets off on pleasing me. When I'm happy with her, I give her what she wants and needs. I use her body for my pleasure, and I give her the kind of sexual release she craves. And, I command her orgasms. Do what you will with her then I'll let her orgasm. She loves it when I fuck her."

Jason nodded again, trying to assimilate all he was hearing. He wiped sweaty palms on his jeans and swallowed hard, staring at the beautiful woman waiting for him to do … what, exactly? A tendril of dark desire swirled at the back of his neck and twined its way to his cock. Todd's explanation was convoluted thinking, but it made sense in a bizarre sort of way. Yeah, this is what he'd wanted with Stacey, though he hadn't been able to name it. Submission. Trust. He'd wanted that more than he'd wanted to do kinky things to her.

"What do you want to do to her?" Todd's softly spoken question snapped him out of his thoughts. "What kind of things did you want to do to Stacey?"

Visions of the scene he witnessed earlier popped into his mind, and his cock surged painfully against his fly. His damp palms itched to turn Brooke's perfectly round bottom red, and hear her moan her pleasure."I'd like to spank her ass."

"Then what?"

"Then I want her to suck my cock. I want to bury my hands in her hair and fuck her mouth until I come." Oh yeah, his cock was on board with that plan.

Todd shifted in his seat, and Jason clenched his fists at his sides and ground his teeth. He'd overstepped and his friend was going to throw his perverted ass out.

"Tell her. Tell her exactly what you want her to do." Todd waved his hand toward a piece of furniture along the back wall. "Tell her how you want to see her on the spanking bench. Do you want her to keep her panties on, or do you want her to take them off, or do you want to pull them down yourself? You have lots of options."

He had never been so nervous in his life, not even on his first day in the major's when he took the field knowing forty-five thousand pairs of eyes were watching, waiting for him to make a fool of himself. He turned to the beautiful woman at his feet. She sat meek, awaiting his instructions. She was so lovely, the picture of perfect submission.

"She wants your attention. Don't make her wait too long."

He stepped closer, tilting her face up as he'd seen her Master do. She looked at him with the same trust she'd shown Todd. *No*, he corrected himself. *She trusted him because she trusted Todd.* "I won't hurt you."

"Thank you, Sir. I know my Master would never give me to you if you were that kind of man."

Jason smiled at her. This was what he wanted, this profound connection with a woman. A deep and abiding trust that he'd never let anyone hurt her, that he'd do anything to see to her pleasure and well being. Todd was right. This was where he belonged.

"Your trust is well placed. I want to spank you. Take off your bra but leave the panties and position yourself on the spanking bench."

"Yes, Sir."

As she rose, a power surged through him, so strong it almost brought him to his knees. Working the front clasp of her bra free, she let it fall to the floor. She pulled her shoulders back, flaunting her perfect breasts before she turned and walked to the bench — her sweet round ass swinging back and forth all the way there. Todd snickered from the corner of the room and Jason realized she was teasing him.

Todd knew. He knew what a feisty little sub he had, knew she'd use her wiles to torment him.

She took her place on the bench. He'd never seen anything more enticing than the strip of black lace over those perfect globes presented for him to do with as he pleased.

"A display like that one deserves something special, don't you think?" Todd asked.

"Not yet," Jason said, instinctively knowing Todd was offering him the use of some sort of toy. Not now. He wanted to touch her, to give her some amount of pleasure before he took his own. "Maybe later."

On her knees, bent forward on her elbows over the higher section of the bench, her tits swung free. Jason cradled the closest one in his palm and squeezed. Her nipple was a hard pebble in his palm. "Your breasts are beautiful," he said. "Does your Master clamp them sometimes?"

"Yes, Sir."

"Do you like it when he does?"

"Yes, Sir. Sometimes the pain is intense, but Master knows how to turn the pain into pleasure."

"I'm sure he does." He fondled the other breast. "What else does Master do to your breasts?"

"Master likes to suck my breasts. He's fond of biting my nipples too."

"Is he now?" Jason smiled. He could imagine doing that to this woman. "Rise up on your knees. I want to suck your breasts." She moved and he found her breasts at the perfect height to take one in his mouth. "Hold them up for me," he commanded.

She cradled them in her hands, offering them to him. His cock was so hard it would be a miracle if he could get his zipper down without coming. Stacey never would have done this for him, and this was nothing compared to the other things he imagined doing to a woman. "Thank you."

He settled his hands on her hips and closed his mouth over her left breast.

Shit. She tasted of vanilla and lemons, and he couldn't get enough of her. She moaned as he bit down on her nipple then soothed the pain with his tongue. He did that a couple of times then pulled away, intending to give the other breast the same attention. She whimpered.

"Sir, please," she begged, offering the other breast.

Something in him, some inner devil told him to deny her, to make her wait. "Enough. Resume your position."

"Yes, Sir," she said, a hint of pout in her voice.

Christ, he'd never felt so much power before. He stood behind her, staring at the black lace over creamy skin. He reached out and smoothed both hands over her perfect ass. So smooth and unblemished. She was soft as silk and cool to his touch. He'd soon fix that.

"Lovely," he said. "Black lace is my favorite. He slipped two fingers beneath the lace on either side and yanked her panties to mid-thigh. "Ah, yes. That's what I want to see." He kneaded both globes, parting them to examine her tight rosebud. Beyond, she was wet, swollen, and ready for penetration. "Your master is a lucky man."

He slid his hand between her legs, wetting his fingers and palm with her juices. He brought his hand to his face and inhaled her scent. "Beautiful. The best perfume on the planet." He placed his palm beneath her face. "Isn't that a beautiful fragrance?"

"Yes, Sir." Before he could move, her tongue swiped across his palm, tasting her own essence.

"Christ," he said, remembering how she'd cleaned Todd's fingers in the same way. "You're a tease, aren't you?"

As she licked his skin, he raised his other hand and landed a solid blow to her ass. She whimpered, but her tongue continued to stroke his palm.

Jason spanked her, alternating between cheeks. A moment of doubt crept into his mind as he landed blow after blow. He was enjoying it too much, the spanking and the hand licking. He should be offering her pleasure instead of taking it all for himself. He stopped and she wiggled her ass. "More please, Sir," she begged. "Harder."

He understood then. She needed, wanted more. He jammed his left hand between her legs again, coating it in her juices. He flicked his fingers over her clit, and she pressed herself against his palm. A chair creaked behind him. He glanced over his shoulder. Todd offered a wicked looking paddle.

"Use this. She likes it hard," he said.

He turned to his sub. "Come for him, baby. I want to see you come."

Jason took the paddle, brought his soaked fingers to his face and inhaled. "Come for me," he said, and brought the paddle down on her ass.

My God, she was magnificent. He landed half a dozen hard blows to her already red butt. With each one, he could see her inward focus, and then he landed one more that pushed her over the edge. He dropped the paddle and cupped her from behind. He toyed with her clit until she came all over his hand.

Power. Lust.

He never knew it could be like this. "On your knees, on the floor," he commanded. She scrambled to do his bidding while he unzipped his fly and shoved his pants and underwear to his knees. He took his cock in one hand and wrapped his other around the back of her head.

"Open." Her ruby lips parted, and he shoved his cock to the back of her throat. He wasn't gentle or even considerate, but she took him anyway. "Hold still," he said, securing her head with both fists. "I'm going to fuck your mouth."

He held her head, flexing his hips, driving his cock past her lips and teeth. He closed his eyes against the aching pleasure. When she dug her fingernails into his ass cheeks to support herself, he lost it.

"Sweet, Jesus," he cried and shot his load down her throat. "Sweet, fuckin', Jesus."

"If you're done now," Todd said, "it's my turn."

Jason pulled his cock from her mouth, wiped cum from the corner of her mouth with a trembling thumb, and on watery knees, stumbled to the chair in the corner.

Todd lifted his obedient sub from the floor, laid her out on the padded table in the center of the room, and spread her legs. "I'm proud of you," he told her. "So fuckin' proud of you." He unzipped, and filled her pussy in one solid stroke that made her cry out.

Jason couldn't take his eyes off the couple.

Todd fucked her hard, complimenting her with each stroke. "Oh, baby, I love to watch you swallow cock. You're so fuckin' hot."

She writhed. She sought and found handholds. Her tits bounced with her lover's thrusts.

"Come for me, baby, like you did for him." Two hard thrusts. "Squeeze my dick. Now, sweetheart."

Jason fisted his cock as her body convulsed in a powerful orgasm, taking her Master over with her. "That's fuckin' beautiful, baby. Ah, Christ, I love you," Todd said, emptying himself inside her.

Chapter Three

"Thanks," Jason said as the waiter placed their drinks on the table and left. He wasn't sure he could stomach alcohol, so he'd asked for a diet soda. Todd ordered a beer, and Brooke sipped something that looked more like a smoothie than an alcoholic beverage. Clearly, they didn't suffer from the same bout of nerves he did.

"Jason," Brooke said, "you were wonderful tonight."

"Yeah, thanks, man." Todd slid an arm around her shoulder and pulled her in tight. "I don't let her play with other men very often because she likes it a little too much for my taste, but occasionally I get off watching her."

"I should be thanking you. Both of you." He tilted his glass in their direction. "I wouldn't mind doing it again sometime."

"We'll see." Todd took a long pull on his beer then set the bottle on the table. "So, tell me what you thought of the place. How did it feel?"

"I'd be lying if I said I didn't want to go back. I don't know how to explain it, but I feel like a weight has been lifted off my shoulders. I never knew people... Well... I always knew I was missing something. I just didn't know what it was until tonight."

"Yeah, I know exactly what you mean. I'm not trying to pry, but you were very good for a beginner. Are you sure you haven't done anything like this before?"

He glanced around the bar. Even though it appeared no one was within hearing range, he folded his forearms on the tabletop, leaned in close, and lowered his voice. "Jeff and I have been known to share, but no, I've never been what you could call a Dom."

"Who's Jeff?" Brooke asked.

"His twin brother."

Brooke smiled. "Oooohh, twins," she cooed, her lascivious intent written all over her face.

Todd rolled his eyes. "His happily married, twin brother," he clarified.

Jason couldn't help but laugh at her crestfallen face. "Oh well, it was just a thought."

"There was a time we might have taken you up on the offer," he said, "but my brother is happily married, and his wife would kill him, and me, too, if I got him involved in something like that."

"But you think this lifestyle is something you want to explore?" She wrapped her pouty lips around her straw. She sucked the fruity concoction causing her cheeks to hollow. *Damn. What a tease.* Todd had his hands full with this one.

"Yes," he said without hesitation, tearing his gaze away from the blatant seduction. "I know tonight was just a taste, but it felt right. More right than anything I've ever done."

"Well then," Todd said. "We need to find you a sub."

He bolted upright in his seat. His heart rate skyrocketed. "How do you go about something like that?"

"We could take him to the munch next week," Brooke said.

Todd narrowed his eyes in thought. "Yeah, that might work."

"What's a munch?"

"It's kind of a private bar event for people in the lifestyle. A bunch of people meet at a place like this, neutral ground where they can size each other up, see if there's someone they'd like to play with."

"Oh…no. No." He shook his head. "No munches.

No public meet-ups. There must be another way." He glanced at his tablemates. "How did you two meet?"

"A friend introduced us at the Dungeon. We hit it off right away." He smiled at Brooke, taking her hand in his. "The first time I laid eyes on her, she had me by the balls. We'd just gotten through the introductions, and she told me she'd done something naughty and thought she needed to be punished. I asked her what she'd done, and she said she made herself come while watching me from the other side of the room."

Brooke blushed. "I was there with friends. It was my first time at that Dungeon. The moment I saw Todd, I knew I was his. It took some doing to find someone who knew someone who knew him, but I managed the introduction, and well…the rest is history."

"I punished the little minx for stealing that first orgasm from me. Every one since then has been mine," he said, pride evident in his voice.

Jason's heart sank to his toes. "Well, I'm glad lightning struck for you two, but I doubt it happens that way for most people."

"No, it doesn't." She laid her hand on Jason's and squeezed. "That doesn't mean there isn't someone out there for you."

"Thanks," he said, pulling his hand free. Her gentle touch and the conviction in her voice was almost more than he could bear. Todd really was a lucky bastard. "If you ever get tired of this lug…."

"Whoa there! Back this train up."

"Just kidding," Jason said. His wink earned a giggle from Brooke.

"Don't make me regret tonight." Todd finished his beer and signaled the waiter for another. "Spend some time in the social area. Lots of unattached people come to the Dungeon looking for a hookup. You'll find somebody."

Jason shrugged. "Fat lot of good it would do me. I don't know anything about being a Dom. Even if I found a sub, I wouldn't know what to do with her. Besides, until I get this figured out, I'd rather not show my face to a lot of people if you know what I mean. Jeff has a wife now. If someone mistook me for him…."

"I hear you," Todd said. "I hadn't thought about that." He looked at Brooke. "We need to find him someone and keep it private."

"I know someone I think he might hit it off with. We just need to figure out a way for them to meet and keep Jason's identity a secret," she said.

"Even if we could pull this off, I still don't know what I'd do with her."

"You'll learn. The protocol is pretty simple, and from what I saw tonight, you'll pick it up quickly. We'll see if we can figure out a way for you to meet this friend of hers. If it works out, I'll teach you all you need to know," Todd said. He turned to Brooke "Are we talking about who I think we're talking about?"

She nodded.

Todd turned back. "Don't sweat it, rookie. Everything's going to work out fine. Give us a few days to set things up. We'll think of something so you two can meet. If you both want to give it a go, we'll make sure you get off on the right foot."

❦

Jason tossed his keys on the table by the door. He was exhausted but exhilarated at the same time — like after winning a big game. He toed off his shoes and made his way to the kitchen. For the first time in his life, he was alone — truly alone — and it was something he didn't think he'd ever get used to. Up until a few weeks ago, he'd never lived on his own. He and Jeff had been inseparable until his brother had married Megan, and where once they'd been a threesome, he had become an uneasy third wheel. So he'd moved out of the home they had built when they first signed with the Texas Mustangs. He'd bought his current house with the intention of sharing it with a Stacey. Now, its large floor plan and empty rooms echoed his failure with every footstep.

Water bottle in hand, he sank into his favorite chair and listened to the deafening silence. Scenes from the Dungeon and his conversation with Todd and Brooke afterwards played over in his mind. His cock stirred. Damn. If anyone had told him a year, even a month ago he would be turned on by what he'd seen and done at the Dungeon, he would have called him a liar. What did it say about him that he wanted to do it all again?

His dark desires had scared Stacey, and she didn't know a fraction of the things running through his brain, driving him crazy with need. Her words and the fear behind them haunted him to the point he'd thought he was some kind of monster. But if he was such a monster, why was that damned book such a hit? The hero had done things to the female character he had never dreamed of doing to a woman, and it had turned Stacey on. She just didn't want *him* doing anything close to that to *her*. Go figure.

But there were other people like him out there, and thanks to Todd, he knew where to find them. He owed Todd, big time. Not just for taking him to the Dungeon, but for allowing him to unleash his desires on someone who found them exciting, who actually welcomed them. Brooke had been wonderful. Todd was a lucky man.

He couldn't help but wonder about the woman they had in mind for him. The idea of being with someone whose desires and needs mirrored his own, well, if that wasn't enough to get his adrenaline running, nothing was.

ৡৎ

Sweat trickled down his spine as he completed his batter's box ritual. He was zero for three today. Fuck, even the crowd was booing him these days. He needed to get his shit together and start hitting. He dug the toe of his left shoe into the dirt and hitched up his pant legs, balancing his weight on his bent knees. He swung the bat to his shoulder in a casual motion that in no way mirrored the anxiety in his gut. The previous year, he led the league in homeruns, and now he couldn't get a fuckin' base hit to save himself. Much more of this, and he'd lose his clean-up spot in the batting order.

The first pitch sailed in, low and outside. He checked his swing in time. Ball one. He swung at the next pitch, fouling into the net behind home plate. Strike one. The third pitch caught the edge of the plate. He swung, connecting for a line drive foul into the left field stands.

One ball. Two strikes.

He stepped out of the batter's box while the catcher threw a fresh ball to the pitcher.

The trickle of sweat along his spine turned into a river. He missed being in control of his life. Somehow his messed up personal life had spilled over into his professional one, and he didn't have a clue how to fix either. Before he stepped back into the batter's box, he closed his eyes and sucked in a deep breath to center himself. A vision of Brooke on her knees, her ass red from his attentions popped into his head. Blood rushed south.

Ah, fuck! There wasn't any room inside his cup for an erection, not to mention the horrendous timing. He stepped into the batter's box, planted his feet, and focused his inappropriate energy on the next pitch.

The pitcher began his wind-up. He narrowed his gaze to the patch of white barely visible between his opponent's fingers. The moment the ball left the pitcher's hand, he knew in his gut, it was a good one. He tracked the orb's trajectory, innately judging its velocity. Adjusting his grip, he shifted his weight to his back leg and lightning quick, swung the bat into the path of the ball. Wood connected with leather.

Thwack.

A sound to give a guy a hard-on for sure. He'd hit enough to know it wouldn't leave the park, but it was a solid hit, nonetheless. He shifted his focus to first base and put every ounce of power he possessed into beating the throw. His foot hit the bag, followed a split-second later by the smack of leather against leather.

"Safe!"

He came to a stop ten feet beyond the base and doubled over, bracing his hands on his knees. The hometown crowd roared their approval, adding to the excitement by stomping their feet in the Mustangs' signature Thundering Herd rally. He took in two deep breaths then straightened, waving an arm at the fans, thanking them for their support. Never mind they were the same crowd who joyfully booed him minutes ago. He smiled and returned to first base. Fans were fickle. Tomorrow's newspaper would celebrate the end of his hitless streak, and in the next sentence complain it hadn't been a homerun.

He couldn't care less. All that mattered was he was hitting again. One hit didn't make a streak, but every streak began with one.

Following the game, Todd caught up to him in the parking lot. He checked to make sure they were alone. "What were you thinking about when you got that hit tonight?"

His face flushed and he was grateful for the darkness surrounding them. *Shit.* Todd would probably kill him if he knew where his thoughts had been at that moment. "Nowhere in particular. I was just trying to concentrate on the ball."

"That's a load of crap if ever I heard one." Todd jiggled the car keys in his hand. "I'd bet you were thinking about Brooke. Maybe how you'd rather be smackin' her ass instead of the ball? I know that's what I was thinking about when I was at bat."

Jason dug his own car keys out of his pocket as they walked. "Naw, man. She's your woman," he lied.

"That she is. She enjoyed playing with you." Todd pointed his remote key entry toward his car. A chirp sounded, and the locks disengaged. "If she's happy, I'm happy. So, until you find your own sub—"

"Oh no. No." He shook his head. "I don't think so. I appreciate the offer, and Brooke was…is spectacular. But I wouldn't feel right."

Todd opened the car door, rested his forearm on the top. "Then I guess we'll just have to see what we can do about hookin' you up with your own woman as soon as possible."

"Yeah, about that," he said. "I'm not sure it's the thing for me."

Todd stared. "When you hit the ball tonight, you were thinking of your handprint on Brooke's ass, weren't you?"

What point was there in denying it? He obviously could see right through him. "Yeah. But—"

"No buts. You're denying your true nature. Go home. Look at some of the books I gave you this afternoon. We're on the road for the next week. We'll talk then."

Jason nodded and turned to walk to his own car parked a few spaces away. The vintage Mustang wasn't fancy, but it suited him better than a new car fresh off the showroom floor. No one would ever mistake it for a tame ride.

"I've been there, buddy. Where you are right now," Todd called.

He stopped at the sound of his friend's voice but didn't turn.

"I know exactly how you feel," he said, truth ringing in his words. "Trust me. You'll be happier once you accept who you are."

A car door shut. An engine roared. Jason turned, catching the glow of taillights on his friend's Mercedes until they disappeared.

Accept who I am.

Fuck.

He knew who he was. It was *what* he was that he found hard to accept. Okay, so sharing a woman with his twin brother wasn't exactly prudish sexual behavior, but it was a hell of a lot different than being a Dom.

He unlocked his car and sank into the driver's seat. He lifted his warm-up jacket and eyed the stack of books hidden beneath it on the passenger seat. His cock twitched just reading the titles. *BDSM Protocol. The Power Exchange Dynamic. The Dummies Guide to Domination and Submission.*

Maybe Todd had it right. Maybe this was the real Jason Holder. One thing was for certain, he couldn't get the images from the night before out of his mind. Most of the things he'd seen, and everything he'd done excited him.

He pulled from the parking lot into the late evening traffic. The closer he got to home, the more certain he became. Denying his sexual needs wouldn't cut it, especially now that he knew he could fulfill those needs in a safe, private way.

The next morning, he tossed two of the books into his suitcase. He would have plenty of time on the road to read. He wasn't sure he was ready to share this part of his life with his brother, but since they would be roommates, he didn't see any way to hide his reading material from him. He wasn't looking forward to that conversation, but it had to come sometime. No more of that mind reading, twins always know stuff shit. He and Jeff were close, but last year that kind of thinking had almost cost his brother the love of his life. So to avoid future problems they'd vowed to actually voice their thoughts instead of relying on the proven unreliable DNA network.

∾ֆ

"I'm not surprised," Jeff said.

Jason stared at his brother who sat on the other bed in the hotel room they shared, thumbing through a book that outlined a Dom's responsibilities to his or her sub. "What?"

"I said I'm not surprised. You've always wanted your way. In everything, not just sex. Though I can remember a time or two when you insisted on getting your way with Megan. Sometimes I went along if it suited me, too, and if she was okay with it. But there were other times…."

He thought about the year and a half they'd spent in a three-way relationship. His brother had a point. He had tried to control many of their encounters. "I didn't see it then, but I can see it now. Our relationship wasn't ever going to work. She just isn't the kind to follow orders."

"That's true," Jeff allowed, still thumbing through the book, pausing here and there when a photo caught his eye. "Though there's some stuff in here I wouldn't mind trying with her. After the baby comes."

"Here, give me that!" Jason grabbed the book.

"Hey! I wasn't through."

"Yes, you are. I'm not going to have your wife blaming me for putting ideas in your head."

"It's not like she's never been tied up. She likes that kind of stuff."

"I remember, but she always knew she could get loose with a flick of her wrists. This is different." He shifted to hide his instant erection from his brother.

"If I used real handcuffs on her, she'd kill me the minute she was free."

"Damned right she would." Jason stretched out on his bed and opened the book.

"But there are women who like this?"

"Yeah, there are."

"Huh." Jeff pointed the remote at the television. "Whatever floats your boat, bro."

Yeah. He had a pretty good idea what floated his boat, now. Reading the first chapter of the book he'd confiscated from his brother, he realized there was a whole protocol to this kind of sexual encounter he knew nothing about. He tuned out the sit-com rerun Jeff had settled on and read. He wanted to be up to speed the next time he went to the Dungeon. Knowledge was power, and power was something he craved.

Chapter Four

She wasn't going to another munch. Three times was supposed to be the charm—only it hadn't been, so why would she think four would be any better.

Carrie deleted the email, sighing at her dismal mood. She opened the next email, sighing once more. Work. That, at least, was a place she felt comfortable, secure in her ability, confident of her talent and worth. It had taken years, but her reputation as an investigative reporter was rock-solid, providing her a nice income and her pick of stories. She scanned the message, noted the possible story, then moved the email to the folder marked "ideas," and moved on to the next email.

She'd nearly made her way through her inbox when her cell phone rang. She found it across the room, buried beneath a magazine. Working mostly from home had its disadvantages sometimes. One glace at the caller ID and she smiled.

"Hi, Brooke. What's up?"

"Can you meet me for lunch?"

Hallelujah! Lunch with her best friend was just what she needed—time away from the computer, and better yet, time with someone who understood her personal dilemma. Her southern socialite mother constantly asked if she had a boyfriend and had made it clear she didn't understand why her beautiful, talented, successful daughter didn't have a string of men vying for her attention. The truth was she'd turned down dates with dozens of men over the last few years, and not for any reason she was willing to share with her mother. She played the fictional conversation over in her mind.

"What happened to (insert name here)? He was such a nice young man."

"Oh, you know, Mom," She would say, dismissing (insert name here) with a wave of her hand. "He didn't want to spank me."

Yeah, that would go over well. She'd imagined a million ways to tell her mother that not just any man would do—especially not some country-club-going, golf-club-toting, pastel-wearing, pasty skin momma's boy. At sixteen, she had compiled a list of qualities she wanted—no, make that—*required*, in a man, and in the decade since, she'd seen very few who came close to meeting those specifications.

Brooke's Dom, was one of them.

She envied Brooke. The owner of a successful specialty cake bakery, she spent her days making decisions and shouldering responsibility. She was good at what she did, and the success of her business was a testament to her ability. She didn't envy her friend's workload. It was the way Brooke spent her nights that turned Carrie green.

She spent her evenings in subservience to her master. The man had it going on, and the few times he'd invited her to join them, she had obeyed without hesitation. He was thoughtful and considerate, and very much in control. Just remembering his voice commanding her made her knees weak. Being mastered by him had been a pleasure, and she sincerely hoped another session was the reason for the lunch invitation. Her panties grew damp at the prospect.

Happier than she'd been in weeks, she powered down her computer and set out for her lunch date.

Thirty minutes later, she entered the sandwich shop and spotted her friend, who waved to her from a booth in the back. Brooke was one of those rare creatures, as beautiful on the inside as she was on the outside. Her beauty queen looks turned heads, but it was her personality that drew people to her. She gave generously of herself and her time, qualities that earned her respect in the community. Carrie was one of the very few who knew just how much of herself Brooke was willing to give to the right person.

She wove her way through the crowded restaurant and slid into the seat across from her friend. "It's so good to see you," she said. "You look great!"

Brooke beamed, and stroked her shoulder length blonde hair. "You like it? Master says the highlights make my eyes look brighter."

"He's right. The gold streaks match the flecks in your eyes. The man knows what he's talking about," she said, squashing down the slight twinge of envy.

"I know." Brooke sighed. "I'm a lucky woman." Her smile disappeared, and Carrie squirmed under her pitying look. "I wish you could find someone, too."

"Me, too. Believe me, I've tried. I've been to every munch in the last six months and spent more hours than I can count sitting in the social area of the Dungeon, hoping a Dom would come in, take one look at me, and decide I need to be spanked." She waved off the protest on the other woman's lips. "Hey, Marilyn Monroe was discovered at a soda fountain." She shrugged. "It could happen."

"There's another way to meet a Dom," she said. "Todd has a friend."

Her pulse leapt. "Go on."

"He thinks you and his friend might get along. I agree."

"You've met him?" she asked. Brooke's gaze dropped to the menu on the table in front of her, silently telling her how they'd met. "Oh. You've played with him."

Their gazes met and she saw nothing but sincerity in her friend's eyes. "Once. Only once. His name is Jason, and he's new to the lifestyle. Master invited him to join us to see if he was as interested as he thought."

"And was he?"

"Oh, yes! He was masterful. Very much so for

someone who'd never topped before. His commands were clear, and his voice was kind. It seemed very natural for him. He didn't spare me, but he knew when enough was enough. And, Master would never have given me to him for even a minute if he didn't trust him."

Oh God. This could be it. She wiped her damp palms on her skirt and tried to quell the butterflies in her stomach. "And you think he would be interested in a novice like me?"

"I do. Would you like to meet him?"

The butterflies felt more like a flock of seagulls now. She pressed a hand to her midsection in an effort to calm the riot going on inside. This was real. All she had to do was say yes. "I trust you, and Todd has been nothing but kind to me, so…." She took a deep breath and let her answer out with it. "Yes. Yes, I would like to meet your friend."

Her friend's face lit with excitement. "I'll tell Todd, and he'll arrange it." She placed her hand over Carrie's. "I'm so happy for you."

"I don't know how to thank you," she said over the tears choking her. "If this works out…."

"I know. Trust me, I know exactly how you feel. Before I met Todd, I was lonely and so alone with my needs. Then…everything changed. I've never been happier."

Carrie nodded and dug a tissue from her purse to dab at the corners of her eyes. "I'm sorry. I don't know what's wrong with me."

"You're excited, relieved, anxious. I've been there, remember? Look, I have no idea if this will work out, and you have to tell him if you don't feel right about it. He's not the only Dom out there, so don't think you have to submit to him if it's not for you."

"I know," she said on a shaky breath. "If it doesn't feel right, I'll say something. I promise. Tell me about him. I want to know everything."

"I don't know much. Todd is a very private person. He never talks about his vanilla life, and it's not my place to ask."

"I'm not interested in his vanilla life. Tell me what this guy was like as a Dom. Did he…you know?"

"No. Master has rules when he shares me, just like the times you've been with us." She hesitated. "Are you sure you're okay with this? I mean, he played with me. I don't want this to affect our friendship."

Carrie paused. Did it matter? "It won't. I'm actually grateful. I'm so new to this. It's reassuring to know someone I trust can vouch for him. I understand trust is the fundamental issue between a Dom and his sub, but to put myself at his mercy without knowing anything about him? I won't lie. That scares me."

"Don't be frightened," she said. "Let's eat then we'll go somewhere more private and I'll tell you everything about my time with him. You're my friend. I'd never recommend someone I didn't trust myself."

Her stomach was knotted so tight she didn't think she could eat a thing, but she picked up the menu anyway. "I know. I trust you. And Todd has been very kind to me. I can't tell you how much I enjoyed the times he invited me to play." She sighed and dropped the menu back on the table. "It's the memory of those times that keeps me going. I know what it's like to submit, to place my entire self into someone else's hands. It's the most incredible feeling I've ever experienced."

Brooke grinned. "Master enjoyed those times, too. And so did I, but anything that pleases him, pleases me. Once he figured out my desire to watch and be watched, he's made sure to arrange suitable scenes."

Carrie blushed at the frank talk, her mind going back to the Dungeon and the feel of leather landing on her skin, Todd touching her, working her to an incredible orgasm. She swallowed the lump in her throat. "I want that for myself. I want someone who sees my need and will take me there. Someone who won't let my fears stand between me and my pleasure." She worried the edge of the menu with nervous fingers. "Is that too much to ask for?"

"No, it's not. There's nothing wrong with wanting the things you want. We're just like everyone else. We crave intimacy, that special connection with another human being."

"You're right. It's, you know…hard. My other girlfriends don't understand. My family wouldn't understand. They all wonder why I haven't found a guy and settled down by now."

Brooke leaned over the table. "Todd and I have discussed taking our relationship outside the Dungeon," she whispered.

"That's wonderful!" She grabbed both of Brooke's hands and squeezed. "So, this is serious between you two?"

She nodded. "Yes. I love him. I really do. I can't imagine my life without him. But I'm scared, too. I don't know anything about his vanilla life. Nothing."

"Nothing about his personal life?"

"Not a thing," she confirmed. "He's taking me to his house this weekend. He said we'd talk then. I think he may be more nervous about this than I am."

She was glad to see her friend's smile return.

"It's kind of cute, you know? Him being so in control all the time, then being nervous about taking me to his house."

"I'm so happy for you. I want to hear all about it next week."

"Promise," she said, opening her menu. "Now, let's order and get the heck out of here. I want to tell you about Jason."

Carrie flipped open her menu and pretended to read it. She really was pleased things were working out for her friend, but her mind spun with thoughts of this new Dom. Would he like her? Would she like him? She trusted both Brooke and Todd. If they said he was a good match for her, then he was. She shut the menu. "I'm having a salad. No cooking." She grinned.

Brooke laid her menu aside, returning Carrie's smile "We'll be out of here in no-time!"

❧

"I'm not sure I'm ready for this." Jason said, pitching his voice low to be on the safe side.

"Don't worry so much. You handled yourself well the

other night." Todd eased himself into one of the seats they'd commandeered in the rear of the plane. "You have a knack for this. Just focus on the sub's pleasure and you can't go wrong. I've played with this girl. Her needs are pretty straightforward. A little pain will make her wet, and with your looks, you'll have her eating out of your hand, or your pants, in no time."

Jason held his response as a teammate ambled down the aisle to the lavatory in the back of the plane. He glanced over his shoulder to make sure they were alone again. "About that. I've been thinking. I make the rules, right?"

"Right. What you say goes."

"She can't see me. Rule number one, she wears an eye mask all the time. I'll tell her it's to heighten her other senses, and that's true, but I don't want her to know who I am."

Todd shifted his frame in the seat meant for anorexic people and glared at Jason. "How the fuck are you going to accomplish that?"

"I'll figure it out. I just need you to make sure she's blindfolded before I get there tonight. Then you can leave. I'll take it from there."

Todd shook his head, gazing up the aisle, stretching the silence an interminable length of time.

Jason shifted in his seat. Maybe he'd gone too far, but he didn't think so. Until he knew this girl, it was the only way he felt at ease. Besides, he rationalized, it was for her protection as well as his. If thing went wrong, the media would be all over both of them. She couldn't hardly comment on their relationship if she didn't know who she had a relationship with. Todd would see he was right. Eventually.

Jason leaned across the empty seat between them. "You'll do it, won't you?"

"Yeah, I'll do it. What makes you think she would know you anyway?"

He flopped back in his seat, letting out a pent-up breath. "I don't know. Maybe she wouldn't, but I don't want to take that chance right now. My career has two toes over the edge of the cliff already. A sex scandal would do me in."

"So, you're going to ask her for her complete trust, sight unseen literally, and you aren't going to give her even the most basic level of trust?"

"It sounds really fucked up when you put it that way, but she won't regret it. I'll make sure she enjoys every minute she spends with me. I know how to please a woman, and if she's willing to explore the darker edges of her sexuality, I can guarantee her more pleasure than she's ever had, sight or no sight."

Todd smirked. "So, you think you're more than just a pretty face?"

"I know I am." He gazed out the window, trying to find a comfortable position in the cramped confines of the seat. "When I'm sure of our relationship, I'll take the blindfold off, but not until then. If she can't agree to those terms, then I'll find someone who will."

"We're getting the cart before the horse here, aren't we? You haven't even seen her yet."

"You said she's pretty. I trust your judgment. Besides, I've never seen a woman's body I didn't respond to, and that's what this is about. Pleasure. Hers and mine. It's not like I'm taking on a mail order bride. I don't want to marry her. I want to fuck her."

"Okay, okay. I get your point. But aren't you asking her to take a lot on faith?"

"Maybe. She'll have the option to walk away tonight. After that, I'll make sure she has an out if she ever feels she needs it."

Todd stretched his left leg into the aisle, nearly tripping the player returning from the lavatory. He muttered an apology then stuck his leg back out, rubbing his thigh. "Damn, I'm getting too old for this shit. Next time you want to talk, do it somewhere else. From now on, I sit in a bulkhead seat."

Jason smiled at his friend's grumbling. "I'll be there at seven. Tell her to be there at seven-thirty. She's to wear a knit dress — something slinky. No bra, no panties, and high heels. Any color dress will do. She's to leave her hair down. You did say she has long hair, didn't you?"

Todd scrunched his eyes shut. "Yeah, shoulder length. Reddish brown. Real pretty."

"She's to leave her hair down, then. I'll bring the blindfold when I come. Make sure she puts it on and kneels then you can leave. And make sure the observation mirror is uncovered. I want to watch her squirm for a while, waiting for me."

Todd chuckled. "You're a sadistic bastard, aren't you?"

"No, just cautious."

❧

Jason swallowed and shifted to relieve the strain against his zipper. She was the most gorgeous creature he'd ever seen. Luxurious auburn hair fell in soft waves down her back — not her shoulders like Todd had said. Soft black fabric hugged generous curves, covering enough to send his imagination into overdrive and his cock into serious distress. It was an alluring package and that made it difficult to focus on the details.

Her nails were well groomed, her makeup understated. His gaze narrowed to her eyes. Green, or maybe blue-green. He'd have to ask Todd because he wouldn't be seeing them again for a very long time — if at all. Red-tipped toenails peeked from sexy stilettos that practically screamed, "Fuck me now."

He punched the button beside the two-way mirror.

"You're kidding me, right?"

Her sassy words, spoken in that sultry, sensual voice brought a smile to his lips. She tapped one sexy foot in a nervous gesture, and he added the tell to his memory bank, along with the tension in her shoulders and the tight lines along her jaw.

"A blindfold?" She crossed her arms under her breasts and glared daggers at Todd. She might be submissive, but she wasn't stupid. "What is he...a freak? Let me guess, he weighs five hundred pounds." She paced away, giving him a good look at her magnificently shaped ass before she turned and continued her rant. "No. I've got it. He's hideous, disfigured, maimed, and this is the only way he can get close to a woman. That's it, isn't it?"

He smiled. She was melodramatic, but the passion beneath her outrage was something he would enjoy channeling in a different direction.

"No. He's none of that. Take my word for it—you won't be disappointed in his physique, and you have nothing to fear from his touch. He's a gentleman. He could have any woman he wants, but he wants you."

She stopped her fidgeting, placing her fisted hands on her hips, and studied Todd as if she could burrow into his mind and tell whether he spoke the truth. He waited with a patience Jason knew he didn't have, especially with a submissive woman. At last, she stuck her hand out, palm up and wiggled her fingers.

"Okay. Give me the blindfold. I'll do it. But if he does anything weird, I'm out of here." She looked directly at the two-way mirror. No dimwit—she knew he was there, watching her. "You got that?"

He laughed. Oh, he got it all right. And so would she, soon. Very soon. Todd issued orders to her in a calm, authoritative voice, which she obeyed with a hint of defiance he admired. He didn't want a weak woman, someone who would blindly follow without a thought for herself. He chuckled at the irony of his thoughts. That's exactly what he was asking her to do, blindly trust him with everything she was. A thrill shot through his veins, hot and exciting, as she adjusted the blindfold and sank to her knees facing the mirror.

Damn. He was tempted to go to her right then. But he had a plan, one he'd given a lot of thought to, and like stepping up to bat, timing was everything.

He issued the instruction for her to stay put then joined him in the hallway. "What do you think?"

"She's going to be a challenge," he said without taking his eyes off her kneeling form.

"Yes, she is, but worth it. She's eager but wary."

"Intelligent. You can see the wheels turning, even with the blindfold on. Look at the way she works her mouth. She's thinking, assessing, worrying. Did you see that?" He pointed. "That twitch in her thighs? She's anticipating, getting hornier by the moment."

"You've got a good eye."

"It's a batter's skill set. Works for catchers, too. You have to watch your pitcher very carefully, look for details. Finger placement, facial expressions, and subtle body language. I wish I could see her eyes, but for now, this will do. She's a passionate woman. All that passion has to be expressed somewhere, and if she can't tell me what she's thinking with her eyes, she'll use the rest of her body."

Todd nodded. "You're right. I don't know anyone more qualified to judge a person's mood or intentions based on body language than you."

They watched her in silence for a few more minutes then he clapped Jason on the shoulder. "Gotta go. She's all yours. Let me know how it works out."

"Will do, and thanks. I owe you."

"No problem. Maybe you can give me some tips on reading the pitcher. Maybe teach this old dog some new tricks."

"You got it, anytime."

Chapter Five

She'd heard the term "mind fuck," but it hadn't held much meaning. Until now. Blindfolded and kneeling on the hard dungeon floor amidst enough torture devices to please a medieval Lord, she had nothing to do but wait and think. The experience had her brain opening doors she didn't know existed. They were dark doors of longing and even darker doors behind which lurked self-doubt, trepidation and a healthy dose of fear. What was she doing here, waiting for an unknown man to come and claim her, body and soul? What kind of crazy person did such a thing? Despite Todd's assurances, this person could be the worst sort of human being. A predator. A sociopath.

Trust. That's what this was about. Submission.

The room was cool, but a bead of sweat trickled down her spine. The silence in the soundproofed room rang in her ears, and her knees ached—hell, everything ached in one way or another. Time became irrelevant. She tried counting her heartbeats to judge the time, but they proved erratic and inadequate for the purpose. He was fucking with her head — making her think about what she was doing, pushing against her barriers, testing her limits and her commitment to this path, and all without showing his face. Clever. If he knew to test her in this way from the start, what other means would he devise to get into her head once he got to know her?

Could she do it? Could she place herself in the hands of a man she couldn't see? She had assurances from people she trusted. Brooke's words echoed in her mind. "He was masterful. His commands were clear, and his voice was kind."

She'd give anything to hear his voice right now, preferably telling her to stand. The ache in her knees had spread to her thighs and up the curve of her back. She rolled her shoulders, releasing some of the tension settled there. She flexed her hands, held at the small of her back, palms out. She would be sore tomorrow, and not for any good reason she could see. Her muscles sent frantic messages to her brain, urging her to forget this crazy idea and get the heck out of there. Did he have no compassion? What kind of Dom let his sub sit for hours on her knees, alone in total darkness and absolute silence? Couldn't he have turned on some music? She was sick to death of listening to her own heartbeat. What good could come of this?

Brooke's words answered for her, "He didn't spare me, but he knew when enough was enough." Her pussy flooded, reminding her why she was here, and she renewed her resolve to see this first meeting through. The least she could do was hear him out, see if they could come to an amicable arrangement. Her heartbeat shifted to warp speed and her breath came in short, rapid bursts. Is this what he wanted, for her to imagine all the things he could do to her, all the things she wanted him to do to her? Her nipples tingled and each breath caused them to chafe against her dress. Soon, her aching breasts and the throbbing between her legs overrode the discomfort in her extremities and took over her thoughts.

Enough was rapidly approaching enough when the scrape of a door opening startled her out of her erotic musings.

∾⋞⋟∾

She was a magnificent creature. If she'd followed his instructions, she was naked beneath that swath of black fabric that barely covered the essentials. Her nipples stretched the cloth like well placed buttons, announcing her arousal. Her auburn hair fell in soft waves over her shoulders and gleamed in the strategic light. The room's dark décor made her pale skin appear fragile as porcelain, but she was anything but. It took a strong woman to do what she was doing, and if she agreed to his terms, she would have both physical strength and courage.

She knew she was on display, that he was using this time to assess her. How did she feel about that? How would she respond to being put on display for others? He wasn't wild about the idea — what was his, was his. But if it achieved the right result, if it could serve a purpose beyond simply arousing her, then he would consider it.

Watching her was a classic study in psychology, and he loved every minute of it. Though she did an excellent job of remaining still, emotions played across her face like storms across the prairie, fast and furious, one after another. Fear. Anger. Pain. Resignation. And, at last, the one he'd been waiting for. Desire.

She was so much more than he'd ever hoped for. Screwing up was not an option. He was asking a lot from her by denying her sight. She hadn't made a peep, and the silence coming through the intercom was deafening. She'd been on her knees for ten minutes, but it must seem like a lifetime to her. He closed his eyes and shut everything out, much the way he did on the field when the roar of the crowds threatened his ability to think. His job demanded total concentration, total focus on the ball, no matter whether he was crouched behind home plate or standing in the batter's box.

He took a moment, grounding himself in what she must be experiencing — well, as much as he could considering all manner of erotic sounds filtered from the common areas like a cheer through a megaphone, amplified and battering at his psyche. Amazing how much more difficult it was to tune this type of noise out. He sought and found an artificial silence. His thoughts turned inward to his needs, his desires, his doubts.

While standing in the hallway, he could acknowledge his uncertainties, but once he walked inside the room, he couldn't let any of them show. This woman needed his strength, his decisiveness, his command. He wanted to give it to her. He wanted to give her everything he was, and take everything she had to give. He wanted to possess her, to own her, and more importantly, he wanted to know her.

Any woman strong enough to place herself in such a position had to be special. He wondered what she did in her outside life, but he wouldn't go there — not yet, anyway. It wasn't fair to ask her to share information if he wasn't willing to reciprocate. Maybe one day, but not until there was a solid commitment between them. Only then could he expose himself up to the risk involved.

Someone opened a door nearby. He snapped his attention back to the exquisite creature waiting for him. It was time to see if he could forge some sort of bond between them. See if her need matched his. He took a deep, centering breath, like he did before stepping into the batter's box. With a slow exhale, he put his hand on the doorknob. *Batter up.*

۶৶৶ৎ

She instinctively turned toward the sound of the opening door. A shiver ran down her spine. *Oh God. He's here.* She'd passed the first test. He'd liked what he saw enough to take the next step. She quickly corrected her posture, hoping he hadn't noticed the breach of conduct.

The door clicked shut, sealing out the sudden burst of music that had accompanied his entrance. Her pussy throbbed in tandem with her racing pulse. The mind fuck had worked. She was horny and desperate, and with a little luck, he would be, too. Adrenaline kicked in, and giddiness was close on its heels, along with an insane desire to beg him to put her out of her misery.

Heavy footsteps crossed the room toward her… but not quite. What was he doing? She recognized the scrape of curtain rings sliding on the rod. Relief flashed through her. At least no one else would be watching. Perhaps he had a modicum of compassion after all. She licked her dry lips and focused her remaining senses on the man in the room. Goosebumps rose on her flesh as his footsteps made a slow circle around her, pausing directly in front.

He stood close enough she could feel heat radiating from his body. One hot fingertip touched her chin, lifting her face. She gasped at the first contact.

Another digit, perhaps his thumb, stroked her jaw line, sending a bolt of heat to her pussy. So very tender. Did he like what he saw? Did he want her?

"You're beautiful, girl."

Oh God. That voice, like black velvet, smooth and warm with an edge. Brooke hadn't come close to describing the sensual nature of his tone. His thumb stroked over her cheekbone, back along her jaw, and over her lips.

"I like seeing you on your knees." He backed away, and she dropped her chin back to her chest. "Ahh, so you do know something about being a sub. I'm impressed."

She tracked the sound of his footsteps, though she could barely hear them over the blood rushing past her ears. He stopped behind her, fingering her hair then moving lower over the curve of her ass. She shivered at his light touch.

"So responsive," he said in a low, seductive voice that lured her in, made her pussy gush with need. "I like that."

One large hand squeezed her butt cheek. She bit her bottom lip to keep from crying out. It was all she could do not to press her ass into his hand in invitation. A heartbeat later, he jerked her dress up, baring her to his gaze.

"You have a lovely ass, girl. I want to see more. Put your hands over your head."

She raised her arms, and in an instant, her dress was off. Heat prickled beneath her skin, and she knew from experience she'd gone into a full body blush. Mortifying. What would he think of a sub blushing from her toes to her ears?

"Lace your fingers behind your head. I'll want to see all of you."

She followed his orders, grateful to have something to do with her trembling hands.

"You're a particularly delicate shade of pink, my dear." There was a hint of amusement in his voice. "I like it. Do you blush often?"

Carrie licked her lips, struggling to form words.

"Do that again, and I'll give your tongue something much more interesting to lick. Now, answer me. Do you blush often?" No amusement, just his deep voice stroking her skin to a deeper shade of need. Any doubt about her effect on him was gone. He desired her. An insane burst of pride warmed her from the inside out.

"Yes, Sir. I do."

He'd moved close enough his unique scent wafted to her nostrils. He smelled of summer afternoons outdoors and beneath that, raw, elemental male. The combination called to everything feminine within her. Chemistry. People talked about it, but only in vague terms, and now she knew why. There were no words to describe how her body responded to his. It was primal. Essential. Somehow, she knew seeing him wouldn't change anything between them.

"I'm pleased to hear it. I'll make it my mission to bring this about as often as possible if you choose to engage in this relationship."

Choose to engage in the relationship? There was no choice. Her body had already made the commitment.

Blunt fingers brushed across both nipples at once, and she whimpered. It was all she could do to remain still then his fingertips closed tightly over the twin nubs, pinching hard. She hissed in a sharp breath, absorbing the bite of pain. He gave a rough tug and desire flooded her pussy.

"Your body pleases me very much." He released her nipples, pressing warm palms against them, massaging her breasts with strong fingers. "Tell me, are your knees hurting?"

"Yes, Sir." *But I'll stay here forever as long as you continue touching me.*

"I'm going to help you stand. Keep your hands behind your head." He wrapped his hands around her waist from behind and lifted her. "Spread you feet wide."

She shuffled her feet, only to have him kick them farther apart while still supporting her at her waist. One hand remained there, while the other trailed across her hip. She held her breath as one finger slid toward the cleft of her buttocks.

"Relax." He paused in his exploration until her shoulders dropped and she let out her breath. "Breathe, girl. Your body is mine, or it will be soon. I'll know all of it in much more intimate detail than this."

His finger parted her, pausing to test the tight ring of muscles hidden there. She struggled to breathe.

"Has anyone had you here?" he asked.

"No, Sir."

"Never?"

"Never, Sir."

"Your choice, or theirs?"

She shrugged her shoulders. "I don't have much experience, Sir." That was an understatement if she ever heard one.

His finger massaged her anus, making it almost impossible to think. "Tell me. How many lovers have you had?"

She swallowed hard. Oh God. If she told the truth, he would probably send her home right now. His hand left her ass, only to return a second later. This time, he pressed his wet finger harder against her. As he breached the tight ring, she gasped. Her knees buckled.

The hand at her waist wrapped around her, securing her hip against his groin, and all the while, his fingertip remained imbedded inside her. His erection ground against her hipbone, and desire swirled low in her belly.

"The truth, girl. Never lie to me. Ever," he growled in her ear. "I don't care if it's one lover or one hundred. You're mine now, and I need the information in order to plan our time together."

Her inexperience must be obvious to him, so no use lying. "Only two, Sir. But I haven't had a lover in over a year if you don't count the few times I've played with Brooke and her master."

"Thank you for your honesty." His calm voice put her at ease. He extricated his finger from her ass, taking care to soothe her with a gentle caress afterwards. "Can you stand on your own now?"

Her knees were shaky, and she wasn't overly steady in the best of times in high heels, but sensing he expected her to be strong, she focused on regaining her balance. "Yes, Sir. Thank you, Sir, for your support."

He set her away from him, though one palm remained on the curve of her hip. "I'll always take care of you. I can and will push your limits, but I'll always have your safety and pleasure in mind."

"Thank you, Sir."

"I can smell your arousal, girl." His hand moved between her legs, cupping her sex. As his hand met her swollen flesh, she gasped. "Lovely. You're wet for me." His fingers flickered through her folds, found her opening, and tunneled inside. "Tight. Excellent." He wiggled his fingers, discovering the spot inside she knew from self-exploration would bring her to orgasm with a minimum of attention. "You want to come, don't you?" he asked, his breath hot against her ear.

"Yes, Sir." She barely got the words out on a whisper.

His fingers abruptly left her and she cried out.

"Not today."

He switched hands — the one between her legs replacing the one on her hip, which slipped across her stomach to the small patch of trimmed hair on her mound. She bit her bottom lip as he explored until he found her clit, pinching it hard. She groaned at the delicious bite of pain that was gone too soon.

"On your knees." He helped her to the floor, and when she was situated, the scrape of a chair filled the air, and she sensed he sat facing her.

"I'm very pleased, girl," he said, his voice coming from directly in front — not from above as before but more in line with her diminished height. "I realize I have an unfair advantage in that I can see every inch of your lovely body while you're deprived of assessing me in the same way. Physical attraction is a powerful and meaningful part of any successful relationship. I know you don't understand the reason I've forbidden you to look at me, but one day I'll explain. If you would like to hear the rest of my terms, then I'll continue. Afterwards, if you still wish to establish this relationship, I'll strip and allow you to explore my body with your hands. That should put to rest any questions you have regarding my fitness. Would you like to hear the terms of our relationship?"

Her hands itched to touch this man, whoever he was. She no longer cared she couldn't see him. He'd demonstrated his ability to master her in a few short minutes, and if he asked her right now to lie back and spread her legs so he could fuck her, she would gladly do it. Talk about a blind date. This was beyond fucked-up, but she loved it.

"Yes, Sir. I would like to hear the terms under which I might serve you."

"Excellent. These are my terms, in a nutshell. You'll find them all spelled out on a document waiting for you at the front desk. Pick it up on your way out tonight, and read it over carefully. If you have questions, there's an email address you may use to contact me. Feel free to ask me anything. It's my job to see that you understand what you're agreeing to. Is that clear?"

"Yes, Sir."

"Okay, then. Rule number one, our outside lives will not be discussed until such time as I deem it prudent to do so. You may of course contact me if you're going out of town or have obligations that prevent you from fulfilling my instructions. My job takes me out of town frequently, for up to two weeks at a time. I'll make sure you know my schedule, but only as it pertains to our relationship.

"Rule number two, I'll email you with instructions on what you're to wear and at what time you're to meet me here. You'll follow my instructions to the letter, and when I arrive, you'll be as you are now, waiting for me.

"Rule number three, You'll address me as Master or Sir.

"Rule number four, You'll provide me with a safe word, and if you use it during a scene, all play will stop immediately. We'll discuss at that time whatever caused you to safe word out. I promise to respect your hard limits, but I will push your soft limits every chance I get. I would never discourage you from using your safe word, but I do urge you to think very hard before you use it.

"Rule number five, if you agree to this relationship, you'll have no right to deny me use of your body. I don't care if you have cramps, you're bleeding, or if you have a fucking headache. It doesn't matter to me. There will be times when I'll bring you here for no other reason than to fuck you. I promise to see to your pleasure before or after I take my own, but you will orgasm. I'll see to it. I'll achieve this by any means I deem necessary or pleasurable at the time. Be aware, that may include the use of any manner of toys or available dungeon equipment. By agreeing to this relationship, you agree to this as well.

"And, the final rule, rule number six. You, at no time will remove your blindfold until I have left you. When I leave the room, you'll be on your knees as you are now, and after counting slowly to ten, you may remove the blindfold, dress, and leave.

"Do you have any questions?"

Her head spun. The only question in her mind was the one that formed when he said he would strip and let her touch him. "May I touch you now, Sir?"

Chapter Six

Jason groaned. He'd just given her a list of rules most women would have slapped his face for, right before they stormed out of the room. But not this one. His admiration for her swelled along with his cock. He stood, unzipped his pants as much to relieve the pressure as to remove them. "A promise is a promise."

He shucked his clothes, draping them over the chair he'd moved back to its spot in the corner. It was well designed, perfect for restraining a sub, sturdy enough to do the job and allow for all manner of wicked activities at the same time. He'd have to give it some thought.

He ran a hand over his face and took a centering breath. Her scent lingered on his hand. Damn. She'd gotten to him like no other woman ever had, and now he was going to let her touch him? His dick was so hard, he was sure he'd go off like a rocket at her first touch. He glanced over his shoulder. She waited for him, still in her subservient pose — perfect in every way. He went through his pre-batting ritual three more times before he moved to stand before her.

"Let me help you up," he said, reaching for her.

"Please, Sir, I'd like to start at your feet if that meets with your approval."

He reached for her, dragging her up by her armpits.

"No. It doesn't meet with my approval. I won't allow you to decide how we go about things. Not now. Not ever. Is that clear?"

"Yes, Sir. I'm sorry, Sir. I meant no offense."

"Apology accepted. You may touch me now with your hands only. Don't touch my cock until I tell you to."

"Thank you, Sir." She reached a hand out and touched his chest, measuring the distance between them before taking a tentative step closer.

He closed his eyes, absorbing the shock of her touch, reveling in the flowery scent that seemed perfect for her. He'd never look at a rose the same way again. Damn, this was so not a good idea. He forced his eyes open. He needed to observe, see her reaction to his body as she trailed her hands up and over his shoulders, kneading and testing each defined muscle. He managed to remain still while she explored his upper body, front and back, his face, arms and hands. When she traced the long scar down the middle of his chest with her fingertip, he froze. A frown turned her lips down and wrinkled her forehead.

"What are you thinking, girl?"

"What happened, Sir?"

He never talked about his scar with anyone, but he saw no reason not to tell her how he'd acquired it. There were only a handful of people in the world who knew the whole story, and they kept quiet at his insistence, so the information wouldn't be an automatic connection to his identity.

"Heart surgery when I was a kid," he said.

"I'm sorry, Sir."

"No need to be. It only made me stronger."

"I'm glad, Sir. Your body is magnificent. I'm honored you have asked me to serve you."

"Your opinion pleases me. For that, you may continue. Anywhere except my cock."

"Thank you, Sir." Her smile sent a fresh supply of blood rushing to his groin.

He steeled himself for her continued exploration. When she had worked her way to his feet, he laughed when she urged him to lift first one foot then the other, so she could explore the soles. "You're very thorough."

"Thank you, Sir. I want to know every part of your body as well as you will know mine."

"That's an admirable goal, and one I'll take into consideration. For now, you may touch my cock and balls. Hands only," he cautioned. Lord help him, he prayed, giving no thought to whether such a prayer was appropriate or not. Her soft hands sought him out, one closing around his cock, the other around his sac. He called up batting stats on every single member of the Yankees in an effort to distract himself from her touch. He didn't make it through the first batter in the order before he grabbed both her wrists and squeezed. "Enough."

She released him, but he held her tight.

"There's one more place you haven't explored, and since you expressed a desire to know my body as well as I know yours, then I think you should explore it today."

The moment she comprehended his meaning, that lovely pink blush covered every inch of her skin. Oh, he was going to love putting that color on her, in so many wicked ways. He gathered both her wrists in one hand and turned around.

"Use your left hand to spread my cheeks, and give me your right," he commanded. When she hesitated, he yanked on her right arm, bringing it around to his chest. He dropped his voice an octave, "Spread my ass cheeks, girl."

Her left hand trembled as she followed his instructions. He sucked her thumb into his mouth, moistening it with his tongue then guided the wet digit behind him. "Touch my asshole."

"Yes, Sir."

As she pressed tentatively against his hole, he forgot to breathe. His stomach muscles clenched while she ventured into virgin territory for both of them. He'd never allowed another person to touch him there, but when she'd explored his ass, obviously avoiding anything between his cheeks, he'd made up his mind to test her one more time before he let her go.

"There. That wasn't so bad, was it?" He stepped out

of her reach and was instantly aware of how much he'd enjoyed her touch.

"No, Sir. I've never…."

He turned and helped her back to her knees. "I know. That's no excuse for your hesitation. If you hesitate to follow any of my orders again, be prepared to safe word out of the scene or accept punishment for insubordination. I decide what you will and will not do. Do you understand?"

"Yes, Sir. I'm sorry, Sir."

"In the future, remember, if your action will require you to apologize to me, the only apology I'll accept will be to punish you. I never want to hear the words, "I'm sorry," from your lips, ever again."

"Yes, Sir."

"We're through today. I know you wanted to come — " And God only knew he desperately needed to himself — "but your orgasms aren't mine yet. Once you sign the contract waiting at the desk, then all your orgasms will belong to me. I suggest you take care of your needs before you sign the contract, otherwise, be prepared to accept whatever punishment I deal you."

"Yes, Sir."

He gathered his clothes and dressed, carefully zipping his jeans over his erection. He could smell her arousal from where he stood, and it was all he could do to keep from breaking his own rules and taking her right then and there. A few short minutes ago, he'd been prepared to let her go if she couldn't accept his conditions. There was something about her that called to him, awakened him inside like nothing he'd ever experienced before. Maybe it was the way she called him sir, submissive but with a hint of her inner strength, or maybe it was the way she held herself, shoulders squared yet head bowed. Whatever it was, he wanted it, wanted her.

He stood over her, hoping and praying she would sign the contract. "Read it carefully. You'll also find a set of instructions for tomorrow evening, provided you sign before then. The email address you may use to contact me is on the cover letter. If you have any questions, I'll be available tonight and tomorrow morning to answer them."

"Yes, Sir. Thank you, Sir."

Walking away unsatisfied, and leaving her unsatisfied, was one of the hardest things he'd ever done. It was beyond stupid, but he pulled his car around into a space across the street from the Dungeon and waited for her to come out. His need to see her existed on several levels. First, he wanted to make sure she was all right, that she hadn't broken down after he left. They'd done virtually nothing, but still, he felt bad that he hadn't cared for her as well as he could have. If she signed the contract, he would make sure it never happened again.

Secondly...well, hell. He just wanted to see her. He wanted to see the way she walked, see how she carried herself in the vanilla world, see what kind of car she drove. He wanted to know everything there was to know about her. That his need violated Rule Number One, at least in spirit, did nothing to change his immediate course. Even though she hadn't signed the contract, he felt a responsibility toward her all ready. He'd just watch and make sure she was okay. Really.

The door opened, and she strolled out, her head held high, her shoulders back in that I-am-woman attitude he admired. Her fuck-me pumps dangled from the fingers of her left hand, along with a large brown envelope he recognized. She was taking the contract home with her. That was a good sign. But she shouldn't be walking across the parking lot barefoot. He should spank that perfect round ass of hers for doing something so stupid, but he couldn't very well do that without admitting to watching her leave.

She aimed a remote key fob toward a late model silver Beamer and slipped into the driver's seat. He clutched his steering wheel in a white-knuckle grip to keep from starting his car and following her. He already knew more about her than he needed. Whatever she did in the real world, it paid well. Her car was expensive, and he'd seen enough women's clothes to know what little she wore didn't come cheap either. When her car was out of site, he relaxed his hold and started his car. He made it home, driving practically on autopilot, his thoughts still back at the Dungeon and the submissive who had the power to bring him to his knees.

❧

She reached for the wine bottle then abruptly switched gears, selecting a diet soda from the refrigerator instead. Her hand trembled, so she set the can on the counter to open it. It was incredible to believe, but she'd only been gone a little over an hour, and most of that had been the trip to and from the Dungeon.

The whole scene, from the time she'd met Todd to the moment her mystery Dom had left had taken around half an hour.

And she was still shaking from the encounter.

She sank onto the sofa and stared at the envelope on the coffee table. She had every intention of reading the contract, but realistically, unless there was something truly shocking in there, she would sign it. Her whole body ached from the physical strain, as well as the sexual. Something about the man made her hormones stand up and sing, or kneel and beg as the case may be. She lifted the soda to her lips and frowned.

Good Lord. She'd managed to drain the entire can without conscious thought, all the while staring at the envelope. She set the empty can aside and picked up the contract. Her hands were steadier, but her body still hummed with sexual tension. For a moment, she considered doing something about it as he'd suggested, but that somehow felt like cheating. In her heart and mind, she'd already signed the contract. Her orgasms were his.

She slipped the papers from the envelope, reading the cover letter first. If she agreed, he would see her tomorrow night. The hour he named was very late, but she could do that. She would nap in the early evening, so she would be rested. As a matter of fact, his orders directed her to do just that. As her Dom, he'd necessarily have a measure of control over portions of her ordinary life, too, as it pertained to their relationship. That would take some getting used to, but since she'd thought of the nap idea before reading his order to do so, she agreed it was in her

58

own best interest.

After reading through the remainder of his instructions regarding their meeting tomorrow, she turned to the first page of the contract.

Clearly, Master Jason was a detail-oriented person. Several times, a full-body blush covered her skin as she read the frank descriptions of the kind of things he promised to do to her, and the things he expected of her.

She amended her assessment. He was detail-oriented and uncompromising.

She briefly reconsidered the wine she'd passed on then decided she needed a clear head. She recognized a bit of herself in the attention to details. In her line of work, details were everything. As embarrassing as it was to read every minute detail of her sexual future with this man, it was arousing, too. Only a few pages into the contract, and she wished she'd done something to relieve the stress earlier. There was even a brief paragraph covering getting herself off.

"You will not, under any circumstances, touch yourself in a sexual manner when I'm not present, or without my expressed verbal or written orders to do so. You will not bring yourself to orgasm by any means if I am not present, or without my expressed verbal or written orders. Breach of this clause will result in the punishment of my choice."

A shiver chased up her spine just reading the clause. She had no doubt he would know what she'd done before she found the words to tell him.

So, no. She wouldn't touch herself tonight, and she would make sure to place her vibrator well out of reach when she went to bed. Besides, no self-inflicted orgasm would be as good as what he could give her. She would wait. After all, how hard could it be to exist in a state of sexual arousal for twenty-four hours?

❦

She was freakin' going to die. She'd never been so horny as to be in actual pain before. The previous night, she'd forced herself to go to bed without signing the contract, and after reading it again earlier this morning, she hadn't hesitated to sign it.

Done. He was officially her Master. And she needed to come so damned bad.

She couldn't wait for him to touch her again — this time with no obstacles between them. Lord, his hands were strong, his touch gentle but firm. She closed her eyes and flexed her hands, remembering the lines of his body. There wasn't an ounce of fat on the man. His skin was as smooth as the fondant on one of Brooke's cakes, flowing seamlessly over his tall frame and roped muscles.

She sighed, melting into the sofa. Yeah, he was worth waiting for.

She added his email address to her contact list and fired off her first cyber correspondence with him, letting her new Master know she'd signed the contract. Her fingers itched to tell him how horny she was, but she couldn't. His reply stunned her.

To: carrie.s.t.@infomail.com

From:MasterJ@infomail.com

Subject: Your disobedience

I'm very pleased you signed the contract. Right now, your pussy is wet and aching, as I am positive you did not take my suggestion to heart about finding relief before signing the contract. From now on, you will follow my instructions, and yes, suggestions are the same as instructions, verbal or written, to the letter. It is too late now — you signed the contract. Be prepared tonight to accept your punishment for not heeding my instructions, and for depriving me of the pleasure of hearing how you accomplished it. Your orgasm will have to wait yet another day. My disappointment knows no bounds, as I was looking forward to both the recounting, and the experience of your first orgasm as my sub.

MasterJ

She wiped angry tears from her cheeks. How she was going to make it yet another day in her state of need? It had never occurred to her that he *wanted* her to get herself off, that he expected her to tell him about the experience before he allowed her to come for him. She thought back over his words the night before and wondered how in heaven's name she was supposed to know a suggestion was the same as an order. She wasn't a mind reader.

As the hours passed, she contemplated retrieving her vibrator and using it. He wouldn't know *when* she used it, but she had no doubt he would know she had. Then she would have to tell him the truth, because thanks to her coloring, she couldn't lie worth a damn.

Frustrated, she could think of only one thing to take her mind off her body, and that was work. Her deadline to turn in an article loomed like a monster on a leash. She might get by with being a day or two late, but if she wanted to continue picking her own stories to investigate, then she couldn't afford even the appearance of tardiness. The competition for column inches and headlines was cutthroat. Someone always had a hot story, just waiting for the right time to fill the void; in hopes of stealing someone else's allotted space. The one she was working on was important. Corruption within the local housing authority was depriving needy people of a chance at affordable housing. If the bureaucrats in charge continued to allocate rent-controlled units to their friends with the means to pay market value, pretty soon everyone on a limited income would be homeless.

Tonight, she would find a way to voice her concerns to Master, but until then…She opened her data file and set to work. *There's nothing like exposing corruption and slaying low-life, morally bankrupt slime balls via the media to take your mind off your troubles.*

❧

Jason moved the cursor to hover over the send button, a smile on his lips as he clicked the mouse and sent the message on its way to his sub. He'd spent a hellish night, wondering whether she would sign the contract or not, and if not, whether he would contact her to find out why. He'd woken to find an email in the special account he'd set up to communicate with Carrie, and found he couldn't sit still. She was his.

As exciting as that was, he'd hoped for a more pleasurable first night together, but she'd managed to disobey him already. Denying her an orgasm for another day might seem cruel, but it was important they began the way they planned to continue. When he told her to do something, he expected her to do it. Of course, that didn't mean he had to deny himself. No, he'd find a way to satisfy his needs and still get his point across.

The Mustangs had scheduled a late game, and he wasn't required to be at the stadium for hours. Sitting around sexually frustrated wasn't an option. A few minutes later, he jogged away from his house, breaking into a full run when he reached the pedestrian path in the park around the corner. He used the time to focus on tonight's game. The season was young, and though his head was filled with stats on all the veteran players, every team had acquired a new crop of rookies he needed to learn.

He ran his usual five-mile loop, returning home tired but more relaxed. After a shower and drinking about a gallon of water to rehydrate, he headed for the stadium. A little time in the batting cage and an hour or so studying videotapes of the rookies the Mustangs might face tonight would keep him busy until the rest of the team arrived for batting practice and the pre-game warm-up.

⇛

Fuck. He spun in the batter's box. Nothing but air. That was fucking wonderful in basketball, but in baseball—not so much. He'd come into the game feeling great. On the last road trip, he'd hit pretty well, or at least better than he had been, and with the prospect of his sub waiting for him, he had every reason to expect a good batting game tonight. His third at-bat, and he was down to his last strike.

He leaned back on his left foot, still outside the chalk line, and took a centering breath. This couldn't fucking be happening to him. Hell, there were kids in the stands who could hit this pitcher. Even the players with splinters in their asses could do it, so why couldn't he? Shaking off the doubts, he swung his foot into the box and raised the bat to his shoulder.

Bring it on, asshole. The pitch went wide. Jason relaxed. If the bastard thought he would swing at something like that, then he had another think coming. He might not be able to hit worth shit, but he damned well knew a bad pitch when he saw one.

The next pitch would have taken his kneecap off if he hadn't gotten out of the box in time. *What the fuck?* He took his time getting back into the box. Shit. There wasn't any need to mess with his head, it was fucked up enough all on its own.

The pitch flew like a missile on a mission. He shifted his weight. Every muscle in his body coiled then released energy. He swung the bat in an arc that should have brought wood and leather together in a violent collision.

"Steeeeriiiike three!" the umpire yelled, punctuating the call with a dramatic hand signal Jason would appreciate if he'd been catching rather than batting.

He racked his bat and helmet and reached for his water bottle. Todd motioned for him to join him on the far end of the bench. After wiping sweat from his face, Jason slung the towel over his shoulder and joined his friend.

"Want to talk about it?"

"Not in particular." Jason wiped his brow again.

"You'll fix it," Todd prophesied. "One of these days."

Jason spoke, his gaze fixed on the batter in the on-deck circle, silently wishing him better luck. They could use a man on base right now. "After last week, I thought I had."

"Did you get the contract?"

He ignored Todd's question, buckling his shin guards in place when the count went to two strikes on the batter. He pulled the chest protector over his head but didn't buckle it. "Uh huh. This morning."

"Congratulations. When does it take affect?"

He shook his head, a small chuckle escaping his lips. "Tonight, after the game." He checked the scoreboard for the count. "Do you always talk in secret code?"

"Nah, only when I want to. I don't really care who knows, but you do."

"Yeah." He leaned forward, his elbows on his thighs.

"I do. Thanks for setting this up for me. I think it's going to work out just fine."

"Glad to hear it," Todd said. "If you have questions, just ask. I've fucked up enough times, I can relate to just about anything."

"That's what I'm afraid of," he admitted. "Fucking up."

"Don't worry about it. Keep your ears and mind open. If you listen with those instead of your dick, you'll be fine."

Chapter Seven

As Jason watched his new sub through the glass, he took a few moments to get his head screwed on right. She'd followed his instructions to the letter. Wearing white lace panties and bra, she looked like an angel, minus the wings. He would have to reward her before he took her to task for disobeying him yesterday.

After tonight's game, nothing would please him more than to give this angel an orgasm she'd never forget then sink his cock into her heavenly heat. But that wasn't going to happen. No orgasm for her, and the one he planned for himself, while fun, would be nowhere near as satisfying as he hoped. He reminded himself he was in this to build a lasting relationship, and in the grand scheme of things, one more day wasn't much to set the right tone. A solid foundation would stand the test of time.

He closed the curtains, affording them privacy. He stripped, folding his clothes and stacking them neatly out of the way, all the time, she remained silent and motionless in the center of the room. He circled around her, admiring the straight line of her back, the curve of her ass, and the pink pads of her toes. No stilettos tonight—or ever again. She wore them to impress last night, but he preferred his women barefoot. She'd be much more stable on her feet for some of the things he had in mind, and she looked softer, more obedient somehow, without the spiked heels.

He admired her breasts. He gave them a squeeze. "Beautiful. I can see your nipples through the lace." He stroked a thumb over each one in turn. "They're hard. Are they aching, angel?"

"Yes, Sir," she said through gritted teeth.

Jason dropped his hands from her breasts. She was aroused, but the tightness in her voice said she wasn't happy about it. With two fingers under her chin, he tilted her face upward. "What's this, angel? Are you unhappy with our arrangement so soon?"

"Yes, Sir. I mean no, Sir. I just…."

She sighed, and he studied her face. He made a mental note to check her expression first from now on. Her every thought was right there in the creases around her mouth and the rigid line of her jaw.

"Anger doesn't become you." He removed his fingers from her chin. "Speak to me. What has you in this state?"

"Permission to speak frankly, Sir?"

"Go on. I don't read minds." He hated the tinge of anger in his voice, and his bad mood returned. She didn't deserve to be the brunt of his misery.

"I don't read minds either, Sir," she said. "Last night, before I signed the contract…well, I remembered what you said about seeing to my needs before I signed, but when I left here, I felt as if I was yours all ready. The contract was only a formality. I read it over, several times, and the clause about not touching myself stood out, Sir. As I said, I all ready felt my orgasms belonged to you, and…it was only a suggestion…."

Jason sighed. "I see. You didn't understand my instructions, is that what I'm hearing?"

"Yes, Sir. I wanted to honor my submission to you, so I didn't touch myself."

"And you didn't email me to clarify my instructions?"

"No, Sir. Perhaps I should have, but I didn't want you to think I was weak, that I couldn't last a day without coming. And I…."

Her body turned rosy pink. He closed his eyes and raised his face to the ceiling. His heart thumped against his ribcage. Had she changed her mind? Damn. He hardly dared to ask. "You what, angel?"

"I wanted to save myself for you."

Her softly spoken declaration made his cock jerk and swell. His shoulders sagged as he let out the breath trapped in his lungs. She was still going to go through with it. He wrapped his fist around his aching dick and stifled a groan as he silently thanked the universe for the blindfold she wore. If she ever got a hint of how she affected him, she'd know exactly how much power she had over him. She topped from the bottom just by existing.

"Are you thinking this heartfelt confession will save you from the punishment I promised?"

"Yes, Sir?" she asked, her voice tinged with hope.

He smiled. She might be submissive, but she wasn't above using feminine tricks to try to get her way. Topping her would be satisfying and fun.

"Well, you're wrong, angel, but I'm willing to compromise. Let me explain. I'm still going to punish you, but not for the reason originally stated. I'll concede my instructions were not as clear as they should have been, and I apologize for any anxiety my mistake caused you. I can see you're upset, and I see my actions are partly responsible. I'll try to make my instructions more clear in the future. I'm pleased you came tonight, even though you clearly were angry with me. But…my other instructions were quite clear. You were to email me for clarification on any point. I waited to hear from you, but you didn't contact me until this morning and by then, you'd signed the contract and were, at that time, completely mine. Had you contacted me last night, we both would have gotten what we wanted. You would have relieved the sexual tension that now fuels your anger toward me, and I would have had the pleasure of hearing ever little detail of how you pleasured yourself." He paused, watching her body language to see how she was taking this bit of logic. Her shoulders relaxed a fraction, and those magnificent lips coated in a soft pink lip-gloss plumped.

"Do you see why I'm still going to punish you?"

"Yes, Master. I should have emailed you. Instead, I

reached my own conclusions, which I see now were incorrect."

"I'm sure you make decisions all day long in your everyday life. Those are your decisions to make. I have no say in them, whatsoever. But when it comes to your body, all those decisions are mine. Do you have any questions?"

"No, Sir. I understand. I was wrong. It won't happen again."

"That's good. Now, let me see you smile."

Her lips curved up in the first genuine smile she'd ever given him. "I like that shade of pink on your lips. You did good selecting it."

"Thank you, Master."

"I'm in the mood to compromise." He strolled slowly around her, stopping when he stood in front of her again. "Do you have a safe word?"

"Yes, Sir, it's broccoli."

"I take it you don't like that particular vegetable."

"Well, I won't be asking for it, that's for sure."

"Then it's perfect, and if I'm ever inclined to feed you, I'll remember broccoli is off the menu. Now, how did you plan to get yourself off last night? With your hand, or do you have a vibrator?"

Her body flushed the darkest pink he'd yet to see. "I-I have a...vibrator, Sir."

"I see," he said. "Describe it. Size. Color. Is it one of those rabbit ones that stimulate your clit, too? Does it gyrate? Pump?"

This was something, judging from her halting speech and the deep shade of pink suffusing her body, she wasn't comfortable talking about. But her body was his now. She would have to get used to discussing intimate details with him. He walked to a cabinet in the corner and perused the contents while she talked. "How long is it, the part you put inside you?"

"Six inches? Eight, maybe. I don't know for certain."

He selected an item, removed it from the package, and laid the empty box with his clothes. He would stop at the front desk and have the vibrator added to his bill on his way out. "Hold out your hands."

She extended her hands, and he placed the giant vibrator across her palms.

"Is yours something like this one?"

"Um...mine isn't this...big."

He took it from her, smiling at the relief that flashed across her face. She thought she was off the hook.

"You can stand now." He assisted her to her feet, gently guiding her to the bondage table. He backed her up to it until her ass came in contact with the padded edge. "Hop up, and lie down." When she was prone, he said, "Push your panties to your ankles, then I want you to raise your knees and spread your legs wide."

Jason stroked her pink, swollen pussy. "You're wet. That's good, but I wouldn't want to hurt you." He selected a tube of lube from a basket on the shelf below the table and squirted a generous amount on her mound. She gasped when the cold gel contacted with her warm skin. "Do you know what I want?"

"No, Sir." Her voice quavered.

He spread the lube over her mound, coating her clit, her labia and dipping inside to swirl a generous glob there, too. "You're going to get yourself off...while I watch."

Her mouth formed a perfect O—she wanted to protest. He'd deliberately selected a vibrator nearly twice the size of the one she'd described. This thing looked like King Kong's mistress could use it. He placed the giant vibrator in her hand, reached for her other, and wrapped it securely around the base, too.

"Hold it up for me." He adjusted her grip so the vibrator pointed straight up in the air above her stomach. Squirting more lube into his palm, he carefully coated the entire thing, making sure to grease every groove. He really didn't want to hurt her. When it glistened with lubricant, he guided her to position it between her legs, snugging the tip against her opening. "Put it in. As far as it will go."

Her hands and legs trembled, but she didn't protest his decision to use the giant vibrator. She tried to work it inside her without much success. He slapped the blunt end of the thing, driving it past the first barrier. She gasped, and he helped her push it farther.

"That's it. All the way in," he crooned encouragement. Her pussy lips stretched thin around the shaft. "Does that feel good? Is that what you wanted last night but were too afraid to ask for?"

"No…yes, Sir."

"I would have been content to just hear about it, angel. But since you made the decision to deprive me of that pleasure, this is my compromise. You get your orgasm, and I get to watch you fuck yourself with a piece of plastic machinery."

He leaned over for a better look. God, he'd give anything to see his cock stretching her, filling her, but that time would come. "He's a big one, isn't he? Does that feel good?"

He wanted words when her body had just been invaded by a giant plastic cock?

She made a gurgling sound he must have taken for a yes. She couldn't think, couldn't manage a coherent sentence if her life depended on it. Frantic protests formed in her brain but never reached her lips. Oh, how she wished she'd given in to her need last night — though even that wouldn't have come without embarrassment. Pleasuring herself in front of him was bad enough, but she wasn't sure telling about her solo experience would have been any better.

Her pussy burned with the stretch, and her skin flamed, knowing Master's gaze was on her. Arousal flowed, molten lava through her veins. He adjusted the clit stimulator, flicking it across her swollen nub. She gasped at the light touch. Heaven help her when he turned the thing on. She'd be rocketing into space in no time. Hell, she was on the launch pad, all systems go already.

"There, that ought to do the trick." Satisfaction and amusement colored his words.

She didn't need sight to know her entire body was flushed with color, and the soft, deep, erotic timbre of Master's voice only made it worse. Every time he spoke, it was like someone waved a magic horny wand over her. Her body responded, anticipated, craved. Good Lord, she was in over her head, and this was her first real encounter with him.

The white lace of her bra stood out against her now rosy skin and drove him half out of his mind with lust. Jason eyed the controls on the giant phallus. His angel was ready to explode. He would have to see about prolonging her pleasure—and his.

"Let's see. How about we start out slow?" He pushed a button, and a low buzzing sound filled the room.

The mammoth device set to work fucking her and her body tensed. She struggled to hold onto the vibrator. This might be punishment, but he fully expected her to find pleasure in it, too. He damned sure was.

"Hold on, angel." He adjusted her grip on her surrogate Dom. "Talk to me. Does it feel good? Do you want him to fuck you harder? Faster?"

Inarticulate sounds gurgled from her throat, past her slackened mouth.

"Damn, that's hot." His gaze traveled from her pussy, past the indentation of her waist to her breasts. He couldn't not touch her. He cupped the nearest lace-covered breast with one hand and palmed her stomach with the other. The vibrator hummed and pistoned beneath his hand. It was ridiculous to be jealous of a sex toy, but he was. His dick throbbed. He needed to be inside her, but everything he'd read cautioned to take baby steps with their relationship if he wanted it to last. She had to understand and accept his control. Her body was his, and he would use it, pleasure it anyway he wanted. If she couldn't live with that, he wanted to know now before he grew attached to her, because growing attached was a real possibility, and he'd never been good at letting go of things he loved.

She was so close. He could see it in the lines of her jaw, in the way she arched her neck, in the way her hips moved, fucking the vibrator as hard as it fucked her. She didn't seem to notice when he freed a nipple from its lace confines, but when he sucked into his mouth, she rose to meet him, offering and taking at the same time. A sexy moan rumbled in her chest, struggling to escape. His first taste of her, coupled with the musk of her arousal and he damned near came right then and there.

Another strangled whimper and he decided enough was enough. He reached between her legs, ramped up the piston speed, and sent her flying.

Sunbursts lit up the darkness behind the blindfold. Her involuntary organs short-circuited, and for the first time she understood the French term, "petite death." She'd died and gone to Heaven. She hung on, unable to let go of the monster between her legs as her body convulsed around it. Her mind focused with laser precision on her pussy. Her internal muscles clenched so hard she was both weak and empowered. With a little luck, her heart and lungs would resume normal function on their own. If not, she would die happy.

Master's lips covered hers, swallowing the unladylike grunts and cries barreling to the surface like freight cars hooked to a runaway locomotive. There was nothing tender about his kiss. He possessed, he took, and demanded more when she thought she had nothing more to give. "Mine," he breathed before swooping in to take the last of her orgasm for himself.

Greedy. She owed him an orgasm, and he was going to take it. He barely managed to cover her mouth with his before she came apart, her body jerking, her muscles rippling across her torso. His hands explored. He took her cries into himself, absorbing the wonder of her orgasm, taking, claiming, demanding what was rightfully his.

Her body relaxed, and he realized he was half lying across her. Crooning ridiculous words of praise, he gently removed the vibrator from her pussy. He kissed up the inside of her thigh to her tender tissues. He inhaled the sharp tang of her arousal and knew nothing would ever smell better. His lips on her clit sent her into another set of spasms, and the way her hips rocketed up to meet his tongue made denying his release worth the sacrifice. He'd brought her pleasure, and he felt like a god.

He guided her legs together then pulled her and into his arms. This particular room was short on comfortable seating, but sitting on the hard chair with her ass cradled in his lap was fine with him.

"Okay?" he whispered against the top of her head.

She sighed, her warm breath tickling his chest. "Um...oh yes, Master." She snuggled even closer if that was possible. "Thank you."

He chuckled. He'd always like this part. Why any man would want to pass on holding a well-satisfied woman was beyond him. They smelled so good after sex, and their muscles were mush after a great orgasm. "I take it my punishment wasn't too harsh?"

"No, Sir."

She sighed again, and he couldn't help feeling smug. He could do anything he wanted to her right now, and she'd take it with a smile on her face. His heart beat out a primal rhythm and his cock joined in. Pressed into her hip the way it was, there was no way it would escape her notice.

"Sir?" She placed one hand on his pec and traced a lazy, seductive circle around his nipple.

"Yes?"

"May I?" Her hand wandered lower, and he shifted to allow her access.

"What would you like to do, angel?" Her fingers closed around his cock. He groaned and bucked.

"I understand why you won't come inside me tonight, Master. I was wrong not to tell you of my confusion, but even in your punishment, you gave me great pleasure. I'd like to do the same for you."

It was damned hard to think with her hand doing wicked things to his dick. He seized her wrist to stop her from jacking him until he came. She was topping again, suggesting another compromise, but damned if he didn't want to hear her out. "What do you have in mind?"

"Anything you want, Sir. I just need to show my appreciation for your kindness. You could have done so much more to me, but through my pleasure I saw the error of my ways."

He struggled with his desire to sink into her pussy and ease himself. He'd made up his mind. She would to have to wait, and so would he, but that didn't mean he couldn't let her ease the pressure. Some would argue she was topping from the bottom, asking him to compromise yet again, but he'd made his point, and she was offering a gift he'd be a loon not to take.

"On your knees," he commanded, guiding her from his lap to kneel between his legs. He cupped the back of her head in one hand and fisted his cock in the other. "Take the bra off. I want to see you."

White lace innocence fell to the rouge red floor, mocking her presence in such a place. She was all sunshine and light on the outside, but deep within lurked a dark, wicked woman with needs that matched his perfectly.

"Open your mouth, girl. You can thank me by sucking my cock."

She smiled, and he nudged the tip against her mouth. Applying pressure to the back of her head, he watched as her pink lips parted and his dick slid inside.

Her tongue swirled and stroked. "Christ almighty," he hissed.

Her cheeks hollowed as she sucked, and those pink lips clamped rhythmically around his cock. If he didn't look away, he'd be shooting cum down her throat in seconds.

"My balls," he croaked, needing to feel her hands on him. "Play with my balls."

She obeyed, holding the base of his cock with one hand, rolling and tugging on his balls with the other. He tilted his face toward the ceiling and threaded his fingers through her hair, holding on for dear life as his angel coaxed him to Heaven.

Chapter Eight

Reliving the previous night over and over was driving her crazy. Master had given her a night she would never forget. She still couldn't believe the way he'd accepted her anger and, with calm reason, had offered a compromise. He could easily have dismissed her feelings, but he'd listened to her concerns—really listened.

Because of the way he'd encouraged her to speak what was on her mind and accepted his part in the misunderstanding, she progressed from resenting his promised punishment, to accepting it—even liking it before it was through. She shook her head. The real punishment had come from within herself. She'd disappointed him, and had he been a less reasonable man, she wouldn't have cared. But he wasn't, and she did care. Very much.

She'd learned valuable lessons last night—lessons about clear communication, about being open-minded, and accepting responsibility for one's actions, and she'd learned to trust her Master. The punishment he'd meted out had been just and fair, based on the level of her misconduct.

She'd also learned something about being blindfolded. Loss of sight heightened some of senses—like touch and hearing, while obliterating others—namely, propriety.

Her skin flamed remembering the things she'd done, and allowed a man, a practical stranger no less, to do to her. The blindfold had rendered her vulnerable but, at the same time, set her free. It blinded her to her inhibitions and took her to a place in her mind where nothing else mattered but pleasure—hers and her Master's.

She'd heard once that punishment was a relative thing. If a person liked solitude, locking them alone in a cell would accomplish nothing. In order to punish, you have to take away something a person values. Master had stripped away her dignity—a punishment befitting her crime. But he'd tempered the harshness with pleasure.

Realization slammed into her. She never wanted to disappoint this man again. But even if she did, he would find a way to gently show her she'd let down herself, too. And she had. Hadn't she known all along she should clarify his instructions? But she'd chosen not to in an effort to preserve her dignity. How embarrassing to email him after their first meeting to ask if it was all right to masturbate. He would know how much he'd affected her, and she didn't want that.

He'd cut to the core of her crime—her pride—and unequivocally demonstrated even that part of her belonged to him. And he'd done it with understanding and compassion. His tender care of her afterwards demonstrated that the offense had been forgotten.

Her Master was an extraordinary man.

She ran her finger across her lips, remembering how they'd stretched to accommodate his cock, much like her pussy had stretched to accommodate the plastic beast earlier. She couldn't believe he'd accepted her gift, allowing her to ease his need. Yes, her Master was an extraordinary man. She couldn't wait to have his cock again—in any way he wanted.

Her cell phone rang, startling her out of her erotic memories and back into the real world. She glanced at the caller ID. The senior editor—her boss—returning her call.

"Hi, George," she said. "Thanks for getting back to me so soon."

"No problem. You saw the email?"

"Yes, I did. I want that story. You can't let someone else have it."

"I know you're passionate about the subject, that's why I sent it to you before anyone else. I want someone on this ASAP."

"I'm in," she said. "Someone has to put a stop to these athletes using steroids. Too many kids look up to them as role models." Cold, hard rage raced through her system. "They don't know how dangerous these drugs are."

"Hey," he said. "You don't have to convince me. I'm on your side."

"I know. Sorry. It's just that I…." Memories flooded through her and her throat tightened.

"You're a good friend to keep after this," he said. "Most people would have let it go a long time ago."

"I can't. Danny was like a brother to me. He did something stupid that cost him his life. Exposing steroid use among elite athletes brings attention to the problem and might convince another teenager of the danger. Save a life."

"Preaching to the choir here," George said. "Take your time on this one. I think I might be able to get you an interview with Martin McCree. I've got a call in to his lawyer."

"That would be fabulous. Let me know. In the meantime, I'll get started on the research right away." She paused and swallowed, "And thanks. I owe you one."

This was the story she'd been waiting for. It had been ten years since her cousin Danny committed suicide. She had no doubt his abrupt withdrawal from steroids was to blame. If only he'd never used them or, at the very least, had understood what they really did to his body, maybe he would be alive today.

Excited to have something to do besides obsess over the previous night, and anticipate tomorrow night, she set to work on her new project.

❧❧

Jason sang along with the radio all the way to the

stadium. He hummed in the locker room and whistled in the dugout.

"Hey, man." Stevens slapped him on the back. "You're in a good mood."

"Yeah, I am," he said, realizing he meant it. For the first time since Stacey left him, he was happy. Really. Truly. Happy. And he owed it to Carrie. She was everything he wanted in a sub. Her body was a work of art, and her mind equal to it. She'd surprised him with her anger. He chuckled to himself, remembering his anxiety upon discovering she was unhappy with his decision to punish her.

She'd been right. He hadn't been clear, and he couldn't blame her for that, but when he pointed out the error of her ways, she'd accepted his punishment with a level of submission that humbled him. And if he was any judge, she'd enjoyed it. He couldn't wait to be with her again. Tomorrow's game was in the afternoon, so he'd booked the Dungeon room for early evening, expecting to use it, and his sub, into the wee hours of the morning.

But first, he needed to get through two games. He was ready. His body was primed for action. It was a feeling he was familiar with, but one that had been elusive this season.

He strode to the plate with more confidence than he'd felt in weeks.

The first pitch came in low and inside. Jason checked his swing and rolled his shoulders to release the tension building there. Last season, pitchers worked hard to keep him off base, and it was good to know a few still respected his ability, despite his dismal showing so far this season. He stepped back into the batter's box. His next swing connected with leather, rocketing the ball foul down the first base line.

God, it felt good to connect again, to feel the sharp bite of energy when two moving masses collided.

He loosened his grip on the bat and repositioned his fingers, searching for the perfect grip. Satisfied, he lifted the bat to his shoulder and focused on the pitcher's hand. His gaze narrowed to the slash of white showing between the pitcher's fingers. He tuned out everything. Nothing existed but the orb hurtling toward him. Four hundred milliseconds to see the ball, calculate speed and trajectory, commit to the swing, and follow through. His brain committed to action, and the bat became an extension of his hands.

He shifted his weight to his back foot then using the muscles in his leg, he lunged forward, twisting first his shoulders then his upper torso, transferring energy from his lower body to his arms to the bat. Simple physics. Point the knob of the bat toward the target, and swing through.

Less than half a second from pitch to impact.

The ball collided with the bat in that elusive sweet spot where eight thousand pounds of force literally crushed the ball before sending in the opposite direction at nearly one hundred ten miles-per-hour.

No sting in his hands. Just a pleasant vibration traveling along his arms, through his shoulders, and down his spine. Every cell in his body responded to the stimulus. Fireworks exploded in his mind. His heart raced. He didn't need to watch, but the miracle never ceased to amaze him. Jogging toward first base, he tracked the ball until it fell into waiting hands in the right field bleachers.

A homerun.

As his foot touched each base in turn, a calm certainty built inside him. He was back in the game. All the doubts he'd harbored since the first pitch of the season vanished. This was his year. Jason Holder was on top — in more ways than one. He crossed home plate into a crowd of teammates gathered to celebrate with him. Over their heads, he caught the gaze of his sister-in-law, Megan, in the stands. Bouncing on her toes, she waved and blew him a kiss. Too bad his brother was stuck in the bullpen and couldn't share this moment with him. Jeff would make it up to him later. Their lockers side-by-side, they always had time together before and after the game.

Jason entered the dugout. The team manager, Doyle Walker, clapped him on the shoulder. "Nice shot," he said. "Glad to see you're back."

"It's good to be back," he said. *And good to have the team manager's favor again,* he added silently.

Doyle had been a good friend to Jason and Jeff since he'd recruited them from the University of Texas almost seven years ago. But his job was to win games, and a player not pulling his weight had to go—friend or not. Today's homerun, though not enough to get him completely out of the woods, bought him time to prove himself.

He shelved his helmet, using the after batting routine to savor the moment privately. It was just one homerun, but he knew it was the first of many. He couldn't really pinpoint the change, but something had shifted inside him. He felt different, more alive, more in charge of his life and body. Until that feeling had returned, he hadn't noticed it'd been was missing. Funny how a person could go through each day without giving a thought to whether they were happy or not. Then—*Wham!* Happiness hit him like a fastball to the helmet, and his whole world had shifted into focus.

An image of Carrie, naked and on her knees, flashed in his mind. She truly was a work of art. A plan formed in his mind for the next time they were together. No punishment, just pleasure. Lots and lots of pleasure. Yeah, life was good.

❧

Carrie waited, none too patiently, to be with him again. Her work had kept her busy the last few days, but she'd found her mind wandering back to her first session with Master, reliving it until her body ached with need and she was tempted to bring the vibrator out. If all her Master's punishments were like the one he'd dealt out the other night, she would have to be a very bad girl. Remembering the disappointment in his voice, she knew she never wanted to hear that tone again, no matter what kind of punishment accompanied it.

She was proud to be his sub and wanted him to be proud of her. So when the email arrived instructing her to meet him at the Dungeon the following day, she jumped for joy. He'd given no indication of what he had in mind, leaving her to dream up scenarios of her own.

❧❧

"Hello, angel."

Her skin tingled at the sound of his voice.

"How have you been?"

He closed the curtains over the two-way mirror, and she followed the sound of his footsteps across the room.

"I've missed you, Sir."

His footsteps halted in front of her. "What exactly did you miss about me?"

"I missed your touch and your voice," she said. *I want to see you.*

"My voice? You like my voice?"

"Yes, Master. Your voice…." Couldn't he see what his voice did to her? Her skin prickled in another one of those damnable full-body blushes.

"Tell me, girl. There's nothing but honesty between us."

She nodded, glad for the blindfold. "Every time you speak, it's like a touch. I feel it on my skin, and it makes me horny."

"Is that so?" A smile tinged his words. "I'll have to remember to speak to you often because I want you horny." He shifted something in his hands, and his knees cracked when he squatted. "Are you horny now?" He flattened his palm over her stomach, nearly singing her skin with his heat "Let me see." His hand slid down to cup her mound. "Spread for me," he said, slipping his fingers between her legs when she complied.

He flicked and played in her damp heat, drawing a whimper from her.

"You're wet," he said, spearing his middle finger inside. "I'm pleased."

She moved her hips, seeking deeper contact.

"Be still," he warned, continuing to play between her legs. His voice, deep and confident assured her, but his words…oh Lord, the combination of the two demolished her self-control.

"Keep still. Tonight I'm going to see and touch every inch of you. I'm going to mark you as mine." She struggled to control her body's natural inclinations, closing her teeth over her bottom lip to keep from begging for what she wanted. With his finger still buried inside her, he leaned in close. "And when I'm through, if you've been good," he whispered in her ear, "you'll get much more than a finger inside you."

A strangled sound gurgled past her lips. Her inner muscles clamped his finger, and she came in his hand. He pulled her to him, cradling her cheek against his solid chest. He cupped her until the last muscle spasm eased, then slipped his finger from her.

He inhaled deeply and let it out audibly. She dared to breathe, taking in the tangy scent of her arousal mingling with the starch from his crisp shirt and the outdoorsy fragrance she was beginning to associate with him.

"I love to smell you on my hand," he said, filling his lungs again.

If he would let her, she would rub herself all over him.

"Open your mouth." He urged her bottom lip down with his index finger. "You taste so good." He inserted his wet middle finger into her mouth. "Taste yourself on me."

She closed her lips around his finger.

"That's good," he said.

Oh, how she wished he'd give her his cock instead, but she'd take any part of him she could get. Her tongue swirled and licked.

"Do you like that?" he asked, pulling his finger free.

"Yes, Sir. Thank you."

"Have you ever tasted another woman?"

"No…no, Sir."

"I think I'd like to see you go down on a woman sometime. That would please me very much."

Her arms, clasped behind her back, trembled.

"Does that disgust you?"

Did it? She'd never thought it a possibility. But for him…."I'm not sure, Sir. It…I…If it would please you, Master, I…."

He stroked her cheek with the back of his hand, bringing her scent to her nostrils. "Maybe one day, but not for a while."

Oh, how she loved the sound of her name on his lips, and she was glad he'd used it now, instead of his usual, "girl"—proof he saw her as a person, not an object.

"I won't lie. I'd love to see you with another woman, eating each other, maybe fucking, sucking tits, but not now. You're mine, and I'm not ready to share. I can see you aren't ready for that either, no matter your brave words." He drew a finger across her mouth, tweaking her plumped lower lip. "I said I would push your limits, and I will. But we have all the time in the world. I won't rush either of us."

"Thank you, Sir."

"No need to thank me. It's purely selfish on my part right now. I want you all to myself." He helped her to her feet. "Hands out in front."

He fastened fur-lined leather cuffs around her wrists, hooking them together with a clasp. Goosebumps rose on her arms.

"Relax," he said, lifting her arms up by the connecting chain. "Keep your hands high."

An electric hum filled the air then he fastened the cuffs to a bar. After wrapping her fingers around the bar, he raised it a few inches so her feet touched the floor, but her torso stretched taut.

"Spread your legs," he said, urging her feet farther when she stopped short of his expectation. "There. I wish you could see how beautiful you are. And you're all mine."

Something plunked onto the floor in front of her. "I need you to remain perfectly still, no matter what," he instructed. "This is a delicate operation. A steady hand is required."

She smiled at the playfulness in his voice. This was a side of her master she hadn't witnessed yet. "Yes, Sir. I'll do my best."

When he lifted one foot to his lips, she clutched at the bar for support.

"Mine." His breath tickled then he sucked her big toe into his mouth, and she would have fallen if not for the restraints. His tongue swirled around the digit, teasing and taunting like she teased his cock the other day. He took his time, tasting, licking, nipping at her toes, across the arch of her foot, to her heel, stopping short at her ankle. She let her head fall back, giving herself over to the sensual onslaught.

He finally released her toe, but replaced the sensation with another. She focused on the feeling.

"What?" she questioned.

"Relax. I'm just claiming what's mine." He resumed his strange work. It took a few minutes, but she figured it out. He was using a marker to draw on her skin. He placed her foot on the floor, and proceeded to do the same with the other. When he finished there, he moved on to her ankles, the slope of her calves, her knees—claiming her body an inch at a time.

❧

He was on a mission to claim what was his in a way she would never forget. On her thighs, he drew arrows pointing to her pussy from every direction, labeling each one with the single word, "Mine."

A yellow daisy sprang up around her navel, its green stem rooted in the neat curls of her mons. So close to her pussy, he couldn't resist a little playtime there, too. He eased the barrel of a marker through her folds until it glistened with her juices. Parting her with his fingers, he slid the marker inside, startling a gasp from her.

"Remain still," he cautioned. "You've been so good…" He added two more markers to fill her. He pumped the plastic tubes in and out, establishing a slow, steady rhythm. Soon her body picked it up, and her hips began to move. He grinned. He'd punish her for that in his own sweet time.

"I can't…oh, God, it feels so…good." She cried out, moving with her body's natural inclinations. "Please," she begged.

"Not yet." He slipped the markers out before he pushed her completely over the edge. She bucked and writhed against her restraints.

Chapter Nine

A solid "thwack" stung her ass.

"I said to be still." His voice came from behind her. When had he moved?

"That hurt," she said, angry with him for denying her what she needed then hitting her for trying to find it.

"You'll learn to do as you're told." He landed another sharp hand on the other cheek. Before she could protest, he cradled her hips in his palms, and his warm breath against her spine documented his descent. His lips soothed where a moment ago his hand branded her flesh.

"God, you are so beautiful." His big hands held her steady while his thumbs brushed over her sore ass. "I wish you could see this. My handprints on your ass." His lips pressed where she imagined his palms must have made contact. "You really should see this."

He began to draw on her ass, and she clenched her cheeks tight.

He swatted her, playfully this time. "Relax. This is too good," he said with childlike exuberance. "You're going to love this one."

Like she had any choice. She consciously relaxed her butt cheeks, trying to envision what he was drawing. He made big loops across her skin, followed by a series of short, choppy lines. A flower? She groaned. Lord, she hoped this would wash off.

When he finished his masterpiece, he parted her cheeks and set to work there, too. Her skin heated. He'd examined that part of her thoroughly before, but this was different. She tried not to think about what he was doing, or what he was seeing. Swirls, strokes, long ones, short ones, all punctuated by the occasional chuckle while he amused himself with her ass, and she silently begged him to go lower, to give her more of what she wanted.

A click signaled he'd capped the marker. His voice came from farther away, maybe a few feet.

"Extraordinary," he enthused.

"How are you doing?" He closed his hand over her ass again, giving it a little squeeze.

"My arms....."

"It's been a while. Let me take you down for a few minutes."

She sighed when he lowered the bar, allowing her arms a respite. He didn't remove the cuffs, but kneaded her sore muscles from just above the cuffs to her shoulders.

"Promise to stay still, and I'll leave your hands down until I finish with your back," he said.

At that moment, she couldn't move if her life had depended on it, so she nodded. "Yes. I'll be still. I promise."

"Good." He moved behind her again, shifting her hair over her shoulders, so he had full access to her back. Marker lids popped, and he resumed drawing. Curves and lines and dots. She couldn't follow it, couldn't discern a pattern. She sensed his total concentration on his art and did her best to remain still, even when the markers veered dangerously close to ticklish spots along her ribs.

"There, all done," he said, capping his markers. They clattered against others near her feet. How many did he have? A scraping sound on the floor, one she'd heard before—a cardboard box perhaps, sliding around in front of her.

The click of a switch and her arms rose above her head again. "A few more minutes, then I'm going to fuck you," he promised.

Her clit throbbed at his raw declaration. "Please, Master."

A laugh rumbled from his chest, just inches from her face. She didn't know this playful Master, but decided she liked him.

"Don't worry, angel. I'm going to spend the rest of the night fucking you."

He stepped away from her and she shivered from the loss of his heat.

"Hmm," he said. "What should I do with those? It's almost a shame to embellish them. Hell, your body's a work of art all by itself, but I've come this far, I might as well finish the job."

"Please, Master."

His laugh almost masked the sound of lids popping. A cold felt-tip slid along her rib cage. He drew and drew on her torso, leaving her breasts untouched. She was just beginning to think he wasn't going to embellish them, when he cradled one in his hand and brushed his thumb across the nipple until it grew diamond hard. Again, she tried to make out the pattern, but like the game she'd played when she was a kid—spelling out words in the palm of a friend's hand—she failed miserably. He took his time with one breast before switching to the other, giving it equal attention. She wanted to arch her back, thrust her breasts in invitation, but she'd promised to remain still.

He lowered the bar again, guiding her to her knees, keeping her arms stretched above her head.

"Open your mouth." Strong fingers clamped her jaw, insuring her compliance, before he thrust his cock inside. "You can do me, while I do you."

She closed her lips around him. The salty tang of pre-cum thrilled her. It was nice to know their play affected him, too. She used her tongue to taste and tantalize, savoring every hiss and curse her actions elicited. He fisted her hair and bucked his hips, controlling the rhythm.

God, he tasted good, like warm sunshine and outdoors. She wondered if he spent a lot of time outside to acquire the scent. His body was firm and well formed, leading her to believe he worked out, or maybe he did some kind of manual labor—construction perhaps. That would account for his physique. She clenched her fingers, wanting to touch him all over.

He tried to concentrate on the artwork he wanted to draw on her arms, but it was an impossible task with his cock halfway down her throat. But damn, it felt good. He finally gave up and focused on the pink angel lips wrapped around his cock. He held her still, pumping his hips, torturing himself with pleasure. God, his balls ached. His little brain argued for coming down her throat while the few remaining cells in his big brain reminded him about his promise to this angel—to see to her pleasure. Punishment aside, he'd vowed to never leave her unsatisfied.

He released her hands from the bar, leaving her wrists shackled together. Her mouth felt like Heaven, but there was a place he needed to be even more.

"Enough," he said, jerking her head back by her hair. Pulling her to her feet, he steered her to the platform bed on one side of the room. "Face down, on your knees."

He stared at her perfect bottom displayed for him. The skin inside the outline of his handprint was faintly pink where he'd spanked her earlier. He framed her hips with his hands. "Beautiful. I love seeing my handprints on your ass."

She groaned, rocking back on her knees, trying to get closer to his touch. "Please, Sir."

He caressed her cheeks. Please what?"

"Fuck me, please, Sir."

He entered her in one swift thrust that caused her to clutch at the edge of the mattress. He withdrew and slammed back in. This is what he needed, to take her on his terms, to claim what was his without reservation. He'd give her what she wanted, too, but she'd vowed to serve him, and she was doing it well.

He traced the curve of her spine with his index finger, slipping between her cheeks to find the tight bud there. She tensed. He gently manipulated her backdoor while stroking her back with his free hand, coaxing her to relax and accept him.

"So tight," he said, pressing his finger harder against her anus. "I was going to wait, but I can't."

Carrie cried out when he withdrew from her and left the bed. She pushed to her elbows, listening to his movements. A zipper. Muffled curses. Then he was back, landing a solid blow to her ass with his hand.

"Did I say you could move?"

"No, Sir." She slid down until her cheek rested on the mattress again.

"Much better," he said, resuming his position between her splayed knees. Heat shot through her when his fingers found her pussy, exploring, driving her need higher with each erotic motion.

"You're so wet, I don't think I'll need the lube." He coated her anus with her own juices, and she groaned.

She couldn't believe how aroused she was, knowing how closely he examined that part of her.

His fingers returned to her pussy, spreading her. "I think the best lube for the beads is your own," he said. Something cold and hard slipped inside her. "Relax, angel. It's just anal beads." A lump formed in her throat, imagining the beads inching their way into her vagina. She'd seen the plastic toys before but never used them. Her butt cheeks clenched, knowing where the beads would go next.

She flinched when his hand came down hard on her ass.

"Relax."

He pulled the beads from her pussy, and spread her wide with one hand. There was a slight pressure against her anus then the first small bead breached her. Her insides twisted and her pussy gushed. Fingers swiped along her slit, collecting her juices and re-depositing them at the point of entry.

More pressure then the second bead joined the first, followed by another, and another. With each one, Master added lubrication collected from her pussy. She counted to herself. Her greedy ass took each bead — six in all.

"Christ, that looks hot. Are you okay?"

"Yes, Master. It feels…good." It did feel good. Better than she'd expected.

He twisted the end protruding from her asshole. The sensation, the naughtiness of it wrenched a moan from her. She sensed his heated gaze on her ass. He played with the beads, tugging gently but not pulling them out, swiveling them around inside her until she thought she might go mad.

"I want to fuck you there," he said. "But we'll work up to that. For now," he said, his cock nudging against her pussy lips, "this will do nicely."

He inched inside slowly, and when his cock touched her womb, he resumed playing with the beads. She buried her face in the mattress, new sensations washing over her. He tugged and swirled the beads in sync with his thrusts. She could only imagine what it would feel like to have his cock filling her there. The beads made her feel full and possessed in a way she'd never experienced before. Her muscles were so weak it was all she could do to maintain her position. As if sensing her weakness, Master curled an arm beneath her waist, supporting her.

"You feel so damned good," he said, pumping into her harder.

With each thrust, his balls slapped against her clit, sending shock waves through her body. The erotic slide of his shaft in and out, the sensation of him possessing her over and over along with the beads in her ass was too much. An orgasm built. Her muscles coiled tight.

"That's it, angel. Come for me." His voice sounded strained but still deep and commanding, triggering something inside her.

Her body shuddered and contracted around his thrusting cock. His balls tapped her clit, the sensation magnified by her orgasm. And with each wave of spasms, Master tugged a bead from her ass. One at a time, the beads popped free, and each one added a new jolt of excitement. She cried out, muffling her screams with the mattress.

The orgasm seemed to last forever. When it subsided, she realized he was still hard inside her, his arms wrapped around her waist, holding her. His cheek rested against her back, his heated breath brushing softly against her skin. She felt safe and...cherished. He nuzzled her nape. One hand slipped to her hip, down her thigh and back again.

"My turn now," he said. "Ready?"

"Yes, Master. Please, fuck me. Fuck me hard."

He couldn't do anything but fuck her hard. What little control he'd managed to hold onto, his angel had sucked right out of him when she came. The anal beads had been the perfect touch for a backdoor virgin, and he couldn't argue with the results. Feeling the ripples of her orgasm clench his dick had almost done him in. Somehow, he'd managed to stall his own release in order to push her further. Now that she knew the delights of anal play, he looked forward to extending her education.

Gripping her hips with both hands, he pulled out and slammed back in. He loved the sound of skin on skin, loved the way her ass cushioned his thrusts, the way his balls flayed against her clit. After her orgasm, her clit had become even more sensitive, and each time his balls had touched her there, she'd moaned and writhed. Letting his thumbs stray to the cleft of her ass, he pushed against the tight rosebud so recently breached and was rewarded with a gasp.

"I'm...going...to...come...again," she panted. "I...can't...stop...it."

Shit. He'd never expected this kind of response from her. The muscles in her thighs clenched, as did the ones across her belly. He slipped a hand beneath her for support.

"Let it come, angel. Let it come." He pushed his thumb past the barrier.

She gripped his cock in a velvet vise. He clenched his jaw tight, grinding his teeth. A fireball ignited in the small of his back and rocketed through his groin, setting his balls aflame.

"Fuck." Pleasure blinded him, and he shot off like

fireworks on the Fourth of July. His body jerked and thrust, each ball of flame erupting from his cock. He fell on top of her, wrapping her in his arms, and she collapsed beneath his weight.

He rolled to his side, pulling her with him. After releasing her wrist cuffs from their restraints , he lazily stroked her breasts, her stomach, her mound. His fingers flicked across her clit.

"Ahh ," she cried, thrusting toward his hand.

He rolled her to her back and settled between her thighs. "Again. I need you again."

"Yes." Her arms wrapped around his shoulders, her legs around his waist,and he slid inside her.

He'd never get enough of this woman.

✦✧

She dropped her shoulder and craned her neck in an effort to see the drawings on her back. Unless she opened the drapes on the two-way mirror, which she wasn't going to do, she would have to wait until she got home. Her legs still trembled from the awesome sex, but she couldn't fault Master for that. He'd held her for a long time following their last fuck—though she had to admit, calling it a fuck didn't feel right.

All the other times, yes, but the last time—that had been more like making love. The way he'd touched her had been different than the times before. It seemed as though he really cared about her, like she were more than an occasional fuck.

Oh, how she wished that were true. Up until today, she would have been happy with their previous arrangement, but after the things he'd done to her, with her…she wasn't so sure. Looking down at the artwork on her front, smeared now with sweat and other bodily fluids, she couldn't help but smile. Along with colorful flowers and hearts strategically drawn all over her, he'd staked his claim in no uncertain terms. She lost count of the number of times he'd written the word "mine."

She belonged to him, in every sense of the word. Whoever this Master was, he owned her, body and soul, and…heart. She pulled on the sweats she'd worn on the way to the Dungeon, slipped the blindfold into her purse, and waved goodbye to Janette on the way out.

"I have something for you," Janette said from behind her desk. "Master J left it for you."

She thanked the receptionist and took the padded envelope she held out. Hand printed on the front was a note—"Do not open until this evening at eleven p.m."

Chapter Ten

Talk about distracted. Carrie closed her eyes then opened them again. Sleep wasn't going to happen. Why try?

But the envelope wouldn't leave her alone. She stood in her walk-in closet, her chin on her shoulder, admiring the red lines on her ass in the full-length mirror. Not the flowers she'd thought, but handprints. Master's handprints. Neatly outlined on her ass cheeks with colorful markers.

Even after all they'd done, the handprint outlines remained. They were smudged in a few places, but were in better condition than most of his artwork. She couldn't bring herself to wash the handprints off—not yet anyway. She carefully removed the stickiness from her thighs and the markings from the rest of her body, but the handprints remained.

She'd never been spanked before. Todd had taken a flogger to her once, but that had felt different—the flogger putting distance between them. The touch of Master's hands on her skin had been personal. She enjoyed a bite of pain during sex—had enjoyed the flogging Todd had given her, but she couldn't remember ever experiencing the intimacy she'd felt when Master spanked her.

Everything her master did seemed personal. She

loved the feel of his callused hands against her skin, abrading but at the same time gentle, as though he knew he could easily overpower her but chose to seduce her instead. Even the slaps to her ass had been delivered with care. He'd reined in his strength, providing her with a measure of discipline she wouldn't forget, then tempering it with kisses and careful handling.

She closed her eyes, remembering the press of wet lips on her hot skin after he spanked her. The kisses were praise for her bravery in accepting her punishment—not a request for forgiveness. He didn't apologize, and he didn't expect her to either. If she did what he said, there would be no need to make amends. And if he performed his duties well as her master, he, too, would have no need to request forgiveness. And he was very good. They both might be novices at the lifestyle, but Master seemed born knowing how to pleasure her.

She eyed the envelope again. Fifteen long hours to wait before the contents were revealed. She'd go mad if she sat around remembering the night before and waiting. She could go into her office and work, but the idea of seeing people today didn't appeal—not that anyone could tell how she'd spent the last two nights by looking at her. But she knew, and here, alone in her apartment the knowledge was a cherished secret she wanted to keep all to herself. One she could examine any time she wanted without anyone asking questions.

The decision made to work from home, she pulled on jeans and a T-shirt. Trying her best to push thoughts of Master and the mysterious envelope aside, she searched the Internet for the information she needed for her steroid article.

She set up interviews with researchers and medical professionals with the credentials to lend integrity to her story. She'd only touched the tip of the iceberg, but it was a place to begin. Once she had the facts, she would tackle the issue of steroid abuse from a more personal side. She compiled a list of athletes, amateur and professional, who'd admitted using the illegal substances, and a few who'd maintained their innocence. Last, she made a list of families who had lost a loved one because of steroid use. She wouldn't contact them until the story was nearly finished. By then, she would have a list of questions to ask based on the latest research.

She worked through lunch, only stopping when she couldn't ignore the rumblings from her stomach any longer. After nuking a frozen dinner, she turned on the television for company and sat on the floor to watch the evening news with her back to the sofa and her dinner on the coffee table.

The lead stories were the usual—fires, murders, and robberies. Not exactly great dinner companions. She was looking for the remote when a name caught her attention. Martin McCree.

∾∾∾

Crouched behind the plate, Jason signaled the pitch to his brother on the mound. One more out and the Mustangs would record another win. The pitch came in low and inside—unhittable, but that hadn't stopped the batter from swinging.

He threw the ball back and grinned. Piece of cake. His brother was better than ever following surgery on his elbow. All that physical therapy and forced workouts had resulted in a world of good for both of them.

At first, Jason accompanied Jeff to his workouts to offer his support, and maybe to keep his brother from giving up, at least on mending his physical self. But he realized early on the extra workouts benefitted him, too. After that, he went because he'd wanted to. As a result, both brothers had never been in better physical shape than they were this season.

Adjusting to the psychological changes had taken them both a little longer. He had to hand it to his brother. Jeff had seen the error of his ways with Megan a lot sooner than he had with Stacey. Marrying Megan had been the final key to Jeff's recovery—and the reason Jeff had returned to the Mustangs' bullpen with a real shot at the record book and the Hall of Fame.

Another swing and a miss brought the Mustangs one pitch closer to the final out. Jason signaled to his brother and raised his glove in readiness. He couldn't have asked for a better throw. The ball came in fast, spinning on a certain trajectory only the two of them knew would shift at the last moment giving the batter insufficient time to adjust his swing. He focused on the ball, not even the arc of the bat cutting through his line of vision broke his concentration. His palm stung as the ball smacked into his glove. Before the plate umpire confirmed the final out of the game, he was on his way to the mound.

"Great pitching," he said, grabbing his brother in a macho hug. "Damn, it's good to have you back."

"I've been back for a while now," Jeff said, returning the hug. "You weren't so bad yourself tonight. Four-for-four with two homers and three RBI's. You're on fire, man."

Jason shrugged. "The season started off shitty, but it's looking up."

The team surrounded them. He smiled and offered his congratulations to everyone for a job well done. This was the fun part, celebrating with his teammates, but a gaggle of reporters waited for him outside the dugout, and he'd have to make an appearance on the local station's post-game show as well.

He'd answered the same questions a dozen times, doing his best to keep a smile on his face and put the credit for the win on the entire team, while his internal clock told him Carrie would be waiting for his call. By now, she would have opened the envelope he'd left for her and found the prepaid cell phone. He'd purchased another one for himself. He hated acting like a drug dealer, using untraceable phones, but he couldn't risk what was shaping up to be the best season of his career on a potential scandal. If the press, who had just spent the last hour building him up as a hero, caught wind of his sexual preferences, he'd go from hero to zero faster than a homerun ball could fly out of the stadium.

Wouldn't they be surprised to learn those same sexual preferences were responsible for his success this season? Like he'd told his brother, the season had started off shitty, despite being in top physical condition, because his head hadn't been in the game. When Stacey left him, his confidence had gone with her. But now he had it back, all because of his angel. Carrie's sweet submission and the way she'd accepted him for who he was without censure or judgment had bolstered his confidence like nothing ever had.

It was a simple formula. He was happy. Correction—he was on top of the world, and that translated into improved job performance. But he couldn't tell the press that. Instead, he credited the improvement in his hitting to those extra workouts with Jeff and good old-fashioned practice. It was true to a degree, and it was all the explanation they were going to get. His private life was just that—private.

๙๑๑

She slit the seal on the envelope and upended it on the coffee table. A cell phone, a tube of lube, and a small pink butt plug slid out, along with a folded note. She clenched her thighs tight to quell the instant need and quiver of nerves that accompanying the sight of the little plug. Unable to sit still, she walked to the kitchen and poured herself a glass of wine, and leaned against the counter to read the note.

Prepare yourself for my call this evening. Remove your clothes and slip into bed. Take these items with you. No need to be nervous, angel. We'll do this together.

Desire and anticipation shuddered through her. His note was as forceful and domineering as he was in person, yet he'd taken the time to address her fears. She dropped to her knees and read the note again, imagining him speaking the words. His voice filled her head, strong, commanding, and reassuring, and her pussy creamed. She could do this. They would do it together.

Clutching the edge of the counter for support, she rose to her feet. Her whole body trembled, and clutching the wine glass with both hands, she took a fortifying sip, then another. She refilled the glass, the bottle clinking against the rim. On shaky limbs, she returned to the living room and the objects on the table.

Grabbing the hem of her T-shirt, she lifted it over her head and dropped it on the sofa. She shimmied out of her jeans, which unceremoniously joined her shirt. Another sip of wine and her bra and panties topped the pile of clothes. Naked, she gathered his gifts and the wineglass and walked down the short hallway to her bedroom.

Between the cool sheets, she sipped the fortifying drink, and waited. With each minute, the need to touch herself grew greater. Master would be disappointed if she did. He might spank her or maybe he would think of another way to punish her. Did she dare defy him? The phone rang, startling her, and put an end to all thoughts of disobedience.

"Master," she said, deferring to him at once.

"Angel."

Her pussy creamed at the sound of his voice and the wealth of meaning in his tone. She was his, even outside the Dungeon.

"I followed your instructions, Sir."

"I knew you would. I wish I could be there tonight to do this for you, but this will have to do. I'm sure you'll accomplish the job to my satisfaction."

Anxiety mixed with anticipation fluttered along her skin, the reality of what she was about to do setting in. "I'll try, Sir. I've never done anything like this before."

"That's not a problem. The plug is small. It won't cause you any discomfort once you have it inserted." He paused, and she thought she heard a sigh. "Angel, before we go any further tonight, I need to let you know...I have to be out of town for the next five days. If you need me, call me using the phone I gave you. My number is programmed in it. If I don't answer, leave a message and I'll return your call. If it takes me several hours, don't think I'm ignoring you. I'm not. I want to talk to you more than you can imagine, so don't worry. I will return your call when I can."

"Thank you, Sir."

"You're welcome. I want to know everything you think and feel while I'm gone. If you're horny, I want to know. If you experience any discomfort from the plug, I want to know."

"Yes, Sir. I promise to share these things with you."

"That makes this trip almost bearable, angel. Now, I'm going to talk you through inserting the plug. I want you to wear it until you wake in the morning, then you may remove it. You're to wear it every night while I'm gone. Each night, I want you to call and tell me when you've put it in. I want to know how it feels—in detail. Remember, I'm not there. I can't read your body language over the phone. I need to know everything you're feeling—good or bad."

"Yes, Master."

"Good girl. Now, tell me about your bed. Do you have a headboard or a footboard?"

"Yes, Sir. I have both."

"That pleases me. I want you on your knees, facing the headboard, close enough you can touch it. Spread your knees wide. Do it now."

She shifted pillows out of the way and moved into position. "Okay."

"Put the phone on speaker and place it on the bed in front of you. Then I want you to open the lube, and squirt a generous amount onto one hand. Don't skimp on the lube. Put the other hand on the headboard to brace yourself while you spread it on your asshole. Do it now."

"Yes, Sir." She could hardly work the buttons on the phone with her trembling hands. She couldn't believe she was actually going to do this. Even though he was miles away and couldn't see her, his voice was in the room with her. Since she had never seen him anyway, did it matter if she was in the Dungeon or her bedroom?

She managed to activate the speaker function and placed the phone on the mattress. "The phone is in place. Can you hear me, Master?"

"I hear you, angel. Now the lube. Describe it to me. I want to make sure you use enough."

She squirted a glob onto the fingers of her right hand. "I'd say it's about the size of a quarter, Sir."

"More. I want your ass wet from cheek to cheek. I

couldn't bear it if you were to hurt yourself."

"Yes, Master." She squirted more on her hand. "I've got twice as much now, Sir."

"That's good. Now, lean over and grasp the headboard. Bend over so your bottom is high and your cheeks are open, then spread the lube on your asshole. Coat it good. Work it inside with your finger."

She braced against the headboard and closed her eyes, imagining Master watching her. The cold gel met her heated skin and she gasped.

"Are you okay?" he asked.

"Yes, Sir. It's cold."

"Tomorrow, warm the tube in hot water."

A cold chill that had nothing to do with the temperature of the lube ran down her spine. She swallowed hard before replying. "That's a good idea, Sir."

"Are you working it inside your hole?" he asked.

"I'm trying, Sir." She pushed against the tight muscles, gathering up the courage to actually do it.

"Just do it, angel. If I was there, I'd have more than my finger up your ass by now."

She imagined Master's cock pushing…demanding entrance and the butterflies in her stomach multiplied. She closed her eyes tight and thrust her finger past the tight barrier. A hoarse moan escaped her throat. "Oh! I did it, Master!"

"Excellent, angel. I knew you could do it. Now, work your finger around. Tell me how it feels."

She wiggled her finger, dared to slide it part of the way out and back in. She'd never dreamed that area could be so sensitive. "It feels good, Sir. Really, really good." She focused all her thoughts on the area. "It makes me weak, but horny, Sir. It's hard to explain."

"I'm glad to hear you're enjoying it. Does it hurt to have your finger there?"

"No, Sir. It feels…good. I never knew…."

"That's what this is about, angel, expanding your knowledge."

"Is that a pun, Sir?"

He chuckled. "Yes, unintentional but a pun. I think

you're having too much fun without me. Take your finger out now and put some lube on the plug."

Carrie obeyed, coating the plug liberally with lube. "Ready, Sir."

"Resume your position. Place the plug against the hole, but don't push it in until I tell you to."

Again, she closed her eyes, mimicking her dungeon experience. She didn't think she would have to nerve to do this with her eyes open, even knowing no one witnessed her actions. "Ready, Sir."

"You sound out of breath. Does this arouse you?"

Her breasts tingled, and the butterflies in her stomach fluttered with anticipation rather than anxiety. "Yes, Master."

"Tell me what you're feeling right now."

"I'm nervous and excited. When I close my eyes, I'm in the Dungeon with you. I can imagine you standing over me, waiting and watching to see me do this."

"Do what, angel? Say it. You're going to have to get over your shyness. When we're together, most of the time I can see for myself what you're feeling, but over the phone, I have to rely on your words and your honesty."

He was right. If she wanted this to work, she needed to get over her shyness. Her face flamed, but she said the words he wanted to hear. "Watching me insert a butt plug, Sir."

"Much better. Now, tell me how that feels against your hole."

"It's cold…and hard. Wet."

"And do you want to push your hips back against it?"

"Yes, Sir. I want that very much. I'm not sure if I'm going to like it. I think I might, based on how my finger felt, but it still feels um…taboo? I think that's what I'm trying to say."

"Anything else, angel?"

"Yes." She hesitated then decided on honesty. "My pussy aches for your cock, Master."

"That's good to hear." The sincerity in his voice reminded her of warm, reassuring stroke along her spine. "My cock aches for your pussy and your ass. As a matter of fact, I'm stroking it right now."

Oh, God. She was dying of horniness, and he was getting himself off. Her mind blanked on a response. "Uhh...."

"Don't worry, little one. Once the plug is in, I'll see to your pleasure, too."

"Thank you, Sir. I don't think I can make it until you come home." *Or even the next few minutes.*

"You can, and you will. Tonight is special. It's your first time to wear a plug, so I'll grant you an orgasm to celebrate. But the rest of the week, the no touching rule applies. If you're horny and think you might touch yourself, call me immediately. Under no circumstances are you to pleasure yourself."

"Yes, Master. I understand."

"Good. Now, press harder so just the tip goes in. Tell me how it feels."

She pressed the plug against her anus. The tight muscles gave way, and she eased the tip of the plug inside.

"It's...in, Sir. It feels, so...oh...." She struggled to recover her equilibrium, her breaths reduced to short, ineffective pants. Weakness stole over her body. And this was only a small plug. Oh God, what would it be like to have Master's cock inside her? "I can hardly breathe, Sir," she managed between panicky gasps.

"Press it all the way in now—hard."

She took a shuddering breath and pressed hard. The plug slipped deep, the tight ring of muscles closing around the shaft.

She grasped the headboard with both hands and held on tight. "Oh, God! It's in. It feels...I don't know...Oh, God." She was babbling, but she couldn't help it. The feelings were too much, too overwhelming to keep inside. "I'm weak, Master. I think all my muscles have turned to jelly. And I'm horny. So damned horny. I need you."

"Is your hand still on the plug?" he asked with a matter of fact voice that coaxed her to come down from the adrenaline mountaintop.

"No, Master. Please...I need." Her arms trembled. She couldn't remember a time she was this desperate for release.

"Shh. Calm down. Breathe, angel. Relax. Concentrate on the plug. Feel it. Tell me what I would see if I was looking at your ass right now."

His calm voice was better than any mood-altering drug. She drew oxygen into her lungs, letting it out slowly. She could do this, but only because he believed she could.

"The plug. The base. It lays flat against my cheeks like one of those brass brads, only its pink plastic. I wish…I wish you could see it, Master."

"Take a picture with the phone and send it to me."

Carrie froze. She'd heard the stories — people sexting their lovers and the photos going viral.

"Now, angel. I want to see your ass."

"Sir…."

"You don't trust me, angel? Your ass is mine, and if and when I show it to someone else, that will be my decision — not yours. Now hold the camera up to your ass and snap the photo."

"Yes, Sir." Her fingers were clumsy on the tiny controls. It took three tries to get a decent picture, but the end result was more erotic than she'd thought possible. That it was her ass in the photo filled her with pride. Master would love it!

"Beautiful, angel. Your ass is simply beautiful. You don't have any idea how hard I got imagining the plug in your ass, but this photo…it brings me to my knees."

Heer breath caught. To hear him so candidly admit how she affected him empowered and confirmed she'd made the right decision submitting to him. Her earlier uncertainty seemed ridiculous, but what was done, was done.

"Your hesitation to follow my instructions will be punished when I return. I promised you release earlier, and I won't go back on my promise. But understand, your disobedience will be punished."

"Yes, Master. I understand."

"I hear the arousal in your voice. Is that for the orgasm I promised, or the punishment?"

"Both, Sir. I just wish you were here to give them to

me in person."

"I wish that were possible, but it's not. Brace yourself on the headboard again. Put your heels together and spread your knees. Then I want you to sit back so your ass rests on your feet."

Carrie got into position. "I'm ready, Sir."

"How does it feel?"

Sexy. Naughty. "My pussy feels exposed, and my heels put pressure on the plug, Sir. It feels like you're there, pushing it inside me."

"Good. That's just what I was hoping you would say. I want you to touch yourself now. Wet your fingers, but don't put them inside. Touch your clit—nothing else."

Sheswiped her fingers along her slit, coating her clit with her juices. "I'm touching it, Sir."

"Take another picture. I want to see."

This time she didn't hesitate. She snapped the photo and sent it quickly.

"Lovely. You're very wet. That pleases me. Now I want you to work your clit. Press down on it, move your fingers in a circular motion. Do it over and over. Talk to me. Tell me how it feels."

For a woman who made her living stringing words together into coherent, meaningful sentences, she could barely get single syllables from her brain to her lips. "This…wicked…um…oh my! Master…I…ohhh…."

"Move your hips. Feel the plug."

She rocked her pelvis, grinding her ass cheeks against her heels. The plug shifted and her clit throbbed in time with each forward thrust. "Uuhhh…Ahh…Oh, fuck, that feels good, Master. The plug… moving inside… Ohh. Master. No idea… so much…. Full. Possessed. Weak and…powerful…at the same time."

"Work your clit, angel. Come for me."

In a matter of seconds, she came. Her inner muscles clamped down on her empty pussy, working the plug lying so close inside her.

"Let me hear you, angel. I need to know what you're feeling."

A garbled scream worked past her lips "Ohh…fuck

that feels…so good."

"That's it, angel. Ride it out. More pressure on your clit. Draw it out, sweetheart."

The orgasm ravaged her body like a summer storm, leaving her wet and completely wrung out. "Master," she sighed, the last tremors rocking her body.

"You are simply magnificent, angel. Thank you. I came with you, you know. I couldn't help it. Because of you, I've got cum all over me."

She smiled at the teasing tone of his voice. She'd pleased her Master. Warmth spread through her body and, along with it, a bone-deep fatigue. She picked the phone up and was surprised to see how shaky her hands were.

"I'd lick it off for you if I could," she said, meaning it with all her heart. She had no qualms about serving him in any way he would permit her.

"You're a naughty little angel, aren't you?" His laugh was rich and deep. "If you were here, I'd rub your face in it, then I'd fuck your mouth until I came again." He sighed.

"A cum facial, Sir?"

He laughed, and she wished she could see the smile on his face from her joke.

"We'll save that for another time," he said with a soft chuckle. "For now, you need your sleep, and so do I. Slide your feet out from under you and pull the covers over your body. Sleep well. In the morning, you can apply more lube and remove the plug. Then you can cleanse yourself. Until then, I want you to sleep surrounded by the smell of your arousal, knowing I gave you the gift of release. Good night, angel."

"Goodnight, Master."

Chapter Eleven

Good God.

Jason sat naked on the sofa, his legs spread wide. His cock was still semi-hard against his cum-spattered stomach. Shit. The woman was abso-fucking perfect. It was tempting to look at the photos again, but like he'd told her, they both needed rest. He headed toward the shower, all the time wondering how the hell he was supposed to sleep after the most incredible phone sex he'd ever had.

Hot water only brought images of Carrie's luscious body to mind. He'd take her every which way and then some if she'd been there in his shower. He rinsed off and finished up with a blast of cold water. It helped but didn't completely obliterate her from his mind. Over the last few weeks, he'd given up trying to block her from his thoughts. It wasn't going to happen. She was the first thing he thought about when he woke up, and the last when he crawled into bed at night. He couldn't believe how quickly she'd come to mean so much to him. No other woman had ever done it. She'd changed his life, pure and simple.

He slipped naked between the sheets, images of Carrie, real and imagined, played through his mind. When sleep claimed him, she was right there with him.

He managed to be ready when Jeff arrived the following morning. Old habits were hard to break—like sharing a ride to the airport with his brother for the team's frequent road trips.

He handed his bag to the limo driver and slid into the backseat. He'd never seen his brother as happy as he'd been these last few months. Shortly after his return to the active roster, Megan announced she was pregnant. Ever since, Jeff had walked around with a permanent grin on his face and today was no exception.

"Man, you look like shit," Jeff said by way of greeting.

"Yeah, and you look like you just got laid."

"Maybe I did." He waggled his eyebrows. Accompanied by the ever-present grin, it was more than Jason could take that early in the morning.

"Can it or I'll tell your wife you're bragging again."

Jeff's face sobered. Jason only felt a little bad about ruining his brother's good mood.

"I only brag to you. She wouldn't mind," he said. "What's wrong with you this morning?"

Jason stared out the side window, letting the question hang in the air. He knew what was wrong. He missed Carrie, and he hadn't even left town yet. "Do you miss Megan on the road trips?"

"Hell, yeah," Jeff said. "I've tried to get her to come along, but the damned stubborn woman isn't going to quit her job until right before the baby comes."

Stubborn women. He'd never let Carrie work…. *Ah, shit. What am I doing?* He barely knew the woman, and his imagination was ordering her pregnant self to quit her job. He didn't even know what the fuck she did for a living. Jeff elbowed him in the ribs, snapping him back to the present.

"You used to miss her, too," Jeff said, reminding Jason of when they'd first met Megan and the three of them had tried to make a relationship work. During that time, he had missed her when they'd been from her, but those memories didn't compare to the current empty feeling in his gut. This was so much more, like he was leaving a part of him behind.

"I did. I still miss her in my own way. You're a lucky man," he said, keeping up his end of the conversation.

"I am," Jeff said. "No two ways about it."

There were disadvantages to having a twin, and one was the way Jeff sensed things about Jason without him saying a word. He could feel his brother studying him. "Leave it alone, bro."

"This new woman has you all tied up, doesn't she?" Jeff asked then quickly corrected himself. "Or rather, you've got her all tied up. Which is it?"

"Just shut the fuck up, will you? I miss her."

"It's only a few days, and there are these things called phones." He pulled his cell from his pocket and held it out. "If you both have one, you can talk to each other from anywhere in the world."

"Aren't you the comic this morning?" Jason smiled at Jeff's attempt to drag him out of the funk he'd been in since he went to bed alone the night before. He batted Jeff's hand away. "Put that thing away before I shove it up your ass."

"That's better." He pocketed his cell phone. "I know how you feel, bro. Being away from my wife is hell, but I talk to her when I can, and focus on how good it's going to feel to hold her again when I get home. It keeps me going."

"I know. But you've had more practice at this than me. Give me a break."

"She makes you happy."

Jason nodded and looked at his brother. "Yeah, she does. I've never been happier, and to tell you the truth, it scares the hell out of me."

"Well, whatever it is she does to you, I hope it continues. Your game is way up, bro. Keep it up, and you'll break the homerun record this season."

"I could," he said, smiling. "Wouldn't that be something?"

"Sure would. I don't know if I have a shot at any records after the stunt I pulled last season, messing up my elbow, but it would be nice if at least one of us got in the record books."

Yeah, wouldn't that be a kicker? "Don't sell yourself short. Your arm is better than new. If you don't go all soft when the kid gets here, you have a shot at the record books and the Hall of Fame."

The flight was undoubtedly the longest of his life. He palmed the cell phone, flipping it over and over in his hand, wishing he could power it up and check for messages. Carrie hadn't called before they'd boarded the plane. If the scene they'd played out last night had affected her as much as it had him, he hoped she was sleeping in.

He turned on his phone the moment the wheels touched the runway and hung back while the others filed up the aisle and off the plane. Bringing up the rear, he listened to the voice message.

"Good morning, Sir." There was a long pause followed by a sigh, as though she wasn't sure she should say what she was feeling. "I miss you."

Damn. The hitch in her voice when she'd said those three little words kicked him in the gut. When he caught his breath, a thrill shot through him. Maybe he wasn't in this alone. Maybe she felt the same way he did. That thought brought a smile to his face while he stood in line to board the bus that would take them first to their hotel, and then to the stadium for tonight's game.

"Hey, Jase."

He looked around for the man belonging to the familiar voice. The short stop, Tanner Haverford, grinned knowingly.

"There's only one thing that will put a smile like that on a guy's face."

He lifted his middle finger at his teammate. "Fuck off, Tanner." He stepped out of line and turned his back to the guys so he could concentrate on Carrie's message.

"Thank you for last night. I…well, it was more than I expected. In a good way," she added hastily.

He couldn't help it, he smiled again. Last night had been more than he'd expected, too.

"I did what you said, Master. I waited until this morning to remove the plug. It still takes my breath away when I think of it inside me. I don't know how to explain it, Master. It makes me feel, vulnerable like I'm giving you more of myself than before. That's a good thing. I wasn't sure about anal play, but last night changed my mind. Once I got past my fear of the plug, I realized how good it felt, and…I felt how much you care for me. It made me all warm inside, knowing you went to so much trouble to do this for me."

He braced one hand against the side of the bus for support. He dropped his chin to his chest and concentrated on breathing while he listened to the rest of the message.

"I can't wait to give you that part of me, Master. Please tell me you'll be home soon. I ache for you."

Holy shit. He saved the message so he could listen to it again, then walked around the corner of the bus out of sight. He parked his ass against the back of the bus with his legs spread for support. *Damn. How the hell did I get so lucky?* He sucked in a deep breath and willed his cock to stand down. The last thing he needed was to walk down the center aisle of the bus with a hard-on. These might be his friends, but they were also grown men with the maturity of adolescents. Traveling with them wasn't all that much different than a road trip to an away game with a bunch of high school jocks.

The back of his head hit the bus with an audible *thunk.* Closing his eyes, he focused on the new distraction. If that didn't work, he might just lie under the bus and let it roll over him. Anything was better than the ribbing he'd take if he stepped onboard in his present condition.

Jeff poked his head around the corner. "You coming?"

"Yeah. Give me a minute."

His brother smirked. "She really does have you hooked." He shook his head. "Man, I never thought I'd see the day."

Jason straightened, adjusting his clothes. For once, he was grateful for the team's travel dress code. The loose fitting trousers and coat would cover the evidence at this stage, where jeans wouldn't.

"Look who's talking." He clamped a hand on Jeff's shoulder and steered him toward the front of the bus. "Megan's going to have you changing diapers before you know it. I'd pay to see that—from a safe distance, of course."

❧

"Fuckin' asshole," Jason muttered. He threw his batting helmet across the dugout. That last pitch had *not* been a strike. He didn't care what the idiot umpire said. He had more hours behind the plate than that yahoo, and he knew when a pitch was out of the strike zone and when it wasn't.

Jerking his batting gloves off, one finger at time, he said, loud enough for everyone to hear, "I hope someone's taking good care of his Seeing Eye dog while he's at work."

His teammates chuckled. They knew. They understood.

"Calm down, son. This isn't the image you want the world to see." The team manager, Doyle Walker stepped up, putting himself between Jason and the TV cameras that were surely trained on him in hopes of capturing a player meltdown. "You know clips like that never die. The networks will play it a million times, then when you die they'll drag it out again and play it in the middle of your memorial tribute."

His shoulders slumped. "I know. But Rankin is blind as a bat. Everyone knows it. I don't know why the league keeps hiring him back, year after year."

"Some things just defy explanation. Remember, you have to go back out there and work with the man. I'm not saying he would, but he could take it out on our pitchers if you cross him."

Someone tapped him on the opposite arm. He took the offered batting helmet and stuffed his gloves into it before shelving them above the bat rack. "You're right. Sorry, Doyle. There's no excuse. I'm just frustrated because I haven't had a hit the entire game."

A big hand clapped him on the shoulder. "They're pitching you careful. A homerun would put us ahead, and they don't want to risk that."

"Yeah." He finger combed his hair. "Doesn't make me like it anymore." He took another calming breath and let it out in a huff. "I was wrong to question his strike zone. I'll apologize to him when I go back out there."

"That's what I wanted to hear. We've got two outs now, better get your gear on."

Fuckin' great.

After the game, Jeff joined him in the locker room. "You okay?"

"Yeah. It's one of those days, you know?"

"Nice hit in the ninth."

"Too little, too late. Maybe if I'd done that earlier, we might have had a chance at winning."

"Hey, aren't you the guy who always tells me the outcome of the game doesn't hinge on a single play or player?" Jeff sat and pulled his cleats off. "Get over it. It's one game."

Jason straddled the bench, facing his brother. "Is that how I sound to you, like a fucking ass?"

Jeff didn't react to the obvious insult. "'Fraid so. Every time I blow a save. You, bro, have single-handedly elevated placating to an art form."

"I'm sorry, man." He shook his head. "I can be a real dickwad sometimes."

"Sometimes," he agreed. He tossed his cleats and socks in the bottom of his locker and unbuttoned his jersey. "But, hey, you're my brother. You can be a dickwad to me all you want." Ever the neat-freak, Jeff folded his jersey and dropped it on top of his cleats. "I'll give you some time when we get back to the hotel. Call her. Get your head on straight for tomorrow."

Jason sighed. "Thanks. You're right, my head wasn't in the game today."

Jeff stood, releasing his belt buckle. "Hard to be in the game when it's so far up your ass." He dropped his pants and stepped out of them and his briefs. The dirty underwear went in his duffle, and after folding his pants, he added them to the pile in his locker. "Find it before tomorrow, okay? I know the team would appreciate it. We need your bat in the lineup, man."

Jason undressed and followed his brother to the shower. Jeff was right about one thing. His head was up an ass, just not his own. He forced that thought away before it traveled south and made his day even worse.

༺ၜၜ༻

Carrie saved the document to her hard drive. So far, so good. With the research done, the article was coming along nicely. Now, all she had to do was add in a few key interviews, and it was good to go.

Balancing a glass of wine and a plate filled with fruit and cheese, she pulled her legs up under her and settled onto the sofa. Hmm. Working from home or sitting in the gray-walled cubby assigned to her at the paper? No contest. If she turned her articles in on time, no one at the paper cared where she did her work, so here, where she could raid the refrigerator and nap on the sofa when she needed a break always won.

Here, she could let her mind wander. That was a good thing—most of the time. She found it difficult to be creative in the bland and noisy atmosphere her newsroom office provided. Yet, today, she had to admit, a little bland and noisy might have been the better option.

She was hyper-aware of her bedroom just a few steps away. She couldn't stop thinking about the small butt plug on her nightstand. She'd even left her computer to go stare at it a few times. Tonight, she would insert it herself, with only the memory of Master's voice coaching her through the process.

She'd kept the cell phone beside her all day, hoping he would call, checking for text messages every few minutes even though it was set to vibrate if a message came in. All day and nothing. Not a peep. Did he receive her message this morning? Maybe she'd been too straightforward, telling him how she felt. But hadn't he insisted on her honesty?

Doubts continued to creep in. Maybe she should email him, or text him, or something to let him know how she was feeling now.

Back and forth. Her thoughts swung from believing she'd done the right thing by telling him her deepest feelings, to fearing she'd said too much and made him angry. She already had one punishment waiting for her when he returned. If she'd earned another, this whole cyber communication thing wasn't going to work out. Even blindfolded, if she listened carefully, she could tell by his footsteps and the way he moved about the room whether she'd pleased him or not. This silence was killing her.

The phone rang, jolting her from her thoughts. Her heart pumped furiously, trying to supply her now alert body with needed oxygen. She picked it up and pressed the answer call button.

"Good evening, angel." The timbre of his voice sent liquid heat to her pussy. She shifted in order to clamp her thighs tight against the ache.

"Master. I'm so glad to hear your voice, Sir. I miss you so much."

"I miss you, too. How has your day been?"

"I worked. I got a lot done, but it was hard to concentrate sometimes. I kept thinking about you, and about last night." She took a breath and plunged on. "Did you get my message this morning?"

His chuckle brought a smile to her lips. "I did. It made me so horny I had to find a place to be alone until I got myself under control."

"I was afraid I'd said too much." She lowered her voice to an almost whisper. "You didn't call me back."

"I couldn't, angel. You shouldn't worry when I'm out of town. I loved your message. I saved it so I can listen to it over and over, just like the photos you sent. They're treasures."

She placed a hand over her heart to keep it from bursting out of her chest. "I'm...no, I-I was about to apologize, but I won't. I'm only human, Sir."

"I'm the one who should apologize. I should have at least texted to let you know how much I loved to hear your voice, and acknowledge your feelings. I won't let that happen again. I don't want you to doubt how special you are to me."

"Thank you, Sir. I knew in my heart, but my brain wouldn't shut up. That happens sometimes."

"I know, angel." His voice changed in an instant.

Gone was the concerned lover, replaced by the Dom in control. "Where are you right now?"

"On my sofa. I'm still wearing the pajamas I put on this morning after my shower."

"Put the phone on speaker and take your clothes off. Put the pajamas away because you won't be needing them tonight."

Blood rushed through her veins so fast it made her dizzy. She laid the phone on the coffee table and removed her clothes.

"Done, Sir."

"Lie down on the sofa and spread your legs. Use your fingers to spread your pussy then send me a picture."

"Yes, Sir." She splayed herself on the sofa. One hand slid through her slick folds while the other positioned the phone and snapped a photo.

"Beautiful, angel. Put the phone down between your legs close to your pussy, and touch yourself with both hands. Use one hand on your pussy, the other on your asshole. I can see from the photo that you're wet already, so spread it around. Don't hurt yourself."

It took some doing, but she found a position that worked. "What do you want me to do now, Sir?"

"Slide two fingers into your pussy, and one into your ass. Then I want to hear you fuck yourself. I want to hear every moan from your lips. Make your pussy talk to me, angel. I want to hear it all."

She closed her eyes and immediately she was back in the Dungeon with her Master hovering near, demanding her submission. She worked her fingers in and out, making sure to repeat any move that created the wet, slurp-smacking sound Master wanted to hear.

"Master, it feels so good. I've never touched myself like this before."

"How deep is your finger in your ass? One knuckle? Two?"

"One, Sir. Ahh, oh, Sir."

"Two knuckles, angel. And work it around, in and out."

"Master. Oh."

"Put your thumb on your clit, angel. Come for me. Now."

"Master," she pleaded. Her body tensed, coiled tight at her core—then exploded, catapulting into a world of pleasure and wrenching cries of ecstasy from her throat.

"Shh, angel," he soothed. "That was beautiful. I love it when you come. I wish it had been my hands on your body, but that can't be right now."

She floated down on a sigh. "Master, that was…thank you."

"Do you remember how to insert the plug?" he asked.

"Yes, Sir. Should I do that now?"

"Go get it and bring it to the sofa. Leave the lube."

Chapter Twelve

Carrie returned, plug in hand. "I've got it, Sir."

"Good, just like last night, but on the sofa. On your knees, legs spread, facing the back, only this time, stick it in your pussy and get it all wet, then put it in your ass. One hard push tonight, angel. It should go in easier."

She assumed her position on the sofa, her breath coming in short gasps. "Here goes, Sir." She brought the plug to her pussy. "I'm going to wet it now."

It slid in easily. She rotated it a little, coating it in her juices. "It's wet," she reported. With her trembling hand, she positioned the plug for insertion. "Here goes…"

"Fast and hard, angel."

With her eyes screwed shut, she pressed hard against the head of the plug. She gasped when it slid into place. "It's in, Master."

"Stay where you are for a minute. How does it feel?"

"Good, Sir. It feels good. I like it. I feel funny sitting here in my living room with my naked, plugged ass in the air. It's so…naughty."

"You are such a horny little thing."

She couldn't help but smile at the humor in his voice.

"Now, don't you go getting too attached to that little piece of plastic. As a matter of fact, there's a new surprise waiting for you at the Dungeon. Ask at the desk tomorrow."

"Yes, Sir. I'll pick it up tomorrow afternoon, if that's okay?"

"No hurry. We'll play with it tomorrow night when I call."

"Thank you, Sir. I feel much better now. I didn't mean to sound so needy earlier."

"You had every right to sound needy. I neglected you today. I thought I was doing it for my own good, because thoughts of you distract me from my job, but I was wrong. I can't think of anything *but* you when I haven't talked to you. I need to hear your voice before I begin my day. I won't make that mistake again."

"You'll call me in the morning, Sir?"

"No. You're going to call me at seven in the morning. I want to be with you when you take the plug out. I promise I'll answer the phone, so do what you have to do this evening, then go to bed. No clothes, angel. I want to picture you in bed naked."

She thanked him again and ended the call.

ॐ

"Times up," Jeff said, letting the hotel room door slam behind him.

Jason set the phone on the nightstand and pulled a pillow into his lap to hide the boner he'd had since he heard Carrie's voice. Not that he had to hide anything from his brother, but he'd taken enough ribbing for one day. He wished he'd had a few more minutes to jack off before his brother came back, but he could take care of that in the bathroom later.

"I just hung up," he said. "Thanks for giving me some privacy." *Time to change the subject.* "How's the little woman?"

"Hormonal. And turning your old room into the biggest, most expensive, nursery in Texas."

"And you wish you were there to help her."

"Damned straight, I do. I hired someone to move the furniture and to paint, but that won't stop her from doing too much."

"She's not sick. She's pregnant. And, she's a nurse.

She won't do anything stupid."

"Fat lot you know. She wants to put a new window in. Says the room needs more light."

"Well, if I know you, you'll do whatever she asks, so you might want to start looking into contractors."

"You're right." He sat on the opposite bed, facing Jason. "I'm her willing slave. Speaking of…how's yours doing?"

"She misses me." He couldn't have wiped the stupid grin off his face if he'd had to. "She's amazing, Jeff. I miss her something awful."

"That's what love does to you. I felt that way—"

"Whoa! Hold it right there." He jumped to his feet and paced the small confines of the room. "I didn't say anything about love."

"Didn't have to. I recognize the symptoms. I had it that bad for Megan almost from the first second I saw her. Why do you think I wrote that invitation on her program instead of just autographing it? She had me from the first moment. It just took me a while to admit it."

"This is nothing like you and Megan. She knew who you were, what your life was like all along."

"But we still kept our relationship a secret. Remember how paranoid we were about the press finding out we were both sleeping with her?"

"That was different."

"How? Look, hiding our relationship hurt Megan. It was wrong. We should have made it clear how much she meant to us from the start instead of pretending she was just a friend. When push came to shove, we denied everything, and that almost cost me the love of my life. Don't be stupid like I was."

"You don't understand. She's never seen me. We talk and email, but when we're together, she's blindfolded. She knows my first name. That's it."

"Who is it you don't trust? Her? Or Yourself?"

That was an easy answer. "Me. I've never been happier, Jeff. This lifestyle feels right, but I can't shake the feeling that it's too good to be true. That it's not going to last. It will be easier on her if she doesn't know who I am if I have to give her up."

"And why would you have to give her up? What are you talking about?"

"I don't have a clue." He shook his head. "I can't explain it."

Jeff shrugged. "Well, until the sky actually falls, can you think positive thoughts and maybe hit a few homers? Preferably with runners on base? And the bullpen would appreciate if you could quit ticking off the home plate umpire."

He accepted the change of subject. Jeff was right. He needed to think positive thoughts and get his head back in the game. "I'll see what I can do. You want me to pitch for you, too?"

"Nah, you can't pitch for shit. I'll handle the hard work, you just swing the lumber."

❧

Talking with Carrie every morning and night had been better than any drug. Jason was pleased with the way the road trip went. He'd posted fantastic stats during the remaining games and he felt it in his bones. He was on a hitting streak and the media was right there with him, discussing the odds of him breaking team and league records this season.

He couldn't wait to touch her, but first, there was the little matter of punishment he'd promised her. Since that first night when she'd hesitated to insert the plug, they'd been through two more plugs, gradually getting larger, and she'd obeyed him without reservation. He had a new plug for her today, one she wasn't going to see until it was too late.

"Good evening, angel." He shut the door behind him. *Damn.* His cock snapped to attention at the sight of her on her knees, waiting for him. Her hair tumbled over her shoulders in shiny waves. He imagined fisting his hands in it while she sucked him off. But that would have to wait for another time. First things, first.

"Are you prepared for your punishment?"

"Yes, Sir. I shouldn't have hesitated to follow your orders. I know you only have my pleasure in mind."

"Yes, that's true. So, let's get the punishment out of the way, then I'll see to your pleasure, and mine."

"Thank you, Sir."

He pulled her to her feet and walked her to the spanking bench. He secured her wrists and ankles so her ass was in the air. "I love to see you like this, angel. I could look at you all day long." He gathered the supplies he needed—a wooden paddle and the new plug from his duffel and lube from the supply in the rack beneath the platform bed. "Since your offense was in regards to inserting the butt plug I provided for your pleasure, it's only fitting that you receive a new one tonight, one of my choosing."

"Yes, Sir."

He spread her cheeks with one hand and examined her anus with his other. After wetting his middle finger in his mouth, he probed the tight hole. "I planned a gentle initiation for you, and you wanted to take that away from both of us."

She gasped and wiggled her hips when he breeched the ring of muscles guarding her entrance.

"Be still, angel. This part of you is mine, and I would never hurt you."

"Yes, Sir. I'm trying, Sir."

"You're still so damned tight, angel." His free hand roamed her body, reacquainting him with her soft curves and silken skin while he allowed her time to adjust to his intrusion. "I love the way your skin feels, and your curves. You're so beautiful, sometimes I can't believe you're actually mine."

Leaning in, he kissed his way down her spine to where his hand rested in the cleft of her ass. He wiggled his finger inside her, startling a moan from her lips. "You don't mind if I take a little time to enjoy this, do you, angel?"

She shook her head once. "No, Sir. My body is yours, Sir."

"Yes, yes it is," he said.

After days of torture, wondering what it would feel like to take this part of her, he couldn't resist a little playtime, now that he was this close. Besides, finger fucking her would only make the next step easier for her in the long run.

He squirted lube on his finger and worked it in and out, massaging her anus. Soon, her hips were moving, thrusting backwards to meet his forward movement.

"You like that, don't you?"

"Yes, Sir," she moaned. "It feels good."

He kept it up, using his finger to gently stretch her. Watching the tight ring pucker and give with each in-out motion, he imagined what it would feel like stroking his hard cock. Soon. One day soon, he would take her there.

"I'd like nothing more than to continue this, but we have another purpose today." Reluctantly, he pulled his finger free.

"This plug is larger than the ones you've used this week." He rinsed his hands at the corner sink then coated the plug with lube. "But I'm bigger." Opening her, he placed the tip of the plug against her hole. "Breathe in, then let it out, angel."

She inhaled, and on her exhale, he pushed the plug past her barrier, all the way to the hilt. She groaned and clenched her cheeks, but he held her open, admiring the view. He stroked along the curve of her back until her shoulders relaxed and her spine dipped low.

"Stunning," he said, gently caressing her hips and trailing his fingers down the sleek line of her thighs. He'd missed her more than he'd ever missed anyone, and now that he was back with her, he knew leaving her behind was always going to be difficult. But knowing she would welcome him back so sweetly would make the trips bearable.

Her slit glistened, and he couldn't resist swiping his hand there to collect the moisture. He held his wet palm to her lips. "Lick, angel. You're so damned wet for me." *And I'm so fucking hard my dick feels like it might explode.*

Her pink tongue swirled over his palm, taking every drop of honey and making him seriously reconsider delaying his gratification. But her disobedience couldn't be ignored. It all came down to trust, and if he failed to follow through on a promised punishment, how could he expect her to trust him to see to her pleasure? He smiled. There was no reason he couldn't combine the two— or her sake, and his.

"I knew you'd like having your ass filled. I know you, angel. There's never any reason to disobey me. Do you understand?"

"Yes, Sir."

Carrie braced herself. The sting of lumber on her ass reverberated through the plug and set off a fireworks display behind her blindfold. She cried out and arched her back—instinctively pulling on the restraints, and tucking her ass under her hips.

"There, now," Master crooned. He palmed her ass, soothing the burn. "God, I love to see your ass red. I can't wait to fuck your brains out."

Two fingers speared her cunt, pumped in and out, stroking a mysterious spot inside that wrenched a moan of pleasure from her lips. She relaxed against his hand. His fingers left abruptly, followed by another stinging slap to her ass that brought tears to her eyes. The plug acted like an antennae, directing the intense vibrations directly to her clit.

"Please, Sir," she begged, choking back a sob.

"That's it, angel." Gentle hands stroked her burning ass cheeks. "You deserve a reward for accepting your punishment so well."

Oh, God. If this was punishment, she might have to defy him on a daily basis! Her ass was on fire, but that was nothing compared to the ache of her pussy. Tears stung her eyes, but they were tears of frustration. That last swat had almost made her come. Her pussy was so swollen, it actually hurt. She needed to come so badly, she'd do anything to make it happen.

"Please. Please. Please," she begged, thrusting her hips high. Then his hand was there, cupping her while one finger played with her clit.

"You want to come, angel?"

"Yes! Please, Sir. Pleeeaaaassseee."

"But I'm not through with you, angel. No coming until I tell you to."

She whimpered.

"Tsk, tsk, tsk." He continued to flick her clit.

She tried to clench her legs together to stop her imminent orgasm, but the restraints prevented any such evasive movement. She clenched her fists, scrunched her eyes tight behind her blindfold and ground her molars. Anything to diffuse the seismic disturbance building between her legs.

"Your control is admirable," he said. "I'm not sure I could stop myself if the tables were reversed."

"Please," she begged through numb lips.

After another flick to her clit, he parted her swollen outer lips. A heartbeat later, his rough tongue scraped across her hard nub and swirled around it. "Now, angel."

Fingers speared her, seeking and finding her sweet spot. He took her clit between his lips and sucked.

Waves of pleasure broke over her, and the sob she'd tried so hard to contain escaped her throat. One large hand clamped her hip in a vise-like grip, controlling her irrepressible need to buck and thrust against his face. The orgasm claimed her, rolling through her body like a thunderstorm over the prairie. His fingers and mouth coaxed her higher and longer until the first sharp pangs of pleasure mellowed to gentle waves he captured with his tongue.

When he unfastened the restraints, she felt like a rag doll. He carried her boneless form to the platform bed and placed her on her side. He stretched out behind her. One hand on her hip slipped to her thigh, then behind her knee.

"Open for me," he said, gently pushing her leg forward. "Stay just like you are, relaxed, sweetheart."

She had no bones or working muscles to move them with, so she lay there, letting him position her anyway he wanted, content to have his hands on her, his soothing words in her ear. His fingers brushed the plug between her butt cheeks, reminding her of its presence. "This has to go now."

She tried to find words to respond, but in their absence, she simply nodded her head in agreement. He gently removed the plug then returned to caress her cheeks. She drifted while he leisurely toured her sated body, soothing and exploring. It didn't matter. After what he'd given her, she'd lie there all night if he wanted. Besides, she loved the feel of his hands on her—strong, but so gentle.

He was the most incredible lover she could imagine. He could be harsh but then could turn right around and give her the most unbelievable pleasure. How he'd come to know her body so well in such a short period of time, she didn't know, and she wasn't inclined to question. It was enough that he had.

In the artificial darkness behind her blindfold, she hovered on the edge of sleep, her face cradled on her hands, her upper leg still crooked at the knee like an outrigger, keeping her balanced on one hip.

"My turn, angel." The words whispered across her cheek.

"Um." She licked her dry lips and rolled her head toward the deliciously seductive voice.

"Just relax. Let me do all the work."

Master. Yes, you do all the work. "Um," she hummed, resuming her slumberous pose. Somewhere in the back of her mind, she registered the telltale opening of a condom, followed by a heavy leg pinning her thigh to the mattress, and the pressure, nudging, prodding.

"So. Tight."

More pressure. A warm palm against her stomach. Her body surrendered to the insistent pressure. She woke with a start, tensing at the invasion of her body.

"Fuckin' damn, that feels good."

Master. Inside her. There.

"Are you okay?" One big hand stroked from her shoulder down to her hip where she registered the close press of his body against hers.

Her heart raced. She focused on the new sensations. His body dwarfed hers and she was helpless against his greater strength. She might have been frightened, but inexplicably, she knew she was safe.

He cradled her ass, stroked her thigh, her back, her shoulder, arm and breasts. No part of her went untouched. His voice soothed in tandem with his hand. His fingers speared through her hair, across her scalp, and down to encircle her neck. A gentle kiss of his fingertips along her lips.

She tried to capture them with her tongue, but he moved again, and all she could do was feel.

Cherished.

"Yes," she whispered, realizing the truth. "Oh, God...Sir...."

She'd known all along he would claim this part of her, but in her wildest imaginings, she hadn't comprehended what it would mean. This was total submission. Even more so than taking him into her pussy. Giving him this part of herself acknowledged his absolute dominion. He owned her body. Completely.

Gentle fingers tipped her chin, lifting her face to his. For once, she cursed the blindfold that separated them. His lips covered hers, his tongue taking up the same rhythm as his thrusts, staking his primordial claim on her. She managed to bring her hand up to cradle his face, trying to convey everything she was feeling through her lips and the touch of her palm on his jaw.

He broke the kiss, laying his cheek against hers. "Thank you," he whispered in her ear.

Until that moment, she hadn't comprehended what her total submission meant to him, but now she knew. He needed her submission, and she needed him to guide her. Two simple words embodied what was between them. She'd given him her body, and now, with this new understanding, she offered him her heart and her soul.

"I'm yours," she said, crooning the words against the shell of his ear.

"Mine." He rocked his pelvis hard against her ass.

She relaxed in the safety of his care, giving her body over to him. He leaned away—for better leverage she supposed— and his thrusts became more forceful. He fisted a hank of her hair and jerked her head back. His other hand dug into her hip, anchoring her. He was hard everywhere she was soft. Flesh slapped against flesh. He took and she gave.

He rode her hard, but in her darkness, there was peace knowing she could give him what he needed.

"Ahh, angel. I. Can't…."

His cock grew impossibly harder inside her. She willed her body to soften, to become a pillow to catch him when he fell. He stilled.

"Christ almighty!" His hips ground against her in short, forceful thrusts. Then he was coming, claiming her.

She sighed, savoring his release, knowing in her heart it represented a bond that couldn't be broken.

He loosened his hold on her hair, wrapping himself around her again from shoulder to their joining. He placed a single kiss on her lips. A benediction. An affirmation. A single kiss that said he understood the significance of the moment.

Christ. He couldn't move. Didn't want to move. His heart pounded against his ribcage—a sure test of its strength. If the repair he'd undergone when he was nine was going to fail, it would have tonight. He made an effort to move. She was soft beneath him, so perfect in her submission. He'd let his libido run wild, taking what he wanted from her long before he'd planned. But there'd been something about the way she'd cuddled against him when he'd laid down beside her that called to him to stake his claim now. To demand her complete submission. No. To *take* her complete submission.

He'd given her little choice in the matter, breaching her defenses while she slept. He'd been wrong to do it that way, but he couldn't regret it now. He would have withdrawn had she asked, when she'd become fully aware of what he'd done, but she hadn't. He'd never felt anything like it—he way her body had yielded to his, offering him complete dominion. It's what he'd dreamed of since his first erection—owning a woman's body. Christ, he'd yearned to give her pleasure, to see her lose control under his tutelage. To have a woman trust him so completely was humbling.

He tipped her face to his, wishing he could offer her the same level of trust she'd given him and remove the blindfold, but he couldn't do it. Not yet.

"Angel?"

"Yes, Sir?" Barely a whisper.

"Are you okay?"

"Mm-hmm," she purred.

"I didn't hurt you?"

"No. Never," she sighed.

Jason allowed himself to relax. He arched, watching his cock slide from her. Good God, he couldn't believe what a lucky bastard he was to have found this woman. She whimpered and clenched her cheeks together.

"Shh. Let me take care of you." He rolled her to her back and lay beside her.

"Hold me," she whispered, nuzzling her cheek against his chest.

He wrapped her in his arms and held her until she drifted off to sleep again. Then he held her some more.

His brother was right, damn it. He'd gone and fallen in love with her. It was such a foreign feeling; he hadn't recognized it right away. He'd loved women before, but he'd never been *in* love. His love for Carrie filled his heart, and felt so right he almost couldn't remember what it felt like not to love her. He didn't really know anything about her, but he knew she was his. Cradled against his body, she was a perfect fit. He had to find a way to tell her who he was. Todd and Brooke said he could trust her, that she wasn't the kind to shout his personal business to the world.

Damn, he hoped that was true because he couldn't imagine his life without her, and he damned sure couldn't keep her blindfolded for the rest of their lives. He slipped a finger beneath the elastic band securing the eye mask, toying with it. All he had to do was remove it while she slept, and when she woke he would be looking into those incredible blue eyes of hers.

He made sure the elastic band was once again in place, and scooted away, extricating himself from their embrace. With a fresh condom in place, he returned, settling himself between her thighs. Pushing her wide, he swiped his tongue along her slit, sucking her clit between his teeth.

Carrie woke with a jolt to total darkness and someone—her Master—between her legs.

"Sir," she moaned, lifting her hips to meet his playful tongue. A strong hand on her stomach pressed her back down.

"Be still." His tone conveyed the unspoken words "or else".

She raised her hands over her head to grip the edge of the mattress. It was torture to endure without responding. His tongue swirled and dipped, laved and lapped and drove her out of her mind. Firm hands held her thighs wide, exposing her completely. Desire, dormant following their earlier session sprang to life, rising like the tide at full moon, fast and high.

"So beautiful," he breathed against her moist folds. His tongue swooped low to tease her backdoor. She bit her lower lip to keep from protesting his actions.

"Are you sore there?" he asked.

"A-a little, Sir.

He massaged her gently, coating her with her own juices. "Relax, angel. No more there tonight. You were very brave. I can't tell you how much it means to me to have claimed this part of you."

She willed her body to relax and accept his touch.

"Nice, angel. Tell me how you felt having me inside you here." His finger pressed softly against the rosebud.

"I felt…weak…defenseless. Safe. It's hard to explain, Sir. I was scared at first, but then…." He fingered her again, and she lost her train of thought. "I can't think when you do that, Sir."

He chuckled and flicked his tongue over her clit while he toyed with her backdoor.

"Go on. What were you going to say?"

"I, um…I felt…conquered, possessed. I knew it before, Sir, but somehow, giving that part of me made me yours. Completely. I lo—"

He covered her with his mouth, stopping her declaration before she could utter it. This time, she couldn't control her hips, and he didn't ask her to. She met his kisses, offering her body to replace the words he'd stolen from her.

Her orgasm came fast. He drank it in, taking all she offered, demanding more with well-placed kisses until the last tremors left her sated and soft. Only then did he move over her. He pinned her wrists above her head and rode her hard, claiming every inch of her body. Her surrender was complete and absolute. After a few thrusts, she wrapped her legs around his waist, allowing him to go even deeper.

He couldn't get enough. Couldn't possess her enough to sate his need. Her lovely body was flushed with color. Perspiration aided the slip and slap of flesh battering flesh. Each thrust wrenched soft moans from her lips and drove him past the point of reason. She. Was. His. Always. Forever.

"Master." The word was both affirmation and plea.

"Come," he said, answering the unspoken request.

Her uninhibited response propelled him over the edge.

Sweet Jesus. Liquid fire shot through his veins, sparked an inferno in his groin, sending a flash flame from his balls to his dick. He ground against her, the primal urge to mate, to give her his seed, blinded him to everything but his physical need. No other woman had ever robbed him so completely of his ability to think, to have a care for his partner. Nothing short of a knife to his balls would stop him from possessing this woman.

A monosyllabic mantra punctuated each grinding, blinding thrust. *Mine. Mine. Mine.*

He collapsed, his face buried in the crook of her neck. Her scent filled his nostrils, and he fought to bring his major body systems back to a sustainable rhythm. Her legs fell to the mattress, bracketing him in her soft warmth. He lifted his head. Her cheeks glowed. Her ruby lips were parted, her breast rising and falling beneath him with each breath.

"Mine," he said.

"Yours."

He lowered his lips to hers, sealing the bond.

Chapter Thirteen

Jason lowered the newspaper and pushed it across the bar. He sipped the coffee Megan had placed in front of him while he'd been reading. "They can say it all they want, but it won't change the way I play. If I break the homerun record this season, I do. If I don't, I don't. I'm not playing for the record I'm playing for the win. One game at a time."

"So says the man just a few homeruns short of breaking the Mustangs' record and on track to break the major league record for homeruns in a single season," Jeff said from the other end of the bar.

Megan slid a stack of pancakes across the bar. He poured a generous stream of syrup over them and dug in. Since he'd moved to a house of his own, these moments with his brother and sister-in-law had become rare. The woman sure could cook. He missed coming home to one of her meals, but he gave up the right to her cooking—and more—when he'd recognized her love was only for Jeff. But that hadn't stopped him from bumming a meal when he could.

"Yeah, well…." He downed another forkful of syrup-coated clouds. "I can't think about the record and play the game. If I tie it or break it, then I do."

He stopped chewing to watch Megan hoist herself

and her burgeoning belly onto the barstool next to him. She was a beautiful woman, and now that she was pregnant, she glowed. A pang of envy shot through him, but he quickly dismissed it. He'd had his chance with her. They were friends now, brother and sister. The child she carried would be his niece or nephew.

"Think the kid will be able to tell us apart?" he asked.

"Sure he will." She reached for her glass of orange juice. Her basketball-sized belly hindered her, so he slid the glass closer. "Thanks. And yes, anyone who knows the two of you can tell you apart. Jeff's the closed off one, you're the open book. Though I'm having a hard time reading you right now. Not that you aren't welcome anytime, but what brings you here so early on your day off?"

"I'm going to tell her," he said. He'd come close to telling her that night a few weeks ago when he realized he was in love with her, but something cautioned him to take his time. In the last few weeks, he'd introduced her to more adventurous play, and tested her in every way he could think of until he was sure her sexual needs matched his. Now, if only he could be as certain she wouldn't bolt when she found out who he was. If they were ever going to take their relationship out of the Dungeon, she'd have to accept everything that came along with being publicly linked to a celebrity.

"It's about time," Jeff said.

"He's right, Jase. You should have told her a long time ago."

Jason glared across the bar at his brother. "Thanks for keeping my confidence, bro."

"Hey, Megan's family. If you didn't want me to tell her, you should have said so."

Before he could argue, Megan cut in. "I'm here for you, and for her, Jase. If she needs to talk to someone afterwards—"

"Thanks." Jason straightened. "I guess I just needed to remind myself that it can work. Look at you two, all happy and pregnant. I want that, too, and I think she's the one, if she doesn't hate me when she finally sees me and finds out why I've kept her in the dark so long."

"She won't," Megan said, laying a hand on his arm. "You're a good man, Jason Holder. She'll understand your reasons. Who knows? Maybe she won't even recognize you."

He lifted an eyebrow at his sister-in-law. "You've got to be kidding. Since I've gotten within range of the record, my face is all over the place. The Mustangs even put me on buses. And there's that giant building wrap you can see off I-35. She'd have to be blind not to have seen my face around town."

"Well, I'm sure it won't make a difference to her, but if it does, send her to me. I'll set her straight," she said.

He left his brother's house feeling better. Carrie had proven her commitment to him over and over, but still he'd put off the inevitable. Every time he'd introduced another scene devised to test her boundaries, she'd come through, trusting him completely. It was time he did the same. He just needed to come up with the right words to explain why it had taken him so long.

Cowardice? Yeah, that pretty much covered it. At first, he'd feared for his career and Carrie giving him up to the tabloids, but he couldn't imagine her doing such a thing now. She was committed to their relationship, and from their post-scene conversations, he knew she, too, wanted to keep that part of her life private.

But he was still an ass for not telling her the truth. Except now, he feared she wouldn't want to be involved with a celebrity. Right now, she could see his face plastered on the side of a bus and not think anything of it—because she didn't know the man on the side of the bus was the same one who restrained her and administered doses of pain and pleasure to her on a regular basis. He'd done things to her polite society would never understand, and she'd loved it. Guaranteed, she'd never look at his face on a billboard again without some kind of reaction. He only hoped to God it was a positive one.

❧

Carrie read the email, memorizing the instructions for that night, hating that work would keep her away for the next several days. She would miss him terribly. She always did when he was out of town. He'd only be a phone call away, but somehow, this was different. He'd be the one at home, waiting for her to come back, instead of the other way around. Two days. Three, max. That was all. She would survive. They'd been apart before. She could do this.

She typed her reply, informing Master she would be waiting for him tonight, as he'd requested, but adding the news she had to go out of town for her job. Why did this feel so awful like she was cutting herself off from oxygen? She squared her shoulders, lifting her ribcage. Flattening her hand against her midsection, she took a deep breath and let it out slowly. It was perfectly ridiculous the way her finger shook hovering over the computer key that would send her message.

What would he think? He'd said at the beginning he wouldn't interfere with her outside life, and this was her life. Her livelihood. Her job. This interview was all she needed to complete her article, and she'd waited a darn long time to get it. Still, she hesitated. In her heart, she belonged to her master. She loved him, had even come close to saying the words on several occasions.

Insecurity. Doubts.

He'd never said he loved her, but she wanted to believe his actions. The way he cared for her, took her to places she never dreamed she would go spoke of his feelings for her.

In the beginning she'd promised to be honest, but she hadn't exactly done that. He'd insisted she share her feelings with him, and she had…to a point. She had no trouble now telling him how her body hummed with arousal when he clamped her nipples or flogged her. He was always careful, using the pain to bring about the most amazing orgasms. She gave her body freely, and took his in return. But she'd held back the one thing she most needed to share with him, the fact that she loved him.

She needed to tell him, even if it was more than he wanted to hear. It wasn't fair to either of them to keep it to herself. But now wasn't the time, not when her outside life demanded she take herself away from him, even for such a short time. When she returned, she'd tell him how much she loved him, and beg him to open himself to her. If he rejected her because of her feelings, she would deal with the pain of losing him.

Heart pounding, she pushed the key and waited.

❧

"Fuck." Jason swore at the computer. Okay, he could deal with this change of plans. He couldn't tell her tonight, not with her going out of town. If there was fallout, he needed her nearby, not God-only-knew how many hundreds or thousands of miles away. If she rejected him, he wanted to be close enough to convince her otherwise.

He paced his home office, rubbing a hand over his nape. A few more days wouldn't matter. He would continue with his plans for tonight, only he would leave the blindfold in place. When she returned from her business trip, he'd tell her and, if necessary, beg her to become his forever.

Stopping in front of his desk, he ran a finger over the box resting there. The white velvet reminded him of her skin. Unable to decide what one gave to a sub when asking for a lifelong commitment, he'd designed a set that said it all, he thought. The platinum collar, more of a solid necklace, represented her submission, the matching bracelet, a more subtle way for her to declare his ownership, and then there was the flawless diamond ring to symbolize she'd given her heart and her body to him.

He sighed. A few more days wouldn't matter in the great scheme of things.

He sat and typed his response.

❧

She waited, blindfold in place for him, counting heartbeats to judge the time. She'd asked him once how long he watched her before he came to her.

"Not long," he'd said.

"How long is not long?"

"I watch until I see your pussy clench then I know you're aching for me."

"I do that?"

"Yes, angel, you do. That's one of the reasons I like

your pussy shaved, so I can see the way the muscles move when you try to control your need."

Since then, she'd tried to control her body, but it was a game she always lost. He never came to her until he saw those little ripples between her legs. Sitting on the hard chair with her legs splayed, she remembered the other times Master had bound her to a chair like this one, and she couldn't stop her body's reaction to the memory. No sooner had her pussy clenched, than the door opened and Master's familiar footsteps crossed to the two-way mirror.

She sighed when he closed the curtains over the mirror. He promised one day soon to leave them open so anyone passing by, "could see how sweetly she submitted," he'd said. Today was not going to be that day. Thank God.

"Angel," he greeted her.

"Master."

Words were few as he lifted her legs, strapping her knees over the padded risers to expose her pussy. He took his time, carefully lacing the leather sleeves binding her arms behind the chair. To ensure she couldn't move, he fastened a leather strap around her waist, anchoring her hips.

"I understand you have a life besides the one you have with me, angel. Anytime I've gone out of town, I've left you well satisfied, have I not?"

"Yes, Sir. You always see to my needs."

"This is no different. I can't accompany you on this trip, but I'll always be here for you. You'll call me daily at the times I specified in the email I sent a few minutes ago. At such times, you're to be in a place where you're free to follow my instructions to the letter. If you choose to do this in the middle of a restaurant or the privacy of your hotel room, it doesn't matter to me. I've chosen the times to see to your physical needs, and you'll obey."

"Yes, Sir."

"So you don't forget that your body and your orgasms are mine, I've prepared this reminder for you."

Cold metal slapped against her palms and she instinctively curled her fingers around it.

"If you can't go on, drop the bar."

"Yes, Master."

"Open your mouth." The ball gag made her mouth water. She swallowed hard.

"Okay?" he asked.

Carrie nodded. Some sounds had become familiar and expected. Fabric rustling. A zipper. The thud of his shoes when he tossed them aside. She strained to make out the less familiar ones as he prepared for this scene. Her pussy flooded in anticipation when the zipper ground open on the duffel he used to carry their personal toys to and from the Dungeon. So caught up in wondering what he'd brought this time, she almost missed the soft footfalls of his bare feet crossing to her.

His hand on her breast startled her.

"Relax, angel." He gently squeezed and massaged. She gasped when he closed his mouth over her nipple and sucked. She arched her back against her restraints, in an effort to encourage more.

"So beautiful," he crooned, plucking her nipple between his thumb and forefinger. The pinch was hard and fast. The nipple clamp bit down on her distended nub, and stars lit up the darkness behind her blindfold.

"Breathe through it," he urged, cradling the abused breast in his palm. "Shh, angel."

The initial pain subsided and her breathing evened out. He moved behind her, stopping to knead the tension from her shoulders. His touch was magic, reminding her he wouldn't push her beyond what she could bear.

"You know what comes next, angel," he said in that hypnotic voice of his. "Nod if you want me to continue."

She nodded.

He clamped the other nipple, allowing her time to absorb the pain before attaching a chain between the two and looping it up to hook to the ball gag so the clamps pulled her nipples toward her chin. There was no way to move her head without causing more pain.

"Simple, but effective," he said, massaging her shoulders once more. "If I ask you a question, I expect an answer. Do you understand?"

She nodded. The clamps eased, then pulled tight in

tandem with the motion of her head. Once. Twice. The pain was mild, but enough to know if she did anything more, the result would be exponential.

"Excellent." His hip brushed her shoulder when he moved around her.

The slight contact sent her breasts in motion side to side and drew another gasp from her lips. His hands smoothing along the inside of her thighs, stilled her scattered thoughts.

"Remember our first meeting?"

Oh Lord, was this going to be twenty questions or more? She nodded, and two fingers entered her, probing, sliding in and out.

"I examined you then, much like this." His other hand spread her lips. Cold air brushed heated, moist skin. "This is much better. I can see all of you."

Her whole body shuddered when he flattened his tongue over her clit. "I can taste you, too. As a matter of fact, I can do anything I want to you."

He withdrew his fingers, replacing them with something cold and hard that stretched her wide. A keening cry died against the gag.

"Do you like this cock, angel?" He pulled it almost all the way out and inserted it again, twisting as he went.

Holy cow! She twitched her hips in a primal reaction to the invader.

"I asked a question, angel."

She nodded, jerking her nipples in the process. The pain was more welcome this time, distracting her from the giant cock in her pussy.

"It's stainless steel, and so damned big," he said. He kissed a line up the inside of her thigh and down the other, fucking her without pause.

"Do you want it harder?" he asked.

She shook her head, creating a shockwave of pain in her clamped nipples.

"Ah, Christ. You almost made yourself come that time, angel." The cock slipped from her. "Can't have that, now can we?"

Another headshake. She groaned and tried to think of

something, anything to stop her impending orgasm. Grasping at straws, she thought about the trip she would take tomorrow, but it reminded her this scene was a direct result of her announcement that she was going out of town.

"Don't," he commanded. His hand clamped on her jaw. "Not until I say so. Is that clear?"

She nodded. Twin pinpoints of pain shot straight to her pussy, and tears formed behind the blindfold. Callused fingers brushed the moisture from her face.

"If it's too much, drop the bar," he reminded her.

If only she could tell him they were tears of frustration and dropping the bar wouldn't make them go away.

"I see," he said. "Let me tell you what I see then I'll let you have what you want." He slowly circled her. When he spoke, his voice came from behind her.

"I see the most beautiful woman I've ever laid eyes on," he said, his voice coming from behind her. "She's totally at my mercy, exposed in such an intimate way that her trust humbles me. Her lovely body is flushed, calling out for release. She absorbs physical pain and mental servitude and turns them into sexual desire. She's a temptress with her quiet submission and her welcoming body."

Footsteps rounded her, stopping between her legs. "I hear the call. My body is hard, primed to take what's offered, to give what is needed."

The steel cock reentered her, startling another gasp from her lips.

"But this lovely, offered pussy won't have my body tonight. I'm saving that for when she returns to me. Incentive to make that sooner rather than later."

A familiar buzz filled the air.

"Until then, remember I command your orgasms. I decide what fills your pussy. Your body is mine."

He pressed the vibrator to her clit, holding it there with practiced precision. He'd forced her orgasms before, but never with her pussy full of metal. Never like this. Her body reacted, trying desperately to escape. Her head whipped side-to-side. Shooting stars of pain burned through her breasts, morphing to pleasure when they melded with the vibrations pulsing through her pussy.

Her nostrils flared, fighting for each breath. Just when she didn't think she could take anymore, he released one clamp, then the other. The rush of blood to her nipples robbed her lungs. She fingered the bar in her hands, considered dropping it, then his voice broke through the screaming in her brain.

"Come. Now."

She let go. Behind the gag, her cries became whimpers. Her hips moved in a primal dance as her body clutched at the imposter buried inside her.

He'd taken her to some wonderful highs in their time together, but this time, mind-blowing was the only term that came close to describing her orgasm.

As the violent contractions quieted to mild ripples of pleasure, he eased the phallus from her pussy and removed the vibrator. Her body slumped in exhaustion. She hovered on the edge of sleep when she realized he hadn't turned the vibrator off. It hummed between her legs, closer, then farther away, but not touching her. Nowhere close she judged by the height from which the sound originated. She listened for the slightest hint of what he was doing.

A hiss. A curse. "God damn."

Holy crap. He was getting himself off with the vibrator. Her heart sank to the pit of her stomach. He wouldn't give her that part of him tonight, but he'd show her what she'd done to him, how her absence would torture him.

His thigh vibrated against hers when he reached behind her head to release the gag. He fisted his hand in her hair and held her head still.

"This is what I am without you, angel. A lonely, desperate man." Deep, masculine grunts followed. Hot cum splattered her face and chest. She lapped at it, trying to capture a fleeting taste of his salty essence.

Chapter Fourteen

"What are you saying, Mr. McCree?" God, she'd hated this man on sight. He could be a poster child against steroid use with that thick neck and those biceps only a comic book superhero should have.

"I'm sayin' I got the steroids from Jason Holder, the Mustangs' catcher. Hey, I didn't want to do them at first, but he kept after me, telling me all the other big hitters in the league were doing them, and if I wanted to keep up, I had to do them too. I don't see why I have to be the only one going down for using. Just look at the guy. Last year he hit okay, but not like he is this year. If you ask me, he's using the stuff himself—going after the record."

"Why are you coming forward with this information now, Mr. McCree?" *What's in it for you?*

"Because. I know who turned me in. It was Holder. He wanted me out of the way so he could go for the record all by himself."

"You're saying, not only did Jason Holder provide you with illegal steroids, but he somehow convinced you to take them, then he turned you in so he could pursue the homerun record himself?"

You couldn't go anywhere in Dallas these days without seeing Jason Holder's likeness on something, and you didn't have to be a baseball fan to know the local team was taking advantage of the hitter's run for the record to sell tickets. But was Holder using and/or pushing steroids? She'd never seen the man in person, but if the photos plastered on everything from buses to buildings around town were current, then he didn't *look* like he was using. He was the best-looking man she'd had ever seen—bar none. It would be a shame if what McCree said were true.

"Yeah, that's exactly what I'm saying."

She glanced to McCree's lawyer, a sleazy guy with expensive taste in suits and absolutely no style whatsoever. "What does your client hope this information will accomplish, if anything?"

"Mr. McCree has turned over a new leaf. He's seen the error of his ways and wants to set the record straight, so professional athletics can purge itself of the unscrupulous people who enable steroid use from within these organizations. Steroid use is on the rise among teenage athletes in this country, and as long as their professional counterparts persist in using these illegal drugs, teenagers will continue to emulate their behavior."

"That's exactly why I'm writing this article," she said. "Thank you both for meeting with me."

Carrie stood, extending her hand. "I appreciate your time. Speaking of which, I have to be on my way." If traffic wasn't too bad, she could make it back to her hotel room in time to call Master. Blood rushed to her pussy at the thought of hearing his voice.

Nearly an hour later, she hung the Do Not Disturb sign on the door and dropped her purse and the bag containing her laptop on the foot of the bed. Precious minutes ticked by while she shed her clothes and dug through her purse to find the phone Master gave her.

"Come on. Come on," she chanted, urging the power up process to go faster. Damn. She was going to be late. She should have thought to power it up right after she got off the plane, but she'd been exhausted and nothing went as planned from the minute the wheels touched the runway. The rental car agency lost her reservation, and when they'd found a car for her, they were out of GPS units to rent. She'd arrived at the hotel behind a busload of tourists, all checking in individually, just to learn the only room left was a smoking room, even though her reservation specified non-smoking. After a fitful night, she'd begged to be moved and they'd agreed to move her to the first non-smoking room that became available.

So, here she sat in her new room, minus her luggage the bell-staff couldn't locate via the claim check they'd given her just a few short hours ago.

The interview with Martin McCree and his lawyer was icing on the cake of her miserable trip. She felt dirty having just been in the same room with them. If it weren't for this phone call, she'd be in the shower scrubbing the invisible taint from her skin.

The screen came to life, and with a sigh of relief, she punched the speed-dial number that would connect her with her master.

"I've been waiting," he said.

"I know. I…this has been a miserable trip, Sir. Nothing has gone right, and I had to wait for the phone to power up. I know it's my fault. I should have thought…."

"Tell me, angel." His voice was a lifeboat, his concern a fresh, calming breeze. "Let me help you."

She told him everything from the flight delays up to and including the night spent in a room that stank of stale nicotine, and ended with, "I hated the people I met with this morning. My hair smells like cigarette smoke, and there isn't enough hot water and soap in the world to get the stench of creepy people off my skin." Drained from the recitation, she flopped back on the bed with a sigh. "I miss you."

"I miss you, too, angel. Feel better now?" She smiled at the humor in his voice.

"Yes, I do. It all sounds so silly, doesn't it?"

"No. Not silly. Stressful. I wish my demands hadn't added to it, but I needed to know you were okay. I want to take care of you, always." His words chased away the last lingering bits of tension. "Did you follow my instructions before you called?"

"Yes, Master. I'm completely naked."

"Good. Put the phone on speaker and go into the

bathroom. Fill the bathtub with hot water. I want to give you a bath."

After acquiring all the things he listed, she placed the phone on a towel atop the closed toilet lid and stepped into the tub. The hot water sapped the last of her energy. "Oh, God, that feels good," she sighed.

"Lie back and rest your head on the edge," he said. "Let the water caress your skin."

The porcelain was cold against her skin, but it warmed quickly. "Ahh, yes," she sighed.

"Let your knees fall open, angel. Let the water caress your pussy."

"This is just what I needed, Master. Thank you."

"Oh, we aren't done yet," he said. "Lather the washcloth, angel."

Pure decadence, that's what it is. She closed her eyes and imagined him there, her sitting in the cradle of his strong thighs while his hands stroked the soapy cloth over her entire body. By the time he instructed her to place it between her legs, she was only minutes away from a soft, languorous orgasm.

"Fold the cloth into thirds, angel, then roll it into a ball so it fits in the palm of your hand."

"Oh, Master," she sighed. "I'm so horny, can't I just rub my pussy without going to all this trouble?"

"No," he chuckled. "No short cuts to orgasm heaven tonight. Just do what I say and roll the washcloth into a ball—something like a roll of dollar bills."

She flattened her foot on the bottom of the tub, and used her raised thigh like a table to roll the washcloth. "Okay. Now what, Master?"

"Lift your knees and let them fall open. Place the rolled up washcloth at the top of your mound and use the palm of your hand to roll it back and forth over your clit. Use enough pressure to do some good, angel. The harder you press, the faster you'll get the orgasm you want so badly."

The water grew cold and she forgot all about the last twenty-four horrible hours. Clean, sated and now pleasantly exhausted, she followed Master's instructions and slipped naked between the sheets of her artificially darkened room for a well-needed nap.

"Sleep well, angel. You'll feel more like working after you rest."

"Thank you, Sir. You take good care of me."

"Always, angel. Always."

❧❧

Three whole days. He was going out of his mind worrying about her. After the first day when she'd sounded so exhausted and had made those comments about the type of people she'd been keeping company with…God, he couldn't stop worrying. He was going to put an end to this torture. When she returned, he would tell her who he was and demand she tell him everything about herself. What kind of job did she have that put her in the company of, in her words, creepy people?

Whatever it was, she couldn't keep it. No way, no how. He couldn't live with the anxiety or the frustration at not being there in person to take care of her. Hell, she didn't need to work. He made enough money to take care of her. He *needed* to take care of her. She was his lifeboat. She'd saved him from drowning in self-pity. Saved him from a living a vanilla lie. He'd never experienced the freedom of being himself, except in her company. She understood. She accepted. And he would protect her. Always.

He'd had no choice the last few days but to channel his negative emotions into aggression on the field. The Mustangs had played three games since she left, a double-header followed by a late game the next day. He added four homeruns to his stats, breaking his own season high, and there were still two months to go in the regular season.

He tried to focus on the report in front of him. Knowing the strengths and weaknesses of every batter on the opposing team was the difference between a decent catcher and a future Hall of Fame catcher. That meant hours studying reports and watching game video, something he'd never minded before, but with Carrie out there somewhere in the great unknown, the numbers might as well have been Greek.

The phone ringing startled him. His heart leapt then plummeted to his toes when he realized the call was his house line, and not the cell Carrie would've contacted him on. *Shit*. Wiping a hand over his face, he reached for the cordless handset. He checked the caller ID. The Mustangs' front office. This day just got better and better.

Within the hour, he tapped on the team manager's office door. "Doyle? You wanted to see me?"

"Come on in, Jason. Shut the door behind you."

His heart was sure as hell getting a workout this season, he thought as his pulse kicked into overdrive. Closed doors were never a good thing when talking with management.

"Have a seat." Doyle waved him to the casual arrangement that boasted a comfortable leather sofa and three matching chairs around a coffee table. If it hadn't been for the massive desk across the room and the walls lined with framed celebrity photos and trophy cases, a person might forget he was in the boss's office.

Jason sat on the sofa, no longer the raw recruit he'd been the first time he'd sat there, but a seasoned professional who had no reason to be as nervous as he was. He crossed an ankle over his knee. "What's up?"

"I've been given a head's up by the local newspaper. They called this morning to ask me for a statement regarding an article they plan to publish in tomorrow's issue."

"And this concerns me, how?"

"Martin McCree says you're the one who sold him the steroids."

So that's what a ton of bricks felt like when it landed on your head. He couldn't move. Couldn't find words. He scanned the room, wondering how this alternate universe could look so normal, but be the polar opposite of reality.

"Jason? Son?"

A block of ice formed in his gut. Like some sort of alien being, it sent out tentacles to his internal organs, flash freezing each in turn. He sat in mute horror while the alien creature gripped his career in its frigid grasp and reduced it to vapor.

"Is that all?" he asked through tight lips.

"He's accused you of using, too."

Bile rose in his throat, the chemical burn almost welcome in the midst of the paralyzing cold. "What did you tell them?" he asked when he pried his jaw from the ice monster's grip.

"I told them the truth. That McCree lied."

"Thank you." Jason nodded, processing the unfathomable. "I'll take a drug test. Hell, I'll take a hundred."

Doyle crossed one ankle over his knee. "That's the first step, but you and I know it won't end there."

"It never does." *Fuck.*

"I don't think we can stop them from printing the article, but I've already contacted our lawyers. They're working on it right now. If there's a way, we'll stop it. If not, then we'll decide what to do depending on the reaction to it."

Jason nodded again. "So, that's it. I'm supposed to wait for some reporter with a hatchet to destroy my career?"

"You're not guilty, son. This won't destroy your career."

Jason jumped to his feet. "Are you fucking kidding me? It doesn't matter if it's true or not. They'll raise the question. That's all it takes. The media will grab on to the lie and every time they repeat it, it'll become truth in the minds of the fans. You know how it works." He forced his legs to move toward the bank of windows overlooking the stadium. Choking back tears that threatened he gazed out at the playing field that had felt like his home. "Who's doing this?"

"I don't know the reporter. He's not from the sports desk."

"What's his name?" *Know thy enemy.*

"Carradine Taylor."

The name meant nothing to him. He should at least be able to look his executioner in the eye.

"He covers random shit, mostly local, but anything that involves scandal or a cover up. Politics, corporate misconduct—that sort of thing."

He counted the squares mowed precisely into the outfield, silently wondering into which category he fell into. Random shit? Definitely scandal. And everyone knew there was always a cover up when steroids were involved. If this Carradine Taylor only knew what kind of random shit, scandal and cover up was really going on in his life, he'd have a golden ticket to every talk show on the planet. *What a cluster-fuck.*

"Look, Jason. Come sit down. The PR people are coming up, then the lawyers. We're all over this. By the time the paper hits the news racks in the morning, we'll have a strategy and a response ready to go. We aren't going to take this lying down."

"You have a copy of the article?" *At least let me view the murder weapon.*

"Yeah, they faxed one over." Doyle crossed to his desk. A moment later, he nudged Jason's elbow. "Here."

Jason turned his back to the view, sank to the floor and leaned against the glass, his knees raised, the only wall of defense he could muster at the moment. He read the article, agreeing with everything the author said regarding the evils of steroid use. Two pages of perfectly good journalism. Then, on the third page, the lies, not even masked in innuendo. Flat-out, blatant, defamatory lies. Each one striking a serious blow to his career. Cumulatively demolishing everything he'd spend his life building.

He closed his eyes, absorbing the hits, each one more painful than the last. A jingling sound roused him. Doyle shook the tumbler he dangled in front of Jason's face. The noise. Ice cube. A chip off the solid block in his gut, no doubt.

"Scotch," he said. "It'll warm you up."

Nothing would do that now, but he took the offered drink, downing it in one gut-searing gulp. He held the glass up.

Doyle tipped the decanter, splashing two fingers of rich amber liquid into the glass. "Don't let McCree mess with your head like he did last year with Jeff. You're going to break records this season, all on your own. We'll get this sorted out."

Yeah, right. Jason downed the amber liquid and held his glass up for another refill.

"Pull yourself together, son." He refilled the glass and corked the bottle. "The PR gurus will be here any minute."

Six mind-numbing hours later—and not a single viable idea to show for it—he escaped the public relations posse and sat alone in the locker room. He'd been desperate to get out of the conference room for while, away from the PR spin and bullshit. Between all those supposed great minds, all they'd managed to come up with was wait and see. Wait and fuckin' see.

"Hey."

He didn't move. At that very moment, counting the flecks of color in the industrial grade carpet between his knees was a better alternative than seeing the pity on his brother's face. "Hey."

Jeff sat on the bench beside him. "They say everyone has their cross to bear. I'd say the name McCree is engraved on the Holder family cross, wouldn't you?"

"There are six hundred fifty-three red flecks in one square inch of carpet," he said. "How many do you think that is in this whole room?"

Jeff sighed. "Forget about the goddamned carpet, and focus. You've got to keep your shit together and fight this. I let McCree get to me last year, and it almost cost me my career. With your help, I fought back and won. The man is pissed, and he knows he's got nothing he can throw at me, so he's going after you. Its delusions brought on by the steroid use. Everyone in the Mustangs organization knows he fabricated every word, and we'll all fight this with you."

Jason nodded— all he could do with the massive lump in his throat.

"We'll get through this."

He nodded again. *Let them have their optimism.*

"Come on." Jeff stood. "I'm taking you home with me tonight."

"I'm not a child." Jason straightened, bracing himself with his palms on his thighs. "I'll be fine. Carrie will be back tomorrow morning. I need to see her."

"You sure, man?"

"I'm sure."

❧

"That's not the article I submitted," Carrie said for what seemed like the hundredth time. She couldn't understand why George wasn't listening to a thing she said. A brick wall would be easier to reason with.

"It's the edited first draft," the editor-in-chief argued. "We all agreed it was better than the final draft you sent in. We're going with it."

"*I* didn't agree," she countered. "Those are unfounded accusations from a man who destroyed what few brain cells he might have had with steroids."

"They are one man's version of the truth. The man is entitled to his opinion."

"And I'm entitled to mine. This is wrong."

"It's called selling newspapers. Get over yourself. This article will make you a household name."

"That's because Jason Holder is going to sue me, and the newspaper, for libel. I'm about to *become* the news. Not a good thing, George. Not at all."

"If it comes to that, we'll provide you with a good lawyer and of course, give your trial a couple of columns above the front page fold."

Carrie disconnected and slammed the handset back into its cradle. *Damned technology. They've taken away the satisfaction of a good hang-up. No matter how hard you punch the off button the person on the other end only hears a soft click.*

This article was supposed to raise awareness of the dangers of steroid use, instead, it was going to ignite a firestorm of controversy, and very likely destroy at least two careers. Hers and Jason Holder's.

She stared at the front-page story. How had something that was intended to do good turn into such a disaster? She glanced at her watch and jumped to her feet. She was due at the Dungeon in an hour. A session with Master would clear her head, allowing her to come up with a solution, a way to make this right. And if all else failed, she'd ask permission to bring her outside life into the relationship. If there was man alive who could help her find a way out of this mess, it was her master.

He always knew what to do. His quite control of every situation always calmed her. He cared for her. She knew he did. He'd said he wanted to keep their vanilla lives separate, but she needed more now. He was her master, and she needed him in all aspects of her life, not just for the few hours a week they were together. With her mind made up to tell him how she felt and ask—beg if need be—for his help, she headed for the Dungeon and the man she loved.

⁂

Jason closed the curtains and stopped in front of her. His angel, so sweetly submissive, waited for him to take what she offered. With one finger beneath her chin, he tilted her face upward. So many plans, now nothing but rubbish. This was the moment he would have taken her blindfold off and asked her, pleaded with her, to be a part of every aspect of his life.

But that was yesterday's plan. Today he didn't have a life to offer her. Linking his angel to him would subject her to media scrutiny of the worst kind. In order to prove his innocence he would have to bare every dark corner of his life to public eyes. Even this one.

He wouldn't drag his angel down into the pits of hell with him. He had to let her go.

"I won't keep you long, angel." He sat on the edge of the platform bed, admiring her perfect body, committing the image of her expectant face to memory. In a few minutes, if he meant anything to her at all, her sweet smile would be gone, replaced by....

No, he wouldn't go there. Sure, she might mourn the loss of their relationship, but she would get over it. She'd move on. It wouldn't be long before another Dom took her under his protection. She was much too special to be alone for long.

If he had a career after this debacle, perhaps he'd ask to be traded. Being in the same town with her, knowing she was on her knees for another man and that he might run into her here would be too much.

"I was going to remove your blindfold today," he said. "But something happened yesterday, and that's no longer possible."

She gasped and turned her head toward his voice. "What happened, Sir?"

"I can't say, angel. It wouldn't be fair to bring you into the mess my life has become in the last twenty-four hours. For the foreseeable future, my career—hell, everything I've ever done is going to be dissected with Draconian precision. I can't and won't let the rumormongers touch. You're everything I ever dreamed of. You'll forever be my guardian angel—the woman put on this earth to show me who I am, who I was meant to be."

Nausea roiled in her gut. *His career. Rumormongers.* Her mind spun like a cyclone, sucking everything into a vortex, scrambling it like pieces of a jigsaw puzzle and tossing it all back to earth in an unrecognizable heap. No matter how she sorted the fragments, they fit together into one inevitable, unfathomable conclusion.

No. It couldn't be. Please, God, don't let it be him. Maybe, sweet God, maybe she was wrong. She forced a plea past numb lips. "Please, Sir. Let me help you."

"There isn't anything you can do. I'm a public figure, angel, and people who have in the past built me up in the public eye, are at this very moment doing their best to tear me apart. I won't bring you into that."

"Who is doing this to you, Sir?" *Oh please, please don't say my name or I'll die right here.*

"I don't know. A newspaper reporter I don't even know. A colleague with an axe to grind. People who don't know me at all."

She was going to be sick.

"Sir, please." She had no idea what she was begging for. Please what? Let me explain? No. There was no explanation for what she'd done. No way to fix it.

"It doesn't matter who, angel."
Oh God. Yes it does!

"Everything I've worked for my entire life will be

called into question, and everything I accomplish from here on out will have an asterisk attached to it. It's the kiss of death in my profession."

She tried to choke back the sob, but it wouldn't be stopped. She doubled over, the pain too much to bear. This was all her fault. If she'd never sent the rough draft of her article, if she'd waited a few minutes, read it over again she would have realized what McCree's wild comments had been meant to do. She'd played right into his hands. *Stupid, stupid fool.*

The cyclone pulled at her, threatening her tenuous hold on sanity. She wrapped her arms around her stomach, doubling over. She lost her grip, and her world spun helplessly out of control.

Jason caught her before she slumped to the floor. He cradled her in his arms, hating he'd done this to her. He'd vowed to protect her, and instead, he brought her to this. It wasn't fair for her to suffer for something she had no control over.

He pulled her onto his lap, tucking her head under his chin. Her tears soaked his shirt. Holding her was pure torture, but he owed her that much. She'd saved his life. He could give her comfort before he severed the invisible cord that bound them.

Her torrential sobs eventually gave way to sobs punctuated by hiccups then she slipped into an exhausted sleep. He sat on the floor, holding her until he was sure she slept soundly. Only then did he ease to his feet and lower her to the platform bed. He covered her with an after-care blanket from a stack in the cabinet. When she woke, he would be gone. If she tried to use the phone he gave her, she would find it disconnected, as was the email address he'd established for her and her alone.

Chapter Fifteen

Carrie shivered. She pulled the blanket tighter, but it was ineffective against the chill that wracked her body from the inside out. This wasn't the first time she'd woken in the Dungeon, but it was the first time she'd done so alone. Master always held her after a scene, staying with her until she was on solid ground again, able to take care of herself. Often, he would even dress her, taking his time, kissing every inch of her skin before covering them up.

Even with his life shattering around him, he'd brought her here to explain why they couldn't be together, proof he thought enough about her to end it in person. His honor prevented him from dragging her into his hell. The irony of that didn't escape her. Some angel she was. His hell was one of her creation and still, he held her, cared for her as best he could. Her fingers clutched the blanket—evidence of his regard for her. He could have left her naked and alone, but he'd taken care to see she was safe and warm before he left. He'd even adjusted the lighting, turning off the harsh spotlights over the platform bed.

Lights. Her hand flew to her face. The blindfold was gone.

She sat up, holding the blanket to her chest and looked around. Her clothes lay beside her in a neatly folded stack—the blindfold atop them, securing a small white square of paper. Her hand shook when she slipped the note out from under its tear dampened black satin anchor.

Three words. Three nails driven straight into her heart.

I love you.

❧❧

It was a nightmare. A living, freaking, cluster-fuck of a nightmare. She hand delivered the retraction she'd spent the better part of the night crafting, but George refused to run it. Newspapers were flying of the shelves. Her article was the most viewed post ever on the Globe's website and had already been picked up by papers across the country. Any other time, she would have been ecstatic. It was a reporter's dream to have his byline on a piece that garnered so much attention.

She stood ramrod straight. This was no place to cower, and she would never bow down to the likes of these people. They had no honor—unlike Jason Holder, the man they were intent on crucifying for the sake of an increased print run.

"If you aren't going to print the retraction," she said, "then here." She handed over the other document that had kept her awake all night. "I quit."

George took the paper, scanned it, and dropped it to her desk. "The Globe won't defend you if you quit."

"I know. There isn't any defense for what I did. I wrote something stupid and irresponsible, and then I was stupid enough to let you see it. I'll take whatever punishment is headed my way."

"Okay, then." He shrugged and shifted his attention to his computer screen. "We're done. I'm sure there are any number of reporters who'll be glad to write the hundreds of follow-up stories."

She stopped at her cubicle on her way out. The few personal belongings she kept there fit in her handbag. A *sign I never belonged here.* Exiting the building, she breathed a sigh of relief. She was leaving a monumental weight behind.

Caught up in her own thoughts, she almost ran into the blockade of reporters on the sidewalk. She raised her arm to shield her eyes from the camera lights.

"That's her. That's the reporter who broke the story." Someone stuck a microphone in her face. "Carradine Taylor, have you had any contact with the Mustangs organization or Jason Holder since your story hit the newsstands?"

Contact? Yeah, you could say that.

But she couldn't tell them that a few short hours ago she'd sat naked on her knees, listening while Jason told her how some person he didn't know was out to destroy him. And then he'd held her in his arms while she bawled her eyes out. *I love you.* If he ever found out she was the one who wrote the article, he'd hate her, and she couldn't blame him. She hated herself plenty right now.

"No." *Liar.*

She tried to shove her way through the crowd of reporters, videographers, cameramen, and sound techs. They presented a solid, impenetrable wall, so she changed tactics. Spying a gap between them and the building, she made a dash for it only to be stopped by another solid wall. This one wore a uniform.

"Carradine Taylor?" the man in uniform asked.

"Yes."

He shoved a large envelope at her. She instinctively reached for it.

"You've been served, ma'am."

She looked down at the papers in her hand. That didn't take long, she thought. Of course. George had to have given the Mustangs a heads up about the article. That's how he had known about it the day before it went to print, and explained how the lawyers had time to sue her. Her heart sank. There was no way to keep Jason from putting her face and name together, especially after this. She tucked the envelope into her purse, along with the relics of her career, and shoved past the reporters.

❧

Fuck.

Jason stared at the screen. It couldn't be. He shook

his head to clear the buzzing in his ears. Had he missed something? No. No, they were still talking about him and that damned article in the Globe. But...Carradine Taylor was a woman. And not just any woman. She was *his* woman.

Or she had been until he'd let her go.

He hit the pause button, freezing her face on the screen. It was her. No doubt about it. Carrie. His angel. Thoughts and possibilities formed like fireflies in his brain, flashing on and off so fast he couldn't grasp a single one. He braced his elbows on his knees and clutched his skull to keep it from exploding. One thought flared brighter and longer than all the rest—had she known who he was all along? Had it all been an act, a chance to get material she could use against him?

Good Lord. Was she going to tell the world about his sexual preferences, too? And he'd thought his life couldn't get any more fucked up.

By God—he was her *master*!

He was on his feet before he realized he no longer possessed her or the title, and perhaps he never had.

He dialed her number then remembered he'd cut off that line of communication. He'd cut *all* lines of communication with her. He squeezed his fist and the edges of the phone bit into his flesh. There had to be a way.

Todd. He knew her. Switching phones, he located Todd's number and placed the call.

"Hey, Jason. How ya doin', man?" Todd asked.

"I've been better. Look, Todd, I need Carrie's home phone number. I really need to see her, and I can't explain, but I don't have any other way to get in touch with her."

"Hey, I heard about the article. I'm sorry, man. I didn't know she was reporter until Brooke recognized her name in the byline."

"It's not your fault. I knew I was taking a chance."

"You think talking to her is a good idea?"

Jason was fresh out of good ideas, but he needed to know how deep her betrayal went. "Probably not, but I'm going to do it anyway."

"Okay. Give me a minute. I'll get it and call you right back."

"Thanks. I owe you."

Precious minutes ticked by. Jason scrounged around for something to write with. He found a pen and a stained takeout menu in the drawer of the end table next to his favorite chair. At last, Todd called back. He scribbled Carradine Taylor's home number down. His very own, fucking guardian angel straight from Hell.

He was due at the stadium in a few hours—not enough time to handle Carrie properly. He punched in a familiar number.

"Doyle," he said when the team manager answered. "Take me out of the lineup tonight."

"You know I can't do that. The media would read all kinds of shit into you not being on the field. You have to be behind the plate tonight and in the batting order. And, by God, if you don't come up with a couple of decent hits, I'll personally kick your ass. Is that clear, son?"

"Yes, sir. Crystal clear." He sighed. "It was a stupid idea anyway. Sorry I asked." He'd have to wait until after the game to confront his demon angel, but confront her he would.

◈

She couldn't believe she was at the Dungeon again. Ever since she received the curt message on her answering machine she'd come up with a million reasons not to follow his orders.

He obviously knew who she was since he'd called her home phone. He knew she was responsible for everything. If he was using steroids, she might be putting herself in a dangerous situation. Combining roid rage with a naturally dominant nature could only spell disaster. But in her heart, she knew her concerns weren't valid. The man she knew wasn't using steroids; she'd stake what remained of her reputation on that.

She paced the Dungeon room. Each piece of equipment held special memories. Over the last months, they'd tried them all. Determined not to cry, she wiped telltale moisture from her cheeks with the back of her hand. It was inconceivable that their relationship was over, but it was true. She would never feel the things Master made her feel again. There wasn't anyone else for her, and there never would be. She'd freely given her body to Jason, and he'd taken her heart. Stolen it right out of her chest.

She could only imagine why he'd asked, *no* told, her to come here tonight. His odd schedule, the late nights and early mornings he'd brought her here, made sense now— as did the long absences when he'd patiently seen to her needs via the phone. Master had a way with phone sex— she'd give him that. Other than the physical contact, it hadn't been much different than what they did when they were together. Either way, he hadn't allowed her to see him.

That didn't mean she hadn't *seen* him. A person didn't need sight in order to see. She knew his body, knew the touch of his hand—sometimes soft, sometimes administering pain or punishment, or both, but always with care.

She knew Jason Holder and she knew the kind of man he was. He was fair and compassionate. Confident and capable. Trustworthy. He was a man of honor. And he loved her. Once.

What remained of her heart crashed headlong into her ribcage then staggered back to land at her feet, battered and bruised—mortally wounded. Yet somehow, her body continued to function without it. Proof miracles did happen.

He'd given no clue about the reason for this meeting. All she knew was, she had another chance. It was too late to keep their outside lives out of the relationship, and in truth, it was probably too late for the relationship. If it died, it was because of her, and she would accept responsibility. She'd accept any form of punishment he deemed appropriate.

Carrie checked the clock. He'd be here soon. She knelt, fully clothed, facing the window. She adjusted the blindfold, a completely symbolic gesture now, and displayed her offering across her open palms. If there was a future for them, she'd know it soon.

❧❧

Jason parked in the lot across the street from the Dungeon and, opening the trunk, removed the bag he kept there. He should be home sleeping, or at least attempting to sleep, but this couldn't wait. He needed to know how deep the betrayal went. Not that he expected her to confess, but there were ways to get a sub to talk—if she really was a sub. Perhaps she had acting talents to go along with her journalistic skills.

He tightened his grip on the bag, its solid weight grounding him. She was here. The sight of her on her knees, waiting for him was a kick to the gut, and he'd racked up more than his share of those the last two days. He took a moment to compose himself. Let her wait. Let her wonder if he would take the flogger from her hands and use it on her. He had every right to. She belonged to him.

He thought he'd known her. He knew her body— every inch of it. He knew the sound of her voice when passion ruled her. He knew the exact shade of red her ass turned following a spanking. He'd buried his cock in her body countless times—given her pleasure and accepted it in return. Was it just yesterday he'd given her the words he knew she longed to hear?

But that was before. Before—when he would have moved Heaven and Earth to keep from dragging an angel into the pits of hell with him. This was now. He knew his angel hadn't been sent from Heaven to save him. Time to find out just how deep into Hell she planned to drag him.

"Hello, Carrington," he said, closing the door behind him.

"Master."

He closed the curtains. Stopping in front of her, he dropped the bag to the floor beside him. "For God's sake, get off the floor," he said. "You aren't my sub anymore."

She didn't move. "Please, Sir. Might I explain?"

"Get off the goddamned floor then I'll listen. And take that damned blindfold off. I think we're past that now, don't you?"

She stood, pulling the blindfold off as she came to

her feet. Her eyes met his for the first time ever. Clear and without guile, her gaze twisted his gut and weakened his resolve to see his plan through. But, he reminded himself, he wouldn't be the first chump to fall for a woman's sweet lies hidden behind innocent eyes. He'd stick with the plan. If she had nothing to hide, he'd know it before the night was over.

"I brought this for you, Sir. If you'll let me explain, I'll gladly accept any punishment you feel is appropriate."

He ignored the flogger she held out to him, backing away. Images of how her lovely skin would look after a good flogging flashed in his mind. Call him sadistic, but he loved to see his marks on her, and heaven help him, his angel really was a demon in bed afterwards. His groin tightened at the unwanted thought. God, how could he still want her? That he did only fueled his anger. He leaned against the wall and crossed his arms over his chest to keep from reaching for her, dragging her into his arms, and paddling the shit out of her ass for doing this to him—to them.

He shouldn't have told her to remove the blindfold. Her eyes…dear God, the way she looked at him…. How many times had he imagined her looking at him that way, pleading, receptive, expectant? That she finally was angered him, too. So many lost opportunities.

"I'm listening," he said.

She squared her shoulders and conviction flashed across her face. "There's no excuse, Sir. I wrote the article, and I stand by what it says—except the lies about you. In fact, I asked to write it."

"Why?" he asked. "Why that subject?"

"Steroids are dangerous. They kill people and professional athletes who use them make it seem like it's okay. It's not okay."

"At least we agree on something. But you still haven't told me why you wanted this story enough to ask for it."

Moisture glimmered in her eyes. She brushed it away with trembling fingers. He stopped himself before he reached for her. He was here for answers, not to comfort her.

"My cousin Danny committed suicide. He'd been using steroids, and when his parents found out, he quit. None of them knew you couldn't just quit taking them, that there were physical and psychological changes that occur when you do. He was only seventeen." Tears brimmed in her eyes. She turned her face away. The leather strands of the flogger swayed when she swiped at her cheeks.

Jason held himself in check. Okay, so she had a legitimate, and a personal, connection to the story, but that didn't excuse the unprofessional journalism that had landed him in his present predicament.

"That's the Danny you mentioned in the article?"

"Yes, Sir."

Well, shit. He took a deep breath, studying her posture—submissive but hinting at the inner strength that had intrigued him from the start. He couldn't let her emotional connection to the story cloud his judgment. He needed answers, and he was going to get them.

"Why drag me into it? Why drag an innocent person into this mess?"

Once again, she squared her shoulders and faced him with the resolve of the last batter in the deciding game of the World Series with two outs and the winning run on third base. He had to admire her guts. Not many people would stand up for their convictions the way she was.

"The article wasn't supposed to be printed—not like that anyway. I sent it as a first draft. I knew it was wrong almost as soon as I sent it. I told my editor not to bother editing it, that I would send a corrected copy. I did send one. It only took a few minutes to remove the defamatory comments and accusations that creep made about you, and I sent the new article right away. I didn't know George had rejected the new one until I got back to town. I begged him not to publish it, but he wouldn't change his mind."

"Did you know who you were writing those things about? Did you know it was me?"

"No, Sir. You have to believe me," she pleaded. "I didn't know my master was Jason Holder until yesterday. I figured it out when you told me what was going on in your life. I wanted to tell you then, but you ended our relationship, and I thought maybe, just maybe, you would never know. I knew it would hurt you to find out I was the one who wrote the article. Disappointing you is the worst kind of pain." She cast her gaze to the floor and her last words trailed off on a whisper. "I can take anything but that."

"So, you thought it would be easier for me to see you on TV a few hours before I had to face the media at the stadium?"

She snapped her eyes back to his. "You have to believe me, I didn't plan that. If I'd known the camera crews were there, I would have found another way out of the building." She lowered her gaze to the floor again, submitting to him. "I know it was wrong, Sir. I can only tell you what was in my heart. I hoped there was something I could do to fix it."

He closed his eyes. Damn it all to hell. Her voice rang with sincerity, and her story had the ring of truth to it, but could he trust his judgment where she was concerned? *Hell no.*

"Did you mean it?" she asked, jerking his attention back to her.

"What?"

"That you love me," she whispered.

The memory of all he'd lost dropped like an acid ball into his stomach. Carrington Taylor sure looked like the angel he'd fallen in love with, but she wasn't the same person he'd meant those words for. He ground his molars.

"I loved a woman who didn't exist." Straightening, he took the flogger from her. "Strip."

It was time to find out how much was real, and how much of what they had was an act. And by God, if she wanted punishment, he was just the man to give it to her. But if she thought all would be forgotten, her betrayal forgiven as if it was nothing more than a minor transgression, then she had better think again. She'd soon find out, this punishment wouldn't change anything.

Carrie folded her clothes, as he preferred her to do,

placing the neat stack on the shelf she'd used so many times before. She dared a glance in his direction while he readied the suspension apparatus. She'd seen him on television, and lately, his face was plastered all over town on buses, billboards and even on the side of a building. For once, she wondered if she would have given herself to him so freely had she known who he was from the beginning. Perhaps not. He was stone cold sexy and handsome, and a hotshot celebrity athlete. She never would have believed he truly wanted her—not when he could have any woman out there. Dressed in slacks and a crisp button-down shirt the same shade of blue as his eyes, he didn't look like the kind of man who played games—of any kind. She probably would have run for her life after their first meeting. But now that she knew him, had glimpsed the real man inside, she could only mourn the loss of a love she'd never find again.

Standing naked, exposed, she wished he too would remove his clothes, but like always, he didn't want her to see him. He moved with grace and economy of motion as he arranged the suspension equipment. The mental images she'd formed of his body didn't come close to the real thing. His face and hands were tan from hours in the sun and she couldn't help but wonder if the coloring extended to the rest of him.

A vise squeezed her heart when she realized she'd never have the opportunity to find out. She closed her eyes briefly, calling to mind the fantasy image she'd created for her lover, adapting it to the new data. The new image was still a fantasy, but closer she supposed to the real thing. She knew the width of his shoulders and chest—he'd allowed her to touch him plenty of times, but now that she could put them into proportion, they seemed so much larger. Everything about him seemed larger, more intimidating.

He took his time, arranging the suspension cuffs she was familiar with, and another apparatus she couldn't remember using. Her heart ached, knowing she was responsible for the hard lines on his face. She'd put them there with her betrayal.

"Stand here," he said, tapping the floor in front of him with his shoe.

She eyed the leather cuffs swaying lightly on a chain lowered for easy access. This was what she wanted. This was what she'd asked for. She'd earned her punishment, welcomed it. She always felt better afterward knowing his administering, and her acceptance of the punishment cleansed them both and allowed the healing to begin. She hoped, but deep down inside, she was afraid there wasn't enough punishment in the world that would allow these wounds to heal.

She stepped into position, keeping her gaze lowered, offering herself without reservation. She knew this man— knew his heart. He'd already hurt her in the only way he could. Whatever he inflicted on her physical body could never equal the pain of losing his love. Offering herself to him, allowing him to work through his anger, to transfer it to her where it belonged was the only gift she could give him now.

His touch was familiar, and she drew a measure of comfort from that. He bound her wrists and lifted them over her head, adjusting the suspension so only her toes touched the floor. He worked in silence. No music. No words of assurance to let her know her safety and comfort were uppermost in his mind. Tears clogged her throat as she watched his hands contact her skin for the first, and perhaps the last, time. She couldn't look away. They moved over her body—at first, lightly skimming the surface, as if examining a delicate porcelain vase, then having determined its solid nature, his touch became more assertive. If she closed her eyes, she would recognize feel of his hands, but seeing it for the first time made it new and exciting all over again. Silently, he stroked her body to a fevered arousal, ignoring the part of her most in need of his attention.

When he cupped her breasts, squeezing and kneading, she was mesmerized at the contrast between her softness and his hard masculinity. He rolled her nipples between callused fingertips, pinching to tight peaks.

She hadn't expected this tenderness, so the pain when

it came, took her by surprise. He clamped her quickly, no open-mouthed, bone-melting kiss followed to make her forget this time. She bit her lip and closed her eyes, concentrating on breathing through it.

"Open your eyes," he commanded. "No more hiding."

She lifted her watery gaze to his, determined to give him what he needed, no matter the cost to herself.

"You think you know who I am, Carrington?"

"I know you won't hurt me," she said, infusing her words with more bravado than she actually possessed.

"You don't know shit about me then. But I know you." He flicked the chain hanging from one nipple and then the other, sending lightning bolts of pain straight to her pussy. "I know you like pain, or was that a lie?" He cupped her sex, fingering her swollen, wet folds. "No, that much was the truth. You're a slut for pain, and I'm man enough to give it to you." He reached for another chain hanging beside her. "But first, I'm going to see to it you have no choice but to accept whatever I want to do to you." He trailed a length of rope from her chin, between her breasts to her mound. "Does that frighten you, Carrington?"

"No, Sir," she whispered the lie. This wasn't the man she'd given her body to so many times before. He'd always gone out of his way to reassure her she was safe.

He methodically knotted the rope, rigging an additional suspension system he placed beneath her thighs to lift and spread her legs. Hanging by wrists and thighs, there was no part of her he couldn't access with ease. He'd seen it all before, but then, she'd been hidden behind the blindfold. No longer in darkness, she felt more exposed, more vulnerable.

Jason bent to the bag he'd brought with him. She took a shuddering breath at the sight of the riding crop he drew out. He moved around behind her and swept her hair over her shoulders. Her skin tingled as he skimmed the leather end of the crop from her nape, slowly along her spine to the tight entrance she'd given to no other man. He tapped lightly there—just hard enough to remind her he could take that, too, if he was of a mind.

She closed her eyes, absorbing the feel of the leather as he traced her shoulder blades and each rib until it disappeared around her torso. Drifting on the decadence of the sensual play, she dared to hope there was more pleasure in store. If this was punishment, she'd take it any day. A hard slap to her pussy startled a cry from her lips and put an end to her romantic notions.

Her eyes flew open. He stood in front of her, a solid wall of angry male.

"Eyes up here," he said, using the riding crop to tilt her face. "No matter what, don't take your eyes off mine."

She met his gaze. Her whole body trembled, knowing she'd underestimated. There was no forgiveness there. None at all.

Eyes locked with hers, he used the riding crop to slowly taunt and arouse. Despite her fear, her body reacted, craving his touch, the bite of pain that led to pleasure. He slapped the crop against her clamped nipples. She closed her eyes against the stinging pain.

He repeated the slap, admonishing her, "Look at me."

Her breasts burned from his attention, ached for him to soothe them with his lips and tongue.

"Do you like that?" he asked.

He didn't have to ask, moisture leaked from her pussy, scenting the air with the unmistakable evidence of her arousal. "Yes, Sir," she said, mortified at how much she liked it, craved it.

The crop traveled the length of her sternum, stopping to dry fuck her navel, then traveling lower, taunting her soft belly, setting of a firestorm of need in her pussy with each stinging slap against her flesh. She flinched, but didn't look away as he coated the end of the crop with her juices, then wedged it between her folds to press against her swollen clit. She twisted against her restraints, straining to get closer to the delicious pressure. *More. Please.* He rubbed her hard there, promising the release she desperately needed.

"How much pain is too much?" he asked. "I wonder. Does Carrington like to have her clit spanked too? Or is that something only Carrie likes?"

The crop slapped against her clit, startling a gasp from her. Once. Twice. Three times—each swat harder than the one before. She bit her lower lip but couldn't contain the moans or the way her body writhed, accepting and absorbing the pain.

His gaze held hers, and in that way he held her captive in mind and body. There was nothing of the kindness and love she'd dreamed of seeing there for the last few months—only cold, hard pain. Her gut clenched. She'd hurt him so badly. He'd worked so hard to get where he was, to earn the admiration and respect of his colleagues and fans, and she'd destroyed it all. She deserved his hatred, but he didn't hate her. She didn't know how she knew, but she did. He didn't hate her. He was hurt, wounded by what she'd done, but deep inside, he still harbored feelings for her. A tiny glimmer of hope kindled inside her.

He demanded her submission, and she gave it willingly. Opening the windows to her soul, she held nothing back, hoping her love for him would burn bright enough to banish the pain and disappointment she'd caused.

Chapter Sixteen

The musk of her arousal filled the air. He inhaled, absorbing the knowledge he could do this to her, that she wanted, needed, him to do these things to her. He'd never dreamed he would find a woman like her. Seeing her like this, needing, taking…submitting…. She was the sexiest woman he'd ever known. Her body was lush and responsive to his touch. He'd made her come so many times, and each time, he'd felt like a god watching her lose control, knowing her pleasure was his to command, that she would beg him, and no other, for it.

Her outer lips were ripe, swollen—inviting. His cock ached to feel her wet heat surrounding him, to pound into her softness, to take what he wanted. She wouldn't deny him. She couldn't, trussed up the way she was. Even if he removed the restraints, she would still spread her legs for him. She'd still take him in, give him her body, let him use her—because she loved it when he couldn't control his need for her. She loved having that power over him.

How many times had he watched for the rosy blush to cover her body, a tell she couldn't control? A few more taunting slaps and she would beg him to fuck her, to let her come. But tonight, she'd find out what it was like to have everything she wanted within her grasp, only to see it ripped away.

"This is the way you like it, isn't it? You like it when you have no choice, don't you?" He clamped a hand over her pussy, fingering her folds. A moan came from low in her throat. Her stomach muscles clenched. "You want it. I can tell. You want to be fucked. You want me to lose control and shove my cock in you. You like it hard and fast." His hand slipped lower. "You want me to fuck you here, too." He pressed a finger against her anus. "In fact, you'd like it if I filled both holes at the same time, wouldn't you?"

She licked her lips. "Yes, Sir. Please."

Her voice was breathless, weak with longing and desire. Time to show her who was on top, who was in charge, who was fucking who.

"Are you going to write about this, too, Carrington? Am I going to wake up tomorrow and find my sexual preferences are front-page news?"

"No, Sir. I'd never do that."

"Why not, Carrington? You might just accidentally write another article, like you accidentally wrote this one."

She cried out when he pinched her swollen clit between his thumb and forefinger.

"Please, Sir," she whimpered. "You know I wouldn't."

He buried two fingers in her pussy. Her eyes closed, and he slapped her ass with the crop. "Don't close your eyes again, Carrington."

She met his gaze.

"See, I don't know anything about you, Carrington Taylor. Nothing at all. I thought I did, but you aren't the woman I thought you were. I trusted you with secrets I've never trusted anyone with."

His fingers worked inside her while he spoke. Tears welled in her eyes—a weak attempt to break him.

"And what did I get in return? Betrayal. My heart for betrayal. Is that a fair trade, Carrington?"

A single teardrop slid down her cheek. She shook her head. He slapped her ass again. "Answer me! Is that a fair trade, Carrington?"

"No," she sobbed. "No. No. No."

She struggled against her restraints. He added another finger, controlling her movements easily from within.

"Your body betrays you, Carrington. Right now, your brain is telling you to make me stop. Your safe word is clanging inside your head, but your body won't let it out, will it? Your body betrays you." He pumped his fingers in and out in a merciless rhythm. "You're wet, Carrington. Wet and hot, and while your brain wants me to stop, your pussy is so close. So damned close to having just what it wants. You think you'll break me, that I won't be able to resist this sweet pussy of yours. You think I'll give in and fuck you, don't you?"

He stilled. Tears spilled unchecked from her pleading eyes.

"Well, guess what?" He withdrew from her and stepped back. "You won't break me, Carrington. No matter how hard you try to destroy me, you won't succeed. You see," he fisted his hand on his chest, "I know what it feels like to have my heart ripped out of my chest, and I've got the scars to prove it. I'm not a fucking dope head, and I never will be. Write whatever lies you want, but don't even think about using what we've done here to bring me down, or I'll bring you down with me. We're through."

He pulled a towel from his bag and wiped her juices from his hands, ignoring her sobs. "You won't be telling anyone about what goes on here." He took his cell phone from his trouser pocket and pointed it at her. "If you do, I'll release these pictures." Walking slowly around her, he snapped photos from every angle before pocketing the camera. He reached for his bag.

"Please, Master...Jason...."

He placed the riding crop inside and clasped the zipper pull.

"I...I love you. Please don't do this."

Her words were like a venomous bite, momentarily paralyzing him. He clenched his jaw tight and forced the zipper to move. He straightened, and without a backward glance, left her hanging there.

He stepped into the hallway and closed the door, sealing Carrington's sobs safely inside.

"Done?" Todd asked.

"Yeah. She won't be revealing anything to anyone," he assured.

"Is she okay?"

Jason turned a cold stare on his friend. "I didn't hurt her any more than she hurt me. You know me better than that. Give her a few minutes then let Brooke take care of her."

"Hey, I didn't mean it like that. I know you wouldn't really hurt her—you know…I heard her crying when you opened the door. That's all."

"She'll get over it. Ten minutes, no more. Then Brooke can see to her."

"Okay," Todd said. "See you at the stadium tomorrow."

Jason waved goodbye over his shoulder. Her sobs echoed in his brain, and he was deathly afraid if he didn't get out of there soon, he might turn back.

❧

She couldn't stay away. Not one to follow sports, Carrie had become a baseball convert over the last few weeks, following Jason's progress toward a homerun record with the tenacity of a rabid fan. Her rational mind knew her relationship with him was over, but her heart wouldn't listen to reason. He loved her once, and she loved him still. She wouldn't give up on them easily.

Handing her ticket over to the gate attendant, she followed the early crowd through the concourse toward a square of daylight that promised a view of the field. She'd learned about batting practice via pregame interviews on the local TV station. A little research had yielded the information that a game ticket allowed you into the stadium early enough to watch, if one was so inclined. Judging from the number of people filing through the gates, this was a popular event.

She followed the line of fans through the tunnel, her pulse kicking up a notch with each step she took. She stopped short at her first glimpse inside a major league ballpark. Jason's world. For a woman who made her living with words, she couldn't find a single one that encompassed all she saw. The sheer size of the stadium overwhelmed her. Tens of thousands of blue seats sat mute, their silence deafening. Arriving fans seemed to respect the quiet, their voices conversational as they picked their way down steps toward the railing. Players trickled out of the dugout in practice gear, stretching and flexing while the grounds crew moved equipment into place. Fans settled into seats to watch their favorite players or lined up along the rail with cameras and autograph pens at the ready.

She slipped into a seat behind a large man, using him to shield her from view. Not that Jason would see her, but it was a chance she didn't want to take. This close, and one among perhaps a hundred, if he looked closely....

He'd made it clear he didn't want to see her again. She understood. Really she did, and she'd tried to quell the impulse, but today was special. One more homerun would break the team record, and perversely, she wanted to be there to support him when he reached a milestone in his career.

The media had continued to speculate on the validity of McCree's accusations, and Jason, with the Mustangs organization beside him, had continued to deny them with quiet dignity while he slowly chipped away at the record. If kids needed a role model to emulate, they couldn't do any better than Jason Holder. He exhibited character and honor, despite the efforts to undermine his career.

Watching him the past few weeks only confirmed what she had known in her heart. Jason wasn't guilty. How she was going to prove it was the question.

He'd voluntarily taken every drug test known to medical science and released the findings to the press. Scandal hungry reporters had gone undercover to show how easy it was to cheat on a drug test, using the roundabout way to suggest that perhaps Jason had done the same.

Never in a million years.

Even at his angriest, he'd gone out of his way to care for her following their last scene together. He could easily have left her hanging there until someone had come to check on the room, but he'd calculated the time, knowing how long it would be before she realized he wasn't coming back, then he'd sent Brooke in to take care of her.

Cheat on a drug test? No way. Besides, she knew the physical side effects of steroid use, and none of those applied to Jason. Sure, his body was solid muscle, but she'd bet her life it came from hours in the gym—not drugs. She'd even seen the ugly side of his temper, but he'd kept that on a tight rein, just like everything else in his life. She had no doubt, if she looked up control freak in the dictionary, she'd find a picture of Jason Holder.

He stepped from the dugout. Carrie sank lower in the seat and peered around the big guy in front of her. Jason paused, hands on his hips to survey the field. He inhaled deeply, his broad shoulders rising and falling. Then he turned to the stands and smiled at the fans. Her heart somersaulted. Lord have mercy, the man was devastating. Another player exited the dugout, hailing him.

Jason held up a finger toward the fans, signaling he'd be over to see them in a minute, and joined the other player. The two men put their heads together to confer. She held her breath. Watching him like this, without him knowing, felt wicked. It was only the second time she'd seen him in person. The first time, she'd had little opportunity to observe him. This was different. His movements weren't calculated or planned. She felt like a peeping Tom looking through a window into his life. This was where he felt at home, relaxed. A place where he was among friends.

His conversation concluded, he turned to the fans, and right beside him stood—his twin. Two identical smiles greeted the onlookers. Together, they signed baseballs, caps, programs, T-shirts, and anything else handed over the railing to them.

The man in front of her spoke to his companion, "How do you tell them apart?"

"Beats me," the other guy said. "If they didn't have numbers on their jerseys, I'd have no idea."

That was rubbish. "The one on the left is Jason," she said.

Two heads craned to look at her.

"How can you tell," the big guy asked.

"It's easy. He's better looking," she said.

They laughed and turned around. She tuned out their further commentary involving the twins and idiot women in general, though she supposed they were referring to her specifically. She couldn't pinpoint what it was that distinguished him from his brother, but she knew which one was which. Just then, a very pregnant woman stepped to the railing and both men smiled up at her. They carried on a conversation she wished she could hear then the woman leaned over. Jason planted a kiss on her cheek, after which Jeff kissed her full on the lips. A lover's kiss.

"See, I told you," she said to the guys in front. "That's Jeff on the right—and that's his wife."

"It better be," smaller guy said, "or he's gonna be in hot water when he gets home."

Jeff's wife said her goodbyes and headed up the stairs toward the concourse. Carrie didn't know why, but as the woman passed her row, she fell into step beside her. At the mouth of the tunnel beneath the upper deck, the woman stopped, leaning against the concrete wall to catch her breath.

She took a couple of steps and stopped. The same impulse that had brought her to the ballpark today took hold of her again, and she turned back. "Are you okay?"

Jason's sister-in-law looked up. "I'm fine," she said with a smile. "You try carrying an extra thirty pounds or so up those stairs and see how you do."

She smiled. "I'll take your word for it." She offered her hand. "I'm Carrie Taylor," she said, wondering if the name would mean anything to her.

"Oh!" Mrs. Holder straightened. "You're her."

Carrie rushed to explain herself, "It's not what you think. I'm not stalking—"

Mrs. Holder shook her head. "You're the woman who has Jason all tied up in knots," she said and winked, "or vise-versa."

Her laugh was spontaneous and infectious. Carrie laughed with her, and before she could protest, she was being led across the concourse.

"Mrs. Holder," she protested. "Where are we going?"

They came to an abrupt stop, the other woman looking around as if she'd lost something. "Hmm. I don't know," she said. "Somewhere we can talk."

"But—"

"I know! I'm sure he won't mind."

Clearly, one didn't argue with Megan Holder. A moment later, Mrs. Holder identified herself to a security guard, who keyed them into an elevator. They stepped out into what had to be the offices of the Mustangs Baseball organization. They passed half a dozen men and women all wearing team polo shirts. Carrie averted her gaze. The last thing she needed was someone else recognizing her, especially since she'd brought a world of chaos to the team. Someone was likely to throw her out on her ass if they recognized her.

They stopped in an outer office occupied by a woman in her fifties, also wearing a team shirt. Mrs. Holder still had a death grip on her hand.

"Hi, Megan," the woman behind the desk said.

"Hi, Cynthia. I need a moment to rest. Mind if we sit in Doyle's office for a while?"

Doyle's office? No. Please, God, not that Doyle.

"Not at all. Go on in," she said. Concern tinted her voice. "Can I get you anything?"

"No, but thanks. I just want to put my feet up." She waved away the secretary's offer. "I'll be fine in a few minutes."

Not wanting to cause a scene, Carrie smiled at Cynthia and allowed her kidnapper to steer her toward a massive set of wooden doors carved to represent the Mustangs logo. A brass plaque announced the office's occupant. *That Doyle.* She almost bolted right then, but that *would* cause a scene, so she followed Mrs. Holder into the office of Doyle Walker, Manager. As soon as the door closed behind her, she grabbed the door handle and prepared to escape.

"Mrs. Holder, I shouldn't be here." She twisted the knob. "I have to go."

"No! Don't go. Please?"

"I'm sure Mr. Walker wouldn't want me here." She eyed the room, and Mrs. Holder's hand pressed against the door to prevent her escape. She didn't know pregnant women could move so fast."

"Humph. That's what you think."

"Mrs. Holder—"

"Please, call me Megan," she said. "Can't we talk? Please. I promise you won't miss the game."

How could she say no? She released the doorknob. "I don't know what we have to talk about, but please accept my apology. I know my actions have affected everyone in Jason's life, and for that, I'm very sorry. I didn't…." Carrie shook her head. "No. There's no excuse for what I did. I'm sorry. I'd take it back if I could."

She expected just about anything except the compassion in Megan's eyes. "Apology accepted." She crossed the room to a seating area that could have been in anyone's living room. "Now that that's out of the way, won't you sit with me a while. I really wasn't lying when I told Cynthia I needed to rest."

She perched on the edge of a chair. "Can I get you anything?" she asked, not that she knew where she'd get it.

Megan laughed again. "Relax, Carrie. Can I call you Carrie?" she asked, but went on before Carrie could answer. "I'm fine. Really. I'm even better now that I ran into you."

She didn't know what to say. This wasn't at all what she'd expected when she followed Megan earlier. She still didn't understand what motivated her to do it. Curiosity? Surely insanity made her speak to the woman.

"I don't understand," she said.

"Jason forbade me to look you up, but since you approached *me*…well, I'm perfectly justified in speaking to you. At least that's the way I see it." Her eyes twinkled with mischief.

"You *wanted* to talk to me?" None of this made sense. The ballpark was a magical place, but this…this went beyond magical into surreal.

"Oh, yes. I've been dying to meet the woman he fell

in love with, but he told me not to contact you, so I didn't. I had to respect his wishes, but now...." She smiled that megawatt smile of hers again. "All bets are off!"

Okay. This was the Twilight Zone, and Megan Holder was clearly insane. In the weeks since she'd last seen him, she'd been forced to face reality. What she'd seen in his eyes had been nothing more than wishful thinking on her part. If he cared for her at all, he wouldn't have left her that way, and he would have contacted her by now. The truth was a bitter pill to swallow. "Jason doesn't love me. He hates me."

"No." Megan shook her head. "I don't know what makes you think that. Well, I can imagine. Jason can be harsh when his feelings are hurt, but he's a good man. Kind. Caring. Generous." Her smile disappeared. " Look, I've known Jason as long as I've known my husband. To say we have a history would be an understatement, but that's a story for him to tell, so just let me say, I know him very well. He was unhappy for a long time. Then he met you, and it was like someone turned on a light inside him. I'd never seen him so happy and, um content. That's it. He seems content. This thing has thrown him, but he's coping. He'll come out on the other side stronger than before, but I want him to be happy, and you, Carrie Taylor, make him happy."

She shook her head. "No, I don't. He was very clear. He doesn't want to see me again."

"And I'm sure he meant it at the time," Megan conceded. "But it's my experience that men don't know how much they want something until they don't have it anymore. Trust me, he'll come around. He's too much like his brother in that respect."

"Begging your pardon, Mrs..., Megan," she corrected, "but I don't think he's going to come around. I betrayed his trust."

"You betrayed the trust of a man you didn't know."

Carrie stiffened at the reference to something the other woman could only know because Jason had told her. Megan waved away her concerns with the flick of her wrist. "Don't get your panties in a wad. I don't know everything, but I know he hid his identity from you. He and Jeff have always guarded their privacy. You should see the security system at our house. The Secret Service could learn a thing or two. Same goes for Jason's new place. Anyway, he told me enough to piece the story together. What I want to know is, would you have written the article if you'd known you were writing about the man you'd grown to know?"

"No. Never." She forced her shoulders to relax. "When I figured out Jason Holder was my mas…." She glanced away as her skin flushed with color. "My master." *Might as well swing for the cheap seats.* "I knew I'd made a terrible mistake. Master would never use steroids. Besides, I knew his body, even though I'd never seen him, I had plenty of opportunity to touch, and there are certain signs. He didn't have them."

Megan nodded. "You can see a lot with your hands."

"Yes, that's true. I tried to stop the article, but my editor wouldn't hear of it." The whole story spilled out then. It felt good to tell it to someone who didn't judge her actions and immediately find her guilty.

"Martin McCree is an ass," Megan said when Carrie wound down. "He used you, and now he's using Jason to dilute the media attention on his own case. Don't let it destroy you. It won't destroy Jason. Maybe set him back a little, but he won't let it ruin him or his career."

"I hope not. He's worked hard to get where he is. He doesn't deserve any of this."

"So…what are you going to do about it?"

"Me?" Carrie squeaked. "I don't know what I can do. I lost my job, and the story has grown into a monster with tentacles reaching out all over the place."

She squirmed under Megan's silent scrutiny.

"Why are you here today?"

"Jason has a chance to break the Mustangs' team record for most homeruns in a single season. I wanted to be here for him, even if he never knows it." She wrung her hands. "Actually, he wouldn't want me here, so please don't tell him you saw me."

"You love him."

No sense denying it. One more truth to face up to. "Yes. More than anything."

"Then you'll find a way to fix this."

"I would if I could. I don't think he'll ever take me back, even if I were able to pull off a miracle and end this for him."

Megan wiggled to the edge of the sofa and stood. "Come over here," she said, leading the way to a plate-glass window on the far wall.

"Wow,"

Below them, the field sparkled like a giant broach—a diamond winked in the center, surrounded by emeralds. The batting practice equipment had been put away, and the grounds crews were busy smoothing the dirt around the bases. Another crew used a template to place the chalk lines of the batter's box where Mustangs history might be made today.

"Did Jason tell you about his heart surgery?" Megan asked.

It took Carrie a moment to adjust to the abrupt change of subject. *No. He never let me get that close.* "He has a scar. He said he was nine."

"Let me tell you a story, Carrie."

Chapter Seventeen

He tried not to think about the record. There was plenty of time left in the season, and unless he suffered an injury or Doyle took him out of the lineup, he'd break the record. If not today, then another day. No sense worrying about it. How many times had players choked trying to accomplish a specific goal? Too many to count. He'd play his usual game, and if the right pitch came along, he'd hit it. That and a little diamond dust would take care of the record. For now, he'd focus on winning the game, because a win for the team was more important than a record for one player. And, if he hit a homerun, then he'd contribute at least one run toward the win. That's what the game was about, all the players contributing. Some did it better than others, but everyone on the Mustangs roster were top-notch players, and they deserved his complete concentration.

Jason stepped up to bat, acknowledging the good luck chorus coming from the dugout with a thumbs up. Bottom of the first inning, two men on, one out. Just another at bat. Forget about Megan and his parents in the stands. They came to lots of games, so no big deal. Just another day at the office.

While the umpire brushed dirt off home plate, Jason allowed his gaze to travel around the stadium. It never ceased to amaze him. What began as Jeff's dream and something for him to hold onto when the going got rough, had become a reality for both of them. But not without a lifetime of hard work. Only a handful of kids grew up to be major league players, and here he was, one of the lucky ones who'd beat the odds. Luckier than most, but that was something he didn't talk about, no matter how much his busybody sister-in-law insisted he should.

The crowd stood, a show of support for his attempt at the record. How many of them believed he'd gotten here by trickery? More than a few, and if he broke the record today, it would be more fuel on the growing bonfire the media had lit underneath his career.

"Tell them," Megan had insisted when she'd come to the rail earlier.

He'd heard the words enough. They were a constant echo in his head these days.

"Scorn or pity. Does it make any difference?"

That usually shut her up. He didn't want either one, so he'd keep him mouth shut, and maybe one of these days they'd believe him. Hell, he could piss in a cup on camera then follow the specimen through the whole testing process, but still, someone would claim the video had been altered in some way. Might as well keep his dick in his pants. They'll think what they want to think, no matter what.

The first pitch was low and outside. Ball one. No pitcher wanted to give up a homerun, much less a record breaking one. Yeah, that'd be a pisser. He lifted the bat to his shoulder and narrowed his gaze on the pitcher's hand—that tiny speck of white showing between his fingers. The windup. The release. He processed the information—arm speed, grip, wrist motion. A slider—impossible to tell if it would come in for a strike. He checked his swing.

Strike one.

Another slider. Jason swung. Funny how sounds meant different things to different people. When he was catching, he loved to hear the smack of the ball hitting his glove, but when he was batting, he preferred the crack of lumber connecting with the ball.

Strike two.

He expected a wasted pitch—something only a man looking for a record homerun would swing at, and that's what he got. High and outside. Jason declined to swing. *I'm not that desperate, buddy.* Bring it on.

Two balls, two strikes.

Two more pitches—both fouled into the net behind home plate.

Another throwaway pitch.

Still not desperate, asshole. Grow a pair, and throw me something I can hit.

Full count.

He forced himself to relax, so he would have something left to hit the ball with if the guy found his testicles and actually pitched to him.

The next pitch veered so far off the plate, the catcher almost dislocated his shoulder trying to catch it. *Fuck.*

The air reverberated with the low, baritone of forty-plus thousand fans booing. Jason tossed his bat toward the on deck circle as he jogged down the first base line. He had no idea how much of the crowd's displeasure was with his inability to drive one out of the park or the wimp-assed pitcher who would rather take his chances with the rest of the batting order. But he was on base, which meant a chance to score if Todd could come up with a hit. A walk was as good as a hit, he reminded himself, but it damned sure wasn't a homerun either. And if the pitcher maintained his control, connecting with one this game, much less two, would be an uphill battle.

❧

Carrie clenched her fists and bit her lip. Her body vibrated with anxiety, or maybe it was from the crowd surrounding her stomping their feet in perfect rhythm. She almost wished she'd taken Megan up on her offer to get her a seat in the family section, but after she had pointed out the block of seats and mentioned she would be sitting with her in-laws, Carrie had politely declined. They were excellent seats, close enough to the field to actually see the players, which meant the players could see the fans, too.

She hadn't come to the game to disrupt Jason's quest for the record, and seeing her in the stands with his parents would certainly do that.

So, she kept her nosebleed seat, doing her best to send telepathic messages of encouragement to Jason. It was almost impossible to concentrate. No wonder this single ticket had still been available. The rows from which her seat had been carved were occupied by a group of ponytailed softball players and their parents. The entire section to her right was filled with underage baseball players on a league outing, judging by their team uniforms, to see the big boys play. If the object of the trip had been to learn something about the game, then they failed miserably. The only education they seemed to be getting pertained to the varieties of junk food available. And everyone in the section was getting a lesson in how to be obnoxious from the group of frat boys occupying the uppermost rows of the stadium.

But Jason couldn't see her, and that was the most important thing. Here, among the anonymous masses, she could cheer to her heart's content, and watch his every move. She knew his body well, could see even from this distance the tension he held in his shoulders. She'd always imagined the players would be relaxed—having fun. Game or no game, baseball was serious business to the players. It was their job. Their livelihood. They played to win, and winning took skill and intelligence, and hard work.

It was impossible to ignore the scattered conversations when Jason came to bat. The scandal she'd created was far from dead. Everyone had an opinion, and they voiced them. She strained to hear a couple of the softball dads.

"You know he's guilty," one said.

"Why? I don't get it. These guys make millions. Why risk it?"

"Endorsement deals if they break the record. A sweeter contract when the current one runs out. Who knows?" the first one opined.

Carrie sipped from her soda, stifling the urge to set them straight, even though the only way she could do that was to reveal who she was and how she knew he didn't take steroids. She'd promised Megan she would try to find a way, but it wouldn't be easy. For now, all she could do was listen to the ill-informed viewpoints, keep her mouth shut, and cheer him on.

"Come on, Holder!" Mr. Stupid Opinion yelled when Jason came up to bat in the third inning. "You can do it. Out of the park!"

Clearly, the man still wanted to see him break the record, steroids or no. *Jerk.* What kind of fan cheered on someone they thought was cheating?

She couldn't sit still. The drunken frat boys behind her didn't seem to care, so she stood tall, subconsciously making herself a human antenna, sending her love and support to Jason via invisible thought waves. Stupid, she knew, but she knew how much the record meant to him— and after what she'd done to him, she couldn't bear to see him fail.

He swung and missed two pitches, and suddenly, she wasn't the only one on her feet. The entire stadium stood. Carrie put her hands over her ears to damp the roar of stomping feet and raised voices. The scoreboard flashed a colorful graphic of horses stampeding. The words, Thundering Herd, scrolled across the electronic banners placed like shiny ribbons around the upper and lower decks, spurring the crowd into a frenzy. Rally towels bearing the Texas Flag on one side and the Mustangs logo on the other, whirled in the air. If someone could find a way to harness the wind energy alone, it would power the stadium lights for a year.

A chant erupted in an outfield section and one by one, the sections joined in. "Jason. Jason. Jason."

How could he not know how much these people loved him? For this one moment, they'd put aside their doubts. They believed in him. They wanted to see him break the record. Accusations and scandal had been forgotten. This was the game at its elemental base. Man against the odds. She had done her homework, knew the probability of bat and ball connecting in the right spot, at the perfect angle and speed to produce a homerun were astronomical, yet Jason did it better than any man alive.

Carrie added her voice to the chant. "Jason." *Please God.* "Jason." *Come on, Master.* "Jason." *Do it. Do it.* "Jason." *Please God.* "Jason." *You can do it.* "Jason."

She stomped her feet and waved her empty fist in the air. She needed one of those rally towels. Her heart thundered. Her stomach tied itself in a knot and grew tighter with each bouncing stomp.

Another pitch. She gasped when the ball whizzed past Jason's chest. No swing.

"Come on, give him something to hit," Mr. Stupid Opinion yelled.

"Yeah, give him something to hit," she echoed.

The cheers continued. Jason stepped into the batter's box again.

Carrie chanted under her breath. "You can do it. I love you, Jason. You can do it. I love you. Please. Please. Please." Her fingernails dug crescent moons in her palms. Blood rushing past her ears all but drowned out the noise around her.

She could watch him all day. The way he moved. The confidence evident in his stance. She could only imagine the level of concentration necessary to tune out the crowd and focus on the ball.

The pitcher began his windup. The stadium held its collective breath, as if the inhale and exhale of forty thousand plus people might affect the trajectory of one three-inch orb. A fraction of a second of silence, over almost too quick to notice it ever existed. The solid, unmistakable crack of wood colliding with leather. A collective gasp, as if one and all suddenly realized they'd ceased to breathe.

Jason paused, his gaze following the ball rocketing toward the center field stands. Before it cleared the wall, he was halfway to second base, raising a clenched fist in victory. The crowd went wild.

As he took his solo lap around the bases, Carrie's eyes watered. The Mustangs dugout emptied onto the field to celebrate with him. He performed a celebratory hop on home plate and disappeared into the clutch of his teammates.

Someone pointed to the outfield. Renewed excitement rippled through the crowd. She turned in the direction of their outstretched arms. A door stood open in the outfield wall. A player appeared, jogging toward the mid-game celebration. Jeff. A moment later, the brothers emerged from the crowd, their arms around each other's shoulders. With his free hand, Jeff pointed to his brother while they turned in a slow circle.

The moment was too much. The half-cheering, half-jeering crowd. The emotions—relief, joy, pride, love, pain—turned her stomach into a giant cocktail shaker. Carrie dropped into her seat. How she wanted to share her feelings with Jason. To tell him how proud she was of him, to kneel at his feet and show him he'd mastered her the same way he'd mastered this game. He owned the game, and he owned her.

When the inning ended, she gathered her purse and picked her way carefully down the steps. Not knowing if she would ever have the strength to come back again, she stopped at a souvenir cart to purchase a rally towel and anything they had with Jason's number or likeness on it. The vendor was all too happy to take her credit card, handing it back along with a bulging bag of Jason Holder loot.

❧✦❧

"Hey," Jeff said when Jason joined him at the kitchen table the next morning. "Glad you could make it."

Staying in bed held a lot of appeal, but so did a well-cooked meal, even if it came with a lecture. He wasn't stupid. Megan's invitation after the game had been couched in terms he couldn't refuse. Before she was through with him, he would be crisper than the bacon sizzling on the grill.

"I never turn down Megan's cooking, even if I have to get up at the crack of dawn and drive twenty miles after a late night." He winked at his sister-in-law, who rewarded him with a scowl and an air kiss.

"You didn't have to come, hot shot," she said.

"Let's not kid ourselves. I know a threat when I hear

189

one." He gave her credit, she hadn't even bothered to deny her invitation to breakfast had been anything other than what it was—a chance to rag on him for something. "So, what have I done now?"

"Nothing," she said.

Jason exchanged a look and a shrug with his brother.

"Well, that's a first," Jason said.

He leaned to the side when Megan reached around him and placed a steaming cup of coffee in front of him.

"Don't be a smart ass," she said, returning to the cook top. "You've got to do something about this mess."

Ah, the mess. "We've been over this a million times. I don't want to talk about it. Not now, not ever."

"You could end all the speculation, Jason, and in the process, do something good for a lot of kids going through the same thing you did. If you'd done it years ago, none of this would be happening now."

Jason sipped his coffee, well aware his brother remained silent on the subject. Jeff understood his reluctance to talk about his scars. Though his brother didn't bear any physical ones, he sported a few of his own from their early years when losing his twin had been a real possibility. A little support would be good right now. "What do you think, bro?"

"I think she's right."

Jason jolted, and his coffee mug clattered against the tabletop. He stared open-mouthed at his brother. *Well shit.* "Don't tell me she's holding out on you until I cave."

"No." Jeff smiled at his wife. "She has a point, Jase. You know I've always supported your decision not to talk about your heart, but that was then. This is now, and the timing is right. You could put an end to the steroid speculation and, in the process, reach a lot of kids and their parents. I think it's great you talk to a few at the hospital here, but there are plenty of others across the country who could benefit from hearing your story."

"I talked to Carrie," Megan said, placing a huge platter filled with bacon and pancakes in front of them.

He ground his teeth. "You did what?"

"I talked to Carrie. She was at the game yesterday."

"I told you not to contact her. What part of that did you not understand?"

"I didn't," she said, helping herself to a generous portion. "She found me at batting practice."

He wouldn't have been more stunned if the bacon and pancakes had jumped up and started dancing on the table. "She was at batting practice?"

"Yep. She saw me talking to you and followed me. We talked, and then she stayed for the game. I tried to get her to sit in the family section, but she wouldn't. Said she didn't want to distract you."

A thrill of satisfaction tingled along his nerve endings followed closely by abject terror. "What did you talk about?"

"You, mostly. She loves you. But you already knew that. She wants to help, Jase."

"I don't need her kind of help, and she doesn't love me. She doesn't even know me."

Megan sipped her orange juice. "Oh, I'd say she knows you very well…Master."

Jason choked on a bite of pancake. *Holy fucking shit.*

"That's what she calls you. She understands why a man like you doesn't want the world in his private business, but she agrees with me. You can't let this media frenzy continue. Have you seen the news this morning? They're already picking apart your record, adding the asterisk to it as we speak. If you don't say something soon, there won't be any way to erase it."

"It's time, Jase," Jeff said. "If you don't tell the story, I will."

"Fuck."

He stood and his chair scraped across the tile floor. "You two think you have it all figured out, don't you? This is my life. My career. My fucking business, and I won't say this again. Stay the fuck out of it!"

His gut churned with the new betrayal. Couldn't they see? Did they not know him at all? Even Jeff—his other half.

He needed to get away. Needed to think. He drove— to where, he had no clue. Anywhere. Away. Alone.

So fucking alone. Just like when he laid in the hospital bed—a kid all alone. Jeff had been at school and his parents had needed to work to pay the hospital bills. They couldn't be there all the time like some of the other parents. Being alone had been worse than being sick. No one to hold his hand, no one to tell him it was going to be all right. Sure, the doctors and nurses said the words, but they couldn't very well tell a scared and lonely kid the truth, could they?

Tears blurred his vision. He pulled to the side of the road and turned on the emergency blinkers. If this wasn't a fucking full-blown flashing light emergency, he didn't know what was. The people he loved most, the ones he counted on to be there for him were going to sell him out. God, he couldn't bear it. That frightened kid inside him wailed. No matter how hard he tried to deny him, the child was still there—afraid of losing control of his life again.

He'd been at the mercy of others then. Everyone had a say in what happened to his body—everyone but him. No control. No opinion. Not even a vote. They'd made the decisions and left him alone to contemplate what they meant to him, to his life.

Jeff had been his lifeline. His dream of being a major league baseball player became Jason's dream. They made plans. Plans Jason had clung to through all the poking and prodding and testing. Even through the surgery, the pain of loneliness had been worse than all the other stuff combined. Jeff would pitch, and Jason would catch for him.

When he'd gotten home from the hospital, Jeff had a specially padded chest protector and a mask waiting for him to go with the catcher's mitt Jason had kept with him at the hospital. He still had that mitt—the one he held onto like other kids on his floor had held teddy bears and favorite blankets. They said he even took it into surgery with him, but he couldn't remember that part. All he knew was he'd had it before, and when he woke up after, it was still in the crook of his arm. They'd probably lied to him, but at the time, he'd been pretty proud of himself for hanging on to it. Control. One little thing he could control.

Control was an illusion. He had no fucking control over anything. He couldn't stop his family from telling his story. In a way, it was Jeff's story, too. But that didn't mean he could open Jason's private pain up to the world without discussing it with him first.

He reached deep for some scrap of control. Inhaling deeply, he counted slow, forcing the breath and a measure of anger out. Again. Each breath was easier than the one before until he was calm enough to think rationally.

He always known he would eventually have to tell his story. Megan and Jeff were right, now was the time. There were hundreds of kids across the country who might find strength in his story, strength they needed to fight for life, and still others who were using steroids or thinking about using. If he could convince any of them to change their course, it might give purpose to his childhood pain— something besides driving him to grasp for control at every opportunity.

First things, first. He glanced in the rearview mirror, checked over his shoulder, and pulled back onto the road. He was going to do it, but he was going to do it his way, or not at all.

Chapter Eighteen

Jason entered his brother's kitchen through the backdoor. Jeff was nowhere in sight, but his blabbermouth sister-in-law was still there.

"What did you tell her?" he asked.

"You know, one of these days you're going to walk in like that and see something you don't want to see." Megan bent to set a plate in the dishwasher.

Jason grabbed the plate, slipped it into place, and held out his hand for another. "Let's not go there. You cooked, so why isn't your husband cleaning? Should you be doing this much stuff?"

"I'm pregnant, not dying, Jase."

"Sit down," he ordered. "I'll finish this."

She gave him a look he was becoming too familiar with—one that meant she didn't have to take orders from him.

"Don't give me that look. Just sit down and let me do this. It's the only apology you're going to get for the way I left here a few minutes ago."

Megan maneuvered onto a barstool. "Okay, since you put it that way."

He loaded the dishwasher and filled the sink with soapy water. "Tell me what's going on in that devious brain of yours so I can tell you what's really going to happen."

"Jason—"

"Stop," he said, turning to lean against the counter. "No lectures. I'll tell my story, but I'm going to do it my way. So, tell me what you and Carrie were planning."

"Okay," she said with a sigh. "Finish the dishes first. You yelled at me, Jason. The way I figure it, you owe me a lot more than a clean kitchen."

"Maybe. It depends on how much meddling you've already done."

She pointed her index finger downward and twirled it around. He got the message, turning to complete the job he'd started.

"I suggested she write an article about kids with PDA. I may have suggested she interview a few specific kids and their families that I know of who've been through heart valve surgery...you know, to get their point of view. I may also have suggested she ask them if anyone had offered them insight or encouragement along the way."

He stopped, hands buried beneath suds, and closed his eyes. "That's all?"

Silence.

"Tell me," he said.

"It's nothing."

He fisted his hands. Damn it. Whenever he used that tone of voice on Carrie, she would do anything for him, so why didn't it work on Megan?

"Okay, don't go all dominant on me," she backpedaled. "I told her the Mustangs would help her get the article out there since she no longer has a job."

Jason dropped his chin to his chest. He locked his elbows and braced against the counter.

"Jeff's talking to Doyle right now...to arrange it."

"Wait." He spun toward her. "What do you mean she doesn't have a job?"

"She argued with her editor about the article. They refused to pull it, so she quit."

Jason turned back around, clutching the granite rim around the sink. *Fuck*. Just when he didn't think this situation could get any worse. He squeezed his eyes shut.

"She asked them to pull the article?"

"That's what she said. You can ask her the details, but she was very upset that they wouldn't listen to her."

He peeled his fingers loose and scrubbed the cast iron griddle. Next, the frying pan. He worked in silence, washing, drying, putting them away. This much he could control. Nothing more. Every other fucking thing in his life was out of his control. *Unacceptable.*

"She shouldn't have written it in the first place," he said, drying the last pan.

"No, she realizes that. You do realize McCree used her, don't you?" she persisted. "He was going to make the accusation, one way or another. If not through her, then some other reporter. None of this is her fault. He had no way of knowing she had a personal relationship with you."

Jason rinsed the sink then wiped the sides and bottom clean with the dishcloth. Megan was right. Carrie got caught in McCree's web of lies. If not her, then someone else. But knowing that didn't make it easier to accept what was happening to him. His life was caught in a vortex, spinning out of control, and the only way to stop it was to grab hold and stop it himself.

"Oh good. You're back," Jeff said, stepping into the kitchen. Jason pulled the drain plug loose. "Doyle says it won't be a problem. He'll arrange everything. A press conference, whatever we need. He said he'd have PR contact Carrie to see what she has in mind."

Water swirled as the drain sucked it down—a metaphor for his life if ever he'd seen one. With one last slurping gulp, the drain consumed the last of the soapy water. Jason squeezed the dishrag dry and hung it over the sink's center divider. He turned to his brother. "Did it ever fucking occur to you to ask me what I wanted?"

"Well…yeah, but you made it clear this morning that your head was still up your ass, so I nixed that idea. Besides, I knew you'd come around."

"You're a controlling son of a bitch, aren't you?"

Jeff smiled. "We're identical twins, Jase. What do you think?"

"I think if I didn't love Megan so much, I'd kill you."

Jeff sidled up next to his wife and gave her a kiss not meant for polite company to see. "It's a good thing you love her then, but she's mine. Go get your own woman."

Maybe he should. Hell, everyone had a say in his life but him. Maybe it was time to go deep and grab onto what *he* wanted. "I think I will. Yeah, I think that sounds like a good idea, and I know just where I can find one."

❧

The first order of business was research. Carrie surfed the Internet for anything on Patent ductus arteriosis, PDA for short. Even if Megan couldn't convince Jason to cooperate and save his good name, she might still be able to freelance the article to a newspaper or magazine interested in children's health issues. She'd just leave out the parts about Jason Holder and the reason he'd have to be insane to use steroids—besides the obvious.

For the first time since she'd walked out of the newspaper's offices after quitting her job, she had a purpose. Bringing attention to this affliction and the kids who survived with the right care could only be a good thing. Hope for the hopeless. Never mind she was one of them—the hopeless, that is. Hopelessly in love with a man who didn't want her, didn't love her. She closed her eyes and took a deep breath, willing the constant heartache to go away. Unsuccessful, she shook her head and resumed work. She couldn't think about what she'd lost. No matter what Megan had claimed, Jason didn't love her.

It was a nice fantasy to have, and one she'd dreamed of often while waiting for the next summons from her master. But like the girl in the fairy tale, the clock had struck midnight, and what had seemed so perfect, so right, had disappeared in a puff of popcorn and hot dog scented smoke. The difference? Carrie's Prince Charming wasn't going to come looking for her.

Maybe something good could come from the mess she'd created. This PDA article could be the beginning of a new freelance writing career. She'd write what she wanted and sell the articles. It wasn't exactly stable work, but it was work, and anything was better than sitting around wishing she could turn the fairy tale clock back.

For a few short months, she'd lived the life she wanted with a man who'd seen the dark needs of her desire and had taken her there. Then the fairy tale had ended, taking her career and her sex life with it. She didn't want anyone else, couldn't imagine giving another man what she had given Jason. Maybe in time….

She shook her head. No, that clock was broken. She couldn't go back, and she couldn't go forward. Not like that. Never like that again.

She refused to watch the news for days following his record-breaking homerun. After leaving the stadium, she'd listened to the remainder of the game on the car radio, sickened by the immediate speculation on how the record was achieved. Hearing the speculation, the thinly veiled accusations had galvanized her resolve to try and fix what she'd done.

The doorbell chimed. She blinked, shifting her focus from her computer screen to the front door. Convinced it had to be a kid selling candy bars or magazines, she ignored it.

The bell chimed two more times.

Persistent bugger, she groused. *Get a clue and move on.*

"Open up, Carrie."

She froze, staring at the closed door. It couldn't be, but she would know that voice anywhere. Her heart hammered against her ribs, and warmth and desire stirred low in her belly.

"I know you're in there."

She swallowed past the lump in her throat. Her brain sent signals to her feet, but they remained beneath the small desk she'd purchased at a flea market.

"Every second I stand out here adds to your punishment, angel. Makes no difference to me how many times I spank you."

Her feet moved faster than she thought possible. She jerked open the door. "Shh! People will hear you!"

"You think I care?"

God, she'd never seen a sexier sight than Jason Holder in her doorway, one forearm braced on the doorjamb, his hips cocked back just so. She didn't know which she liked better, Jason in the tight jeans he wore today, or Jason in those clinging baseball pants. He looked mighty fine in both.

"I'm tempted to bare your ass right here in the doorway and give you the spanking you deserve."

The low, seductive promise in his voice set her internal thermostat to simmer. Her temperature spiked and a familiar heat rushed from her chest to her hairline. She forced her gaze to the floor. "If that's what you want, Master."

He pushed away from the doorframe, straightening. "Invite me in, angel. We'll do this in private."

She stepped back, closing the door behind him. She folded her shaking hands behind the small of her back and waited. She tracked his feet as he walked to the center of her living room and turned slowly to take it all in. There wasn't much to see—just an entertainment center with a TV and a few family pictures on one wall, a sofa took up another. Beneath the single window that looked out on the strip of rocky soil between her apartment building and the neighboring one, sat her desk. She cringed when he moved in that direction, realizing she'd left the Internet browser open to a clinical study on PDA and steroid use.

"I see you've been hard at work, angel." He clicked a few keys on her laptop.

She dared to glance up in time to see her screen saver pop up.

"Well, look what we have here," he said.

Mortification blazed through her system, and what had been perhaps a sweet blush now had to be a blotchy red rash. She loved that picture of him at bat. The photographer had captured his steely-eyed concentration in the split-second before his bat connected with the ball for one of his many homeruns. But what she liked best was the way the muscles in his arms and thighs stood out in the photo. An artist couldn't have asked for more perfect lighting.

She averted her gaze, sucking her bottom lip between her teeth.

"I understand you were at the game yesterday," he

said.

"Yes, Sir."

"And you didn't see fit to tell me."

"I…I thought you wouldn't want me there," she said.

"What I don't want is you or anyone else meddling in my personal business."

She nodded, wishing the floor would open up and swallow her so she wouldn't have to hear another word about how she disappointed him.

"But, as my brother and sister-in-law have pointed out, I've had my head up my ass."

Something like hope blossomed in her chest. He paced away from the desk, glanced around the breakfast bar at the tiny kitchen, and stopped in front of the entertainment center.

"You're right. I didn't want you there."

That tiny, flickering flame of hope died a sudden death.

"But I'm glad you were. It means a lot to me that you came to support me, even if I would have told you not to had I known."

"I couldn't stay away," she admitted.

"Why is that?"

She bit her lip. Loving him was her own private pain, and she wouldn't blurt it out to only to have him squash it like an unwanted bug. She closed her eyes as if closing the drapes would keep the light glowing inside from spilling out into the world for all to see.

"Tell me, angel." His voice—inches from her—was deep and smooth, a sensual caress that invited her to reveal her innermost secrets.

She wouldn't say it. His finger beneath her chin was warm and strong. He tilted her face up.

"Look at me," he commanded.

Carrie sniffed back tears. She looked into his eyes. They were kind and inviting, like his voice.

"Tell me," he demanded again. "Why couldn't you stay away?"

Her lips trembled. The words came forth as if charmed from her. "I love you. I couldn't stay away…because I love you."

He stroked her lower lip with his thumb. His eyes searched hers, then his gaze roamed over her face. She hated the tears that ran unchecked down her cheeks and her lips that quivered in tandem with her legs. Her breasts ached for his touch, and it was all she could do not to lean forward. To just brush against his solid strength would be Heaven.

His lips quirked up on one side, and she thought she might die. He was laughing at her! Oh God, why had she said those words? Her body trembled from head to toe. If only she could move, run far and fast. She stood on the edge of a cliff, unable to plunge over and end the infinite humiliation of not being wanted.

"There," he said, brushing tears from her cheeks with both thumbs. "That wasn't so bad, was it?"

She swallowed, but her thick tongue wouldn't let her answer. *Yes. No. I don't know.* His hands cradled her face. So warm. So strong. His lips descended toward hers. Her eyelids dropped.

His mouth touched hers, tentative at first, like a lover unsure of his reception. She rose to her tiptoes, following when he broke away. His next kiss was more sure. Firm, like a lover who knew he'd be well received. The flicker of hope in her chest burned brighter. She moved her lips beneath his, kissing him back with all the love she had for him.

"Open for me," he growled, nipping at her bottom lip.

The tiny flame became a torch when his tongue plunged past her lips, exploring, tasting, claiming. Their tongues battled. With each gasping breath, they made love to each other with lips and tongues. Her palms itched to touch him, but their only points of contact were his hands holding her still and the mating of their mouths.

He broke the kiss. Carrie whimpered. He dropped his forehead to hers, and still cradling her face, they both fought for oxygen. She had no shame. She wanted him. Wanted to keep on kissing him forever. Wanted to touch him, taste every inch of him. Wanted to open her body to him, to take him inside her, and hold him there forever. No shame. Just longing, and need, and a love so deep, so real, her heart bled.

"I love you, too," he said, startling the breath out of her lungs. "I've been an ass. Please say you forgive me."

Her ears were playing tricks on her. She couldn't rely on her senses anymore. Somehow he'd short-circuited them. Even her eyes, looking into the depth of his, told her she'd heard right, but it couldn't be….

"My God, Carrie, please."

"Say it again." Her lips moved, but she wasn't sure she'd actually said the words.

"I love you. Please forgive me."

"You love me?"

"Yes," he said, a smile in his voice.

He kissed her again. This time, his love filled her all the way to her curling toes and tingling fingertips.

"You know," he said, breaking this kiss, "I could command you to forgive me."

"No," she shook her head. "Please, don't. I can't forgive you, Sir, because there isn't anything to forgive."

"None of this was your fault," he said. "If I'd told you who I was from the beginning, or if I'd told my story years ago when I should have, none of this would have happened. I've been an ass." He released her and took a step back. "It's time for me to fix things, but first, I need to know if you want to continue our personal relationship."

She opened her mouth to answer, but he stopped her with a hand signal.

"Even if you say no, I want you to write my story. All the embarrassing, humiliating details I've kept to myself all these years. And if you say yes, I'm going to spank your ass until you can't sit down, then I'm going to fuck you senseless."

Her palms itched, and her sex tingled. Blood rushed to the region in anticipation of the spanking and fucking. "You want me?"

"Forever," he said with conviction. "In my life, in my bed, at my games. I want you on your knees, at my mercy.

I want to push that lovely body of yours to your limits, and beyond."

Forever. The word echoed in her heart. "Can I see you naked?"

"Hell, yes," he said. "No more blindfolds." He paused, thinking. "Well, maybe on occasion, but I promise you'll see me naked more than you'll see me clothed." He sealed the vow with a devilish smile and a wink.

"Forever might not be long enough," she said.

"Is that a yes?"

"Yes, Sir."

A weight lifted off his shoulder, and for the first time since before his heart betrayed him when he was child, his world was completely right. "Remember what I said I would do if you said yes?"

"You promised to spank me until I couldn't sit down then fuck me senseless, Sir."

"Yes, I did. I was wrong to blame you for this mess, and I've already punished you for your part in writing the article in the first place, so this spanking is for going behind my back to talk to Megan. The two of you conspired against me, and I won't stand for that kind of behavior. Do you understand why I'm punishing you?"

"Yes, Sir. I should have come to you as soon as she confided in me. Instead, I conspired with her against your wishes."

"And, you didn't tell me you quit your job," he said.

"I planned to the day the article came out. I was so glad you wanted to see me. I was going to ask you if we could break the rule about keeping our regular lives out of our relationship. I wanted to tell you what was happening in my life, but then you told me what was happening in yours. Well, then I *couldn't* tell you." Her voice dropped to a whisper. "I didn't want you to hate me."

"I'm so sorry, angel. I should have been there for you, but I was so wrapped up in my own misery that day, I didn't notice how much you needed me. I really fucked this up, didn't I?"

"No, Master. It was all my fault. If I'd taken a few

more minutes and thought before I sent the article…I'm sure I wouldn't have sent it the way it was."

"You were rushed," he said.

"I wanted to get back to you. I hated being away from you," she said. "That whole trip was a disaster, from start to finish."

"I remember. I felt so helpless. You needed me, and I didn't know where you were or what you were doing. You know, I was going to tell you who I was that last night, but when you told me you were going out of town, I changed my mind. I wanted to be close to you afterwards, in case you needed to talk."

"Really?"

"Really. Then all hell broke loose and my career was in the toilet, and I cut you lose. I didn't want to drag you down with me."

"You love me that much?"

"I do. I convinced myself you would be happier if you never knew who you'd been with those last few months. I thought it would be better that way."

She shook her head. "No. I don't care what you do for a living, Master. I never did. I only wanted to be with you."

"Well, now that you know, I promise not to keep anything from you again."

"Thank you." She dipped her head. "If it pleases you, I'm ready for my punishment now, Master."

Ah, she submitted so beautifully. He couldn't wait to give her all he'd promised. "Take your clothes off. Stack them on the sofa then brace yourself against the desk with your ass in the air."

"Yes, Master."

She removed and folded her clothes while he opened drawers on her desk, sifting through them until he found what he wanted. The crack of the old wooden ruler on his palm was a satisfying sound against the quiet backdrop of her living room.

She placed the neat stack on the corner of the sofa. Jason moved her old-fashioned ladder-back chair, indicating with a wave of the ruler she should take its place. Bracing her palms against the front edge, she arched her back and dipped her head.

"Spread wider," he said, tapping her inner thighs from behind with the ruler.

She shuffled her feet apart, baring her pussy to him.

"Better. Lift your chin. Eyes straight ahead," he said.

She lifted her gaze to the dusty mini-blinds covering the window, and he yanked on the cord dangling to her right. The blinds flew up, inviting anyone who might come by to see her punishment.

"It's not quite the open doorway, but it will do. Do you like the idea that someone might see you, angel?"

Cool wood stroked her ass cheeks.

"One of the gardeners I saw when I arrived could decide today is the perfect day to take care of the little patch of weeds outside your window." He pressed the ruler between her legs, applying pressure from her clit to her anus. "He'd be, what, three feet away? No more. He'd see your tits." He tapped her breasts with the ruler and she gasped. "He'd see your hard nipples and your ass in the air."

He fisted one hand in her hair, holding her head so she couldn't look away. "He'd see the look on your face when the ruler lands on your ass."

Thwack!

She gasped at the stinging blow. This wasn't a gentle, playful, arousing spanking. This was punishment. He landed three more blows in quick succession. Releasing her hair, he smoothed his hand over her ass.

"Keep your face up. You know he's watching. Let him see how much you like being punished."

His fingers dipped lower to toy with her gaping slit. "Christ, you're wet all ready." He flicked her clit, and she bent her knees in an effort to press herself closer to his touch. He admonished her with a not too gentle slap to her pussy. "Hold still."

Four more punishing blows landed on her ass, followed by a tender massage, but he no longer roamed between her legs to ease the ache growing there. He repeated the process for a total of twenty licks. He was right, she wouldn't sit easily for days, but at that moment, all she could think about was his other promise—to fuck her senseless. She didn't care if the entire choir from the First Baptist Church was watching, she needed him inside her, needed him to fulfill his promise.

"Please," she begged.

He felt her up, using his fingers to prepare her, pumping in and out of her channel with hard thrusts. "A promise is a promise, angel." He continued to work her while he unzipped his jeans. He left her long enough to protect them both, then he was there, driving into her with deep, forceful thrusts that had her gripping the edge of the desk with white knuckles.

His hands spread her ass cheeks wide. She couldn't think past the glorious wonder of having him inside her. She set aside her own pleasure, reveling in giving herself to him. He took her hard, and when he pressed both thumbs in her ass, the warmth of complete possession melted her bones. She toppled forward, pressing her cheek against the cold plastic of her laptop while his cock supported her lower half.

"Mine." He pounded into her limp body. "Mine. Mine. Mine."

She fisted her hands on either side of her head and closed her eyes, focusing every molecule of her being on her center, where the man she loved possessed her completely. It was the most beautiful thing she'd ever experienced; this giving of herself to a man who in turn gave her everything he was.

Thrust after hard thrust, she took and gave until her body was like a clock-spring wound too tight. "Master," she pleaded.

"Yes. Come for me, angel. Milk my cock."

He'd died and gone to Heaven and his angel had taken him there. Her sweet pussy clenched around him, drenching him in honey. His orgasm felt like she'd reached inside him and pulled his heart out through his dick. He screwed his eyes shut and pumped furiously, the ecstasy almost too much to bear. Fucking amazing. He'd never get enough of her, and he'd never get his heart back from this woman. She'd stolen the wounded organ right out of his chest, and though each time he drove into her he thought he could touch it, he knew he'd never get it back.

He didn't want it back. It had been damaged goods from the beginning. Flawed. But in her care, it was new, whole again. Her love was better than any surgeon's repair. Her love had done what medical science could never hope to do—burrow deep and rejuvenate a busted heart.

❧

They moved to the sofa where he held her across his lap. His quiet strength created an invisible shield that made her feel safe. They'd shared quiet times before, but never had the silence between them been this easy. He held her like he didn't want to let her go, and she couldn't stand to think about being apart from him.

"I love you," she whispered, worried if she spoke the words too loudly she would break the spell.

"I love you, too." His sensual lips brushed the shell of her ear. "I have a game."

"Can I come watch?"

"I'd like that, but you have something else to do tonight."

"I do?"

"You do. You have to pack about a week's worth of clothes and anything you can't live without for a few days then you're going to drive over to my house and put it all away. I want to play tonight knowing you're at home waiting for me."

"I like the sound of that."

Chapter Nineteen

Nothing could spoil his good mood, not even the reporters waiting for him when he arrived at the stadium. Having made the decision to tell his story and put an end to the rumors and speculation, a weight had been lifted from his shoulders. The hype would come to an end soon, and even though it would be replaced with another media frenzy, at least this one had the potential to help people. Megan and Jeff were right. He should have told his story long ago instead of holding on to the painful memories like they belonged only to him, and no one else could understand or sympathize. He waved off the reporters with an impatient hand, promising to answer their questions at a later time.

"Hey," Jeff said with a nod as Jason approached their side-by-side lockers.

"Hey, yourself." Jason sat next to his brother. He returned greetings from the other players nearby then turned to his brother. "You win. I'm going to do it."

"That's great," Jeff said. "It's about fuckin' time, if you ask me."

"For the record, nobody asked you. The two of you stuck your noses in my business. And just because you were right this time doesn't mean you should make a habit of it."

"Point taken." Jeff pulled a practice jersey over his head. "Megan likes Carrie."

"That's good because she's going to be around for a long time." Soon, she would be at his house. "Damn! I forgot the alarm." He dug his cell phone out of his pocket. "Is Megan coming to the game?"

"No. Why?"

"I need her to disarm the alarm at my house. I gave Carrie a key, but I forgot all about the alarm."

"Just call her, dude."

"Can't." He punched the speed-dial for his sister-in-law. "I don't know her phone number. Besides, Megan can show her around, help her get settled in."

"She's moving in?"

"I sure as hell hope so.... Hey, Megan, sweetheart. I need you to do me a favor."

❧

Carrie shifted her laptop case on her shoulder and reached down to get her suitcase from the trunk.

"Here. Let me help."

She almost jumped out of her skin at the woman's voice. Her hand automatically went to her shoulder to protect her precious computer from the woman's grasp.

"Megan?" she said with a half-hearted laugh when she recognized the woman beside her.

"Sorry. I didn't mean to startle you. Jason asked me to come over and turn off the alarm system for you." She reached for the laptop again, and this time Carrie handed it over. "Let me rephrase that. Jason *told* me to come over and turn off the alarm." She made a face. "I honestly don't know how you stand it, having him order you around."

She tugged her suitcase out, closed the trunk and followed Megan up the drive and in a side door. She followed her through a short hallway, past a laundry/utility room into a large kitchen dominated by a black granite bar.

"He used to try that with me. I think that's why we never got past the casual lover stage."

"Wait." She grabbed the edge of the bar for support. "What do you mean, casual lover stage? You and Jason...?"

Megan set the laptop case on the bar and put her hand over her mouth. "Oh no. I thought…well, he didn't tell you about…us?"

Her knees gave out, and she stumbled to the nearest barstool and sat, shaking her head. An image of Megan on her knees in front of Jason formed and wouldn't go away. "No. No."

"Oh my." She settled on the stool next to Carrie. "I'm sorry. I just assumed…." She reached her hand out, but Carrie jerked back from her. "Please, listen to me. It's not what you're thinking. At least I don't think it is."

"You and Jason?" She couldn't wrap her mind around it. "But…you're married to his brother."

"Look, I'm sorry Jason didn't tell you, but please, you have to believe me, it was never anything real between us and we both knew it. He's a fantastic lover, which I'm sure you know, but I was in love with Jeff. I fell in love with him within days of meeting him, but the two of them were…overwhelming."

"The two of them?"

"Um…yes."

She stood, not sure if she was leaving, or what. What does one do when confronted by something like this?

"Please, don't go. Let me explain," Megan pleaded.

Carrie found her tongue. "I get the picture."

"I don't think you do. Please, sit down. I'll make some tea and tell you what Jason should have told you before he asked you to—check that—*ordered* you to come here. That's what he did, right? Ordered you?"

"I don't see that's any of your business," she said, proud she'd found her spine along with her tongue.

Megan moved around the kitchen, finding the teakettle with an ease that spoke of familiarity with her surroundings. "You're right. Sorry. It's just that Jason can be overbearing at times. It drives me crazy." She filled the kettle and set it on the stove before opening more cabinets to set out mugs and a selection of teabags. "He can be easy going about some things, but when it comes to sex…"

"I don't want to hear this," she said, but morbid curiosity drew her back, and she resumed her seat at the bar.

"And I don't want to say it, but you need to hear it." Megan placed the mugs on the bar, then leaned back against the opposite counter and crossed her arms over her baby bulge. "It's a long story, but I met them sort of by accident, and the next thing I knew, they were seducing me. Both of them. At the same time." She shook her head. "It was crazy. Two great looking guys…well, you've seen them, and they wanted me. I guess I lost my mind because before I knew it I was having sex with both of them, often at the same time."

Her gut clenched. Would Jason share her with another man, his brother even? She grew lightheaded thinking about it.

"Whoa," Megan said. "Calm down. Remember, I was in love with Jeff. Jason was…extra, I guess. He was fun. A fantastic lover, but it was never anything other than physical pleasure for him or me. It was his idea to leave the relationship. He realized I'd fallen in love with his brother even before I did. And to tell you the truth, I knew I couldn't ever make Jason happy."

She paused to pour hot water into the mugs. Carrie, working on autopilot, selected a teabag and dipped into her mug.

"I've never seen him this happy. It's like you had the key to open him up or something."

Carrie dunked and stirred and stared at her tea, trying to process what she was hearing.

"I've done things I never thought I would do, but I'm not ashamed. They are wonderful men. They have a special bond that goes beyond the twin thing. I think it goes back to when Jason was sick. They were just kids, too young to have to go through something like that. Jeff was scared to death of losing his brother, and in order to cope, he built a fantasy that included Jason. The fantasy of becoming major league ball players. They became inseparable, Jeff trying to do anything to keep his brother alive, and Jason…well, I think he was grasping at anything he could control." She took a sip of her tea and moved around the bar to sit next to Carrie again.

"That's my theory. Take it or leave it." She shrugged. "Anyway, I wasn't the first woman they'd shared, but I don't know anything about the others. I don't want to know. And I'm sure you didn't want to know about me. But I never meant enough to Jason for him to want me all to himself. It wasn't like that with Jeff. At first, I was just someone he shared with his brother, but it wasn't long before he wished he'd never allowed it to happen. It never will again.

Megan smiled and patted Carrie's hand. "I think Jason has finally found the woman he won't share, the one he wants all for himself."

Could it be true? Just this morning, he'd fucked her in front of the open window, teasing her with the idea of being watched. Would he share her with another man? "I'm not so sure,"

"Trust me, he's very much like his brother in many ways, and I can tell you, once Jeff made up his mind that I was his, he was like a kid on the playground guarding his toys from all the other kids. He wouldn't let another man near me now, not even his brother. Especially not his brother."

Carrie didn't know what to think, where to look. She couldn't look this woman in the face without picturing her with Jason…and his brother. And fast on the heels of those images, were ones that shook her even more—the ones of Jason offering her to another man.

Would he expect her to accept another man? And if he did, would she do it?

"What are you thinking," Megan asked, shaking her out of her thoughts.

"Lots of things. Nothing."

"Has he mentioned sharing?"

"Yes, sort of. He said he'd push my limits. That's one of my limits."

Megan reached out, covering Carrie's hand with hers. "Trust him. He's a thoughtful lover, even if he can be a bit pushy sometimes."

"Pushy?" Carrie laughed. "I don't think I'd exactly call him that."

Megan shrugged, "Well, I think you know him better than I do, so I'll defer to your expertise."

She nodded. "Yes, I think I know him pretty well." She sighed. "All this has taken me by surprise, I guess. I do trust him, but I need to talk to him about my feelings. I don't want…."

"I understand," Megan said. "Talk to him. He loves you, and he's a good listener."

≪৶৹৶≫

Crouched behind home plate waiting for the next pitch, Jason forced the image from his mind long enough to concentrate on the ball speeding toward his face. The batter held up, watching the ball all the way into the mitt for a strike.

Every free second, his mind went back to his house, picturing Carrie there. She would obey him, which meant she was naked, putting her things away in his drawers, his closet, his bathroom. He couldn't wait to get home. He'd have to remember to call the house phone to let her know he was on the way. Maybe they'd have phone sex while he drove so she'd be horny and wet when he got there. He couldn't wait to bury his cock inside her again. Maybe he'd rub lotion onto her ass too. It was probably still red, or at least pink from the spanking he'd given her earlier.

Another strike for the third out.

He moved to the dugout, unbuckling his chest protector on the way. Seated, he removed the shin guards, and gulped down several cups of water from the jug on the bench next to him. Damn, it was hot tonight. He wiped his brow on his shirtsleeve before rising to select a bat and retrieve his helmet.

Standing in the on-deck circle, he narrowed his focus to the man at bat. *Hit the ball. Just hit the fucking ball. Get on base, Reynolds.* Two RBI's would be nice, and he mentally willed Tanner Reynolds to get a hit. The second baseman couldn't be counted on to knock one out of the park, but his on-base percentage was good. He had a pretty good scoring percentage, too, thanks to having Jason batting behind him in the order. *Come on, Tanner. I'll bring you in.*

Jason doubted his feeble attempts at mental telepathy

would do any good. Shit, if his teammates could hear his thoughts, they'd never let him hear the end of it. Just for fun, he sent Carrie a mental message. *You're mine. All mine, angel, and I'm going to taste every inch of you when I get home.* He smiled. Wouldn't the guys on the team shit a brick if they heard that in their heads?

The crack of lumber on leather snapped his attention back to the game in time to see Reynolds digging his way toward first base like there was a pit bull on his ass. Jason strolled to the batter's box. This was his game. Two runs here would be a nice cushion, almost guaranteeing a win if Jeff didn't screw up and blow the save.

He went through his routine, scratching out a foothold for his right foot, then his left. He adjusted his junk and raised the bat to his shoulder. His cup felt two sizes too small today. It was the first time he'd played an entire game semi-hard, and if it became a regular occurrence, he'd have to find a bigger cup. This one was past being uncomfortable, but his semi-rigid state reminded him what was waiting for him at home.

All the more reason to get this game over with. With the image of Carrie, naked, kneeling on his bed, waiting for him, he assessed the first pitch. Too low. He backed out of the box, repeating his routine once the pitcher had the ball in hand again.

Just fucking throw me something I can hit.

The pitch was his from the moment it left the pitcher's hand. Jason tracked the spinning orb with the accuracy of a NASA scientist tracking an asteroid headed toward Earth. Instinct propelled his hands toward the ball, and he unleashed one hundred and eighty pounds of coiled energy along the length of the bat. The only thing that felt better than the impact of a fastball connecting with the sweet spot was his cock sliding home.

It had taken him long enough, but he'd finally found the sweet spot he couldn't let go of, and she was waiting for him. Trotting around the bases, all he could think about was getting home to her.

❧

Long after Megan left, Carrie sat at the bar, her still

packed suitcase on the floor beside her. It didn't matter that the tea in the cup between her palms had grown cold; she just needed to hold onto something solid while the unpredictable world shifted under her feet with each new wave of uncertainty.

Her thoughts were as unsettling as ocean currents, and equally as dangerous. She was in love with Jason, but the fact remained, she knew very little about him. Even though Megan assured her there was nothing between the two of them other than sisterly affection, she found it unnerving to accept assistance from someone who had been intimate with Jason.

Which brought up the question—how many others were out there? Thanks to Megan, she knew he had shared several women with his brother. Would he share her, too? If she believed Megan, it wouldn't be with her husband, so who? Todd? Some stranger in a club?

And what if someone offered him the opportunity to fuck another woman?

She clenched the coffee mug. What right did she have to question his past or current sexual interactions? It wasn't like she was pure either. She'd been with a few men. She'd even been with Todd and Brooke a few times. Each time, she'd walked away physically satisfied, but there'd been no emotional connection between them, and never would be.

Megan had said that was how she'd felt about being with Jason, physically satisfied, but no emotional connection—though clearly, she loved him.

The house phone rang, startling her. She glanced at the clock then to the phone and answering machine on the built-in kitchen desk. His voice filled the room. She shifted on the barstool. Lord, her body even reacted to his recorded message.

She tensed, knowing what was coming next. Jason. For real.

"Angel. Pick up if you're there. I'm on my way home."

That wonderful, commanding voice made her clench her thighs together, which only made her need him more.

"Christ. Please tell me you're there, Carrie."

Hearing the vulnerability in his voice weakened her resolve, but she stopped herself before she did something stupid, like run to pick up the phone to reassure him she was there. If she did, he'd give her instructions on how he expected to find her when he walked in the door, and until they got a few things straight, she couldn't let herself be influenced by his voice or the promise of the best sex she'd ever had.

Coming to his house had been a big step. Hell, he'd practically ordered her to move in. Megan had showed her the empty drawers in his dresser and where she could hang her clothes in his closet. She'd mentioned that Jason had bought the house after she and Jeff were married. That ruled out her possessions occupying the empty space. But had he made room specifically for her, or had some other woman's belongings recently been there?

She had to know where she stood. Perhaps she'd just fallen in love with the great sex. Lord knew, it was almost enough to live on, but she wanted there to be more.

Her head spun. There was more, she knew it, but everything was all jumbled in her head and her heart where he was concerned. Things were moving too fast after months of slowly getting to know each other as lovers.

She didn't know where her insecurities were coming from. Yes, she did. She'd been blind, and blindfolded for so long, she'd never considered other women in his life. She'd never asked about them, and he'd never said. Now, not only was she confronting vague shadows of his past lovers, but an actual one—one he considered a friend, one who'd become part of his family. Megan seemed like a nice person. She even seemed to genuinely want Carrie to work things out with Jason.

No wonder she couldn't make her feet budge. He was asking her to take a lot on faith. Until she got some answers, she'd keep both her suitcase and her jeans zipped.

ॐॐ

"Shit." Talking to his own fucking answering machine. What a pisser. Maybe she was in the shower, or better yet, up to her nipples in the giant Jacuzzi tub in his bathroom. Or maybe she wasn't there at all. Tomorrow he'd reactivate the cell phone he gave her, or at the very least find out what the hell her phone number was so he could reach her.

The drive seemed to take forever, as if the roads had somehow stretched since he'd driven them a few hours ago, or perhaps time slowed. Either way, he was aware of every heartbeat, every breath. He was adrift on a dark ocean all alone, where home and the woman he loved were nothing more than wishful thinking. He knew about anxiety. Had known sheer terror facing the best pitchers in the league in clutch situations, but he hadn't felt this alone, this terrified since he was a kid.

Halfway home he convinced himself he'd screwed up, though he didn't have a clue what he'd done to scare her away. With each mile that registered on the odometer, he considered altering his course to her place, then thought better of it. Maybe he was wrong and she was there. His thoughts bounced back and forth between she was and she wasn't faster than a ping pong ball in a championship tournament, so when he finally pulled into his driveway and saw the lights on in his house and her car in his driveway, he almost wept with relief.

He tossed the duffel containing his dirty underwear into the laundry room and hung his keys on the hook next to the side door. Following the light spilling from the kitchen, his body thrummed with anticipation.

"Angel," he said, stepping into the kitchen.

She turned her head, but her posture was rigid, and if she held that mug any tighter she would crush it into dust. He took it all in, reading the signs. Her suitcase beside her, the fact that she was dressed and kept her body turned from him, shutting that part of herself away. Her full lips were nothing more than a pale slash across her face, and though there weren't any tears, the puffiness around wary eyes suggested there might have been some earlier.

His gut clenched. Had he caused this? If so, he had no idea how.

Aware he was treading through a minefield, he weighed his options. He could walk in as her master and order her to tell him what was wrong. He could get it out of her, even if it meant hours of patient attention to her body. His other option, and the one he leaned toward, was to simply ask like any other clueless guy would.

Just step on the damned landmine and let it blow you to kingdom come. Get it over with.

Chapter Twenty

"What's wrong?" he asked from his strategic position near the exit.

"Megan told me about you…and her…and Jeff."

Kaboom!

There it was, the explosion that rocked his world—not her words, but the single tear sliding down her cheek. Damn. It wasn't one of those artful tears, designed to manipulate, but a tear straight from her heart. He thought he'd been doing her a favor, not telling her everything, but all he'd done was hurt her. The question was, had he done irreparable damage?

"Why didn't you tell me?" she asked, her voice small and unsure, and more deadly than any bullet.

He wanted to cross the room, take her in his arms, and tell her it would be okay, but he wasn't sure he believed it himself.

"A few reasons," he said, stepping carefully to avoid more explosive tears. "One, we haven't spent much time talking, so my past relationships haven't come up, nor have yours. Two, I thought I was protecting you by not telling you. I can see that was a mistake." He inched closer, considered it a victory when she didn't bolt. "And three, it's in my past and has very little to do with my future. Our future." He eyed the coffee pot, decided cold caffeine wasn't a good idea this time of night, and opted for a water bottle from the fridge instead. "Four, my relationship with Megan wasn't real. It was just sex, and not very honest sex at that. She was never what you are to me, and I was never myself with her. And last, but by no means least, she's my sister-in-law. I love her like a sister, and I don't go around telling people about our past relationship. Besides, Jeff can be touchy about the subject, though it was his idea in the first place."

"Really?" she asked, her eyes wide with disbelief or curiosity. He wasn't sure which.

"Honest to God truth." He held up one hand, swearing an oath on it. "His idea. I never would have gone along with it if I'd known the two of them would fall in love. It'd never happened before—the falling in love part."

"She said she wasn't the first."

He nodded. "That's right. There were others. Mostly during our college days. We both felt a few girls up in high school, but we didn't have a clue what we were doing."

She smiled at that, which gave him a glimmer of hope, but the smile faded, and so did her questions. Her gaze dropped to her hands still wrapped around the coffee mug.

"What is it you want to know?" he asked.

She took a deep breath and squared her shoulders. He braced for whatever she was working up the courage to ask. He'd asked her to be honest with him, and he was determined to give her the same consideration.

"This morning in front of the window…I was wondering…now that I know about your previous ménages, is that something you would do with me? I mean…do you want to share me with someone else?"

Jason drained half his water bottle in one swig, never taking his eyes off her. Did he want to share her?

"The truth? No. Not really. But I told you when we first began that I would push your boundaries, and I meant it. Don't tell me you didn't enjoy the idea of being watched because I know you did. Your body doesn't lie. Right now, I want you all to myself, but maybe in the future, if I think it would please you or please me, I would consider sharing your body with another man, or perhaps a woman. You've been with Todd and Brooke. Tell me about your experience with them."

"It wasn't much. Todd likes to tease Brooke, make her watch him get other women off. He never...I mean, it was always just touching, mostly. He'd bind us both then make us watch while he touched us. He used his fingers, and once he used a vibrator."

"He never fucked you?"

"No!" She shook her head. "Never. It was all for Brooke's benefit. It made her crazy to watch him touch me, but crazy in a good way if you know what I mean."

"Yes, I know what you mean." He finished off his water and tossed the empty bottle in the recycle bin under the sink. "Did you watch them fuck afterwards?"

"Yes. She likes having an audience."

"I see," he said, crossing his arms over his chest. "There's something very primal about two men fucking a woman at the same time. Rest assured, I won't be inviting another man into our bedroom anytime soon, but it is something I want you to think about. There are ways I can give you a taste of what it would be like, and you can always ask Megan. I don't think I'd be lying to say she enjoyed it. Very much. I don't think Jeff is ever going to let it happen again, but I don't think he'd mind her talking about it with you. All I'm asking is that you keep an open mind.

"At some point in the future, I may bring another person, or persons to watch or participate in some way, but it would be nothing more than sex, physical gratification. It wouldn't have anything to do with the way I feel about you, other than my desire to give you all the pleasure you can accept."

"I see," she nodded.

"Do you, Carrie? I need to know you trust me to see to your well-being. Yes, I'll push you, but I'll never push beyond your ability to accept. Yes, I'll require things of you that you can't even conceive of right now, but I'll never force you to do anything you don't want to do. You'll always have a safe word, and I'll always respect it. That doesn't mean we won't talk about your reason for using it, and perhaps try again based on that discussion."

"I understand," she said. "I guess I'm just scared. You're asking me to take a big step, coming here."

"You have no need to be frightened. I'm asking a lot, I know, but I want you in my home. More than that, I want this to be our home, a place where we can be ourselves. A place where nothing we mutually agree upon is wrong.

"I want that, too."

Jason inclined his head in the direction of her suitcase. "So, why didn't you unpack like I told you to?"

"I was going to then I got to thinking about you and Megan, and there were the empty drawers. I wondered...."

"If you were just the next one to have a panty drawer at Jason Holder's house?"

"Yes, I guess that's what I was thinking."

He pushed away from the counter. "Come on and bring your suitcase with you."

Jason disappeared into the house. She slid off the barstool and followed like a robot, pulling her wheeled luggage behind her. She caught a glimpse of his back as he stepped inside the room at the end of the hallway—his bedroom.

He stood in the center, facing the door with his hands resting on his trim hips. Waiting. She stopped in the doorway, unsure whether to step inside or run for her life.

"Come here, Carrie."

His voice was all the convincing her feet needed. She took a step forward, then another.

"There, was that so hard?" he asked when she stood before him like a wary child her first day at the orphanage.

She tightened her grip on her suitcase and shook her head.

"Tomorrow, go buy new furniture for this room. Especially a new mattress and linens. My only requirement is that the bed be either four-poster or otherwise have some way to attach restraints. While you're at it, you can replace anything in the house that isn't to your liking." He stepped closer, taking her face between his palms, capturing her gaze with his. "To answer your question...yes, before you, there was a woman named Stacey. She ran for the hills at the mere suggestion that she might like for me to tie her to the bed and have my wicked way with her."

"Were there others?"

His hands fell away from her face, and he stepped back. Carrie shivered. It was like he'd flipped a switch, leaving her cold and alone.

"No. I bought this house and everything in it after Megan, and before you. Stacey was a mistake in many ways, but her revulsion at what she called my perverse ways led me to you, and for that I can be nothing but grateful."

She glanced at the king-sized four-poster bed holding court in the center of the room. "She left because you wanted to restrain her during sex?"

"That's what she said. But in the interest of honesty, I think that was just the last straw. She wasn't happy with the traveling I have to do, and she thought I had a woman in every city. She's a physical therapist and works with professional athletes. She hears stories, some of which I'm sure are fabricated, and others I know aren't. I never could convince her I didn't sleep around."

"Did she know about Megan?"

"Yes, she did."

"How did you meet her?"

"Jeff injured his arm last season. She was his physical therapist."

She eyed the bed again. "You changed the sheets?"

He laughed. "She's been gone since before I met you, so yeah. I have a housekeeper who changes the sheets twice a week."

"Will you tie me to the bed and have your wicked way with me?"

"Yes, but not tonight." He reached for her suitcase and headed for the door. "Tonight, you get your own bed. Tomorrow morning, I'll tell you my whole, sordid life story, then you can go furniture shopping. If you want, you can come to the game tomorrow night."

"But—"

"No." He parked her suitcase at the foot of the bed and wrapped her in his arms. His body heat seeped into her bones, melting and molding them to fit perfectly against his hard frame. "It's enough tonight that you're here, that you waited for me so we could talk."

She slipped her arms around his waist, drinking in his clean scent, the one that reminded her of the out-of-doors. "I wanted to leave, but I couldn't."

"Thank you for staying. It means a lot that we can talk about these things, work them out."

She nodded. Her cheek rubbed against the soft fabric of his T-shirt. She tightened her hold on him, loving the feel of him in her arms. Here in his embrace, her fears seemed juvenile, and she was glad she waited for him to get home. "Sir?"

"More questions, angel?"

"Just one. Will you make love to me tonight?"

A chuckle rumbled through his chest, making her smile. His hands slid along her arms, pushing her away from him. "Is my angel horny?"

"Yes, Sir. Please?"

"Had you been waiting for me in the way I expected, you would have been well satisfied by now, but since you weren't, I think not. You did disobey me, angel. You could have followed my orders and still voiced your concerns before I touched you. I'll always listen to you. I know you don't trust me enough to believe that yet, but you will. I'm a man of my word, angel."

Carrie nodded.

"At the beginning, I told you there were consequences for disobeying me, did I not?"

"You did, Sir."

"I respect your feelings regarding the previous women in my life, but I won't allow them to come between us. Out of my respect, you can refurnish our bedroom, but that's the end of my generosity. Tonight you'll sleep alone." With his hands on her shoulders, he turned her around to face the opposite direction. "That's the bathroom straight ahead. Go get ready for bed, and when you're ready, come back and wait for me to tuck you in. No clothes, angel. You'll sleep naked from now on. I don't want to fight clothes every time I want you."

He gathered the things he needed from his bedroom then took his time undressing. He'd been hard since walking in the door to find Carrie in his kitchen, and it was damned tempting to take what she was offering. But rules were rules. The sooner she understood that, the sooner she would learn to trust his word.

He pulled on a pair of pajama pants that did nothing to hide his erection, but might convey the point she wasn't going to get what she wanted tonight. Of course, he smiled at his thoughts, that didn't mean *he* had to suffer through what was left of the night.

She was so fucking beautiful, she took his breath away. Kneeling on the floor, her hands behind her back to emphasize her perfect breasts, she was every bit an angel. He tossed the items he'd brought with him on the bed and stood before her. Fisting one hand in her hair, he jerked her head up. His other hand tunneled past his waistband to free his cock. Her mouth opened on a gasp.

"Perfect," he said, filling her mouth with his cock. She was hot and wet, and damn if she didn't set his cock on fire. He hissed through clenched teeth. "Mint mouthwash. Fuck, woman, that feels good. Hold still. I'm going to fuck your mouth." He held her steady while he pulled out and thrust back in. "This. Is. For. Me." He punctuated each word with a hard thrust that drove his cock to the back of her throat, savoring the spiced heat inside her mouth and the stinging bite when the mint hit the outside air.

He couldn't look away. He loved watching his cock slip past her lips—loved the way her eyelashes fanned across her cheekbones when she lowered her eyes to watch, too. "God, I've needed you the whole fucking day."

He needed to take the edge off before he forgot his own rules and fucked her good and hard. He'd never wanted a woman the way he wanted this one. He'd never get enough of her, even if he had her night and day for the rest of his life. Even now, using her for his pleasure, she swirled her tongue around his shaft, giving of herself. And if her sexy little moan was any indication, she was enjoying herself, too.

The orgasm shot like lightning down his spine to the small of his back where it exploded into a fireball no amount of willpower would stop. He reached for his cock, yanking it free of her mouth. The first wave of cum spewed forth, hitting her on the cheek. He pumped furiously, guiding the stream to splash against her neck and breasts.

His knees were weak, but he managed to help her to her feet, and after stripping the covers from the bed, positioned her on her back in the middle. She made no protest while he attached the restraints to the bed frame, adjusting them so her limbs had limited movement. When she was spread eagle, he stood beside the bed, admiring her.

"You're lovely," he said. "I can't have you touching yourself tonight. Your orgasms are mine, angel. This is your punishment for disobeying me."

"Yes, Sir," she said.

"You should have enough movement to keep from getting a cramp. He leaned over to place a kiss, tasting himself on her lips. "I'll check on you after a while."

He turned off the light and went to his room, taking no satisfaction in denying her needs.

 си

She slept in fits and starts. She had some room to move her arms, but not enough to touch herself, or even to roll over. He'd left her legs loose enough to bring her knees up, but getting comfortable was out of the question. And on top of it all, he hadn't covered her and she was cold. Every time the air conditioner kicked on, which was every few minutes, her nipples tightened and shivers rippled over her skin. She stared at the bedside clock, counting the minutes and hours until Jason would return to release her.

She'd been through a dozen emotions since he

exacted his punishment. First came resignation and submission. She'd done the crime, she'd do the time. When she realized he meant to leave her there all night, fear and anger took over. Those two heated her blood so she didn't notice the cold so much — until the constant brush of chilled air caused her nipples to tighten and ache. That's when the horniness she'd experienced most of the day came back with a vengeance.

Eventually, exhaustion took over and she drifted into a restless sleep. She'd dreamed of him before, but not like this — so real it stole the breath from her lungs. He came to her, releasing her ankles, massaging the skin where she'd pulled against the restraints. His hands were warm on her chilled flesh, molding her to his will. He kissed his way up her inner thighs. She moaned. *Um...so good.* So close to where she needed him.

"Please," she begged, thrashing against the sheets. She dug her heels into the mattress, thrusting her hips up in desperate invitation.

He stilled her with one strong hand on her stomach then his mouth was on her, his lips kissing her swollen flesh. His tongue teased her opening, thrusting in and out. She'd never had a phantom lover who knew her so well. He lavished attention on her pussy, urging her toward to the edge. She was so close...close enough to see the promise of ecstasy beckoning to her.

"A little further," her lover coaxed. "You can do it."

His voice could seduce a saint to sin. "I've got you, angel. Spread your wings and fly."

Carrie whimpered. So close, he thought. Damn, she was beautiful. Even in the darkened room he knew the color of passion on her skin, could see her holding on, craving the freedom he could give her, yet frightened to give up control and let him push her over the edge. No woman had ever tasted like this one, heaven and earth mingled into a tantalizingly fragrant elixir he needed in order to live.

He could stay here forever with his face buried in her sweet spot, but his angel was hurting. He knew the feeling.

All she needed was one tiny push, and she'd take the freefall. Precious moments plunging headlong into the abyss, facing death only to find her wings at the last moment and soar on the currents of ecstasy.

"Time to fly, angel," he said, sucking her clit into his mouth.

She held on with every muscle in her body. She strained against the woven restraints, and they creaked against the bed frame. *Trust me, angel.* He flicked his tongue over the tight bundle of nerves then gently clamped it between his teeth and tugged.

He sucked on her clit. She took the fall, hurtling into the dark abyss of pleasure, her body clenching and writhing. *You're safe with me, angel.* Holding her hips secure, he provided the ballast she needed to unfurl her wings. *I've got you.*

She gasped, giving up the struggle. She couldn't hang on any longer. The promise was too bright, too enticing.

"Time to fly, angel," he said.

Trust me. She felt the words, rather than heard them, and somehow she knew trusting him was the right thing to do. This phantom lover promised pleasure beyond anything she could comprehend, if only she would trust him.

Pain, sharp and unexpected sent her hurtling into space. She rode a cloud of pleasure, safe in her phantom lover's care.

"Wake up, angel." Jason rolled on a condom, and moved over her, fitting his cock to her pussy. "Let's fly together this time."

Her eyelids fluttered open. He stared into her doe eyes, loving the moment she realized this was real. Reaching for her wrists, he released one then the other. "Do you come in your sleep often?"

Her face flushed scarlet. "No. Oh God, Master…."

"Shh. It's all right. Who were you dreaming about, angel?"

"You, Sir. I needed you so bad."

He nudged her core. She gasped then widened her legs in invitation.

"I needed you, too, angel. I couldn't wait another minute to have you."

He filled her with one sure thrust, going deep, loving the way they fit together perfectly. Braced on one forearm, he angled over her so he could fondle her breasts. He teased the nipples to hard buds then bent to suckle, matching each pull and tug to the tempo of his thrusts.

"You're so fuckin' perfect." He kneaded her breast, wishing he'd turned on a light before he crawled between her legs. He'd heard her, straining against the restraints, moaning, and he'd come to see about her. She'd obviously been dreaming, writhing for her lover in her sleep, and so beautiful all he could think about was walking into her fantasy and taking her to a place she was afraid to go in the light of day.

"Your pussy is so hot and wet. I've never felt anything like it, angel." He pumped harder, and with each thrust, he gave a little more of himself to her.

She wrapped her arms around his neck, her fingers grasping for a handhold in his hair. He stared into her eyes, loving the welcome he saw there. It was inconceivable how he'd denied them both this connection for so long. He took her harder, saw the moment she surrendered everything to him, felt it in the way she softened under him, letting him take what he needed, trusting him to care for her.

He reached between them to find her clit. "Come with me, angel. Share your wings with me."

Chapter Twenty-one

The need in his eyes made her go all weak and gooey inside. How had she missed this vulnerable part of him? Maybe it was because he had never let her see it. This was the real reason he'd kept her blindfolded so long, not because he didn't trust her to keep the secret about his sexual inclinations, but because he didn't trust her to keep this secret — the one he hid from everyone.

His need for her was so deep and primal it ruled him, but along with that need was his fear of rejection he hid away from everyone, including himself. Warmth bloomed inside her. She gave herself to him. He was a powerful man on the outside, but a frightened, lonely boy on the inside. She stroked his back. His firm ass flexed. He drove into her as if he tried to squeeze his entire body into hers. She opened her heart and took him deep.

You're safe. You'll always be inside me. I'll never let go. She cradled his face with her palms so he couldn't look away from her. "I've got you."

He roared like a lion freed from captivity. His body coiled tight then he pushed up with his hands and unleashed his need. He took her, each thrust brutal and punishing. She relaxed her body, absorbing the impact, reveling at the power of the man inside her as he let loose the demons he'd held in check so long.

She cradled his hips, loving the feel of his hard muscles as they slid across her palms. His cock battered into her, filling her, shattering her heart, so all her love for him spilled out. The words were on her lips, but she held them. The slick slide of his cock beckoned her to spread her wings and fly.

His eyes mirrored her need. "Fly with me, Jason."

She raised her arms over her head and arched her body, seeking the pressure that would send her over the edge. He stretched out over her, pinning her hands with one hand, stroking her from breast to hip with the other, grinding against her, giving her what she asked for.

His cock pulsed inside her. The sensation was all she needed. Her heart took wing, carrying them both into the dark abyss and from there, straight into the sunrise.

∽ℐℒ∾

He moved around the kitchen—ostensibly to fix them breakfast. It didn't take a genius to figure out he had no clue what he was doing.

"Want some help?" she asked, sliding off the barstool he'd directed her to when hunger had driven them from their bed.

He stared at the coffee maker. "Uh...yeah, I guess. Do you know how to work this thing?"

She gave him a hip bump. "Step away from the coffee maker," she said in a nasally voice. He laughed. While he watched, she went through the motions, coaxing a burp and gurgle from the machine.

"Excellent," Jason said.

"Food?" She headed toward a set of tall cabinets that looked like they might conceal a refrigerator.

"That would be nice." He tagged along behind her. He looked over her shoulder at the empty shelves.

She nodded. "Yep, it would be. Nice, that is." She opened the drawer labeled meats. Empty. Same with the vegetable bin. There was a tub of soft margarine in one of the door shelves. She opened it, bringing it to her nose for a sniff. "This will do. Now all we need is some bread." She tossed the margarine tub on the counter and opened the nearest cabinet.

Jason crossed to a concealed door on the far wall. "Pantry, I think."

This time, Carrie followed him, stopping short at the empty shelves of a cook's dream—a walk-in pantry.

"This is…."

"Pathetic?" He grabbed the one item occupying the space and held it out to her. "Bread."

She took the loaf, eyeing it for freshness. "I was going to say, incredible, but pathetic works, too." She held the loaf up. "When did you buy this?"

Jason shrugged. "Last week?"

She rolled her eyes and spun on her heels. He followed her out, passing her when she stopped to open drawers looking for flatware.

He opened one in the island behind her. "Utensils are over here."

"Thanks," she said. "Toaster?"

He pointed to a corner cabinet. "Over there."

They sipped coffee and nibbled toast until they'd taken the edge off their hunger. He managed to refill their mugs then he sat back down, tracing the handle of his with his fingertip. She waited for whatever he was getting up the nerve to say.

"I almost died when I was nine," he said.

❧

Carrie sat to one side of the packed media room at Mustangs Stadium, along with Jason's parents, his brother Jeff, Megan, and Doyle Walker, the Mustangs' manager. His teammates formed a solid line around three walls of the room, standing in support of one of their own.

She admired the inner strength it took for him to bare his soul here today. Of course, no one could possibly guess how difficult this press conference was for him. He wouldn't let them. He stood tall, his posture relaxed, his voice confident. He was completely in control of himself, and his welcoming smile insured he controlled the room. She thought her heart might burst with pride.

"Good afternoon," he greeted the crowd. "My name is Jason Holder, and I'm a catcher for the Texas Mustangs, in case you didn't know." A chuckle rose from the assemblage.

"Many of you are aware that a player on another team has accused me of not only using, but also providing steroids to him and other players," he said, his tone indicating how much he disliked the subject matter. "I have remained quiet, under the assumption that lies should not be given credence by speaking of them. I've called this press conference today to tell you a story. There are only a few people who know what I am about to tell you, and they have kept it to themselves at my insistence. First, let me say, the Mustangs organization has known this from the beginning of our association. Actually, since the first scout watched Jeff and me play at a high school tournament.

"When Jeff and I were nine years old we came down with a case of strep throat. It's a common ailment at that age, and we were given antibiotics to combat the bacterial infection. We both recovered, but where Jeff resumed his normal activities, I did not. The infection was gone, but I had very little energy, and things went downhill from there. Weeks went by, and I underwent every test known to medical science. At least that's what it seemed like to a nine-year-old."

The crowd chuckled again. Jason cleared his throat. He looked directly at her, and she saw a lifetime of pain in his gaze. She offered him a weak smile for encouragement. His lips lifted on the corners ever so slightly, then he looked out across the room and continued his prepared speech.

"I was diagnosed with Patent ductus arteriosus, a congenital heart defect. I won't bore you with the details right now, but it was something I was born with, and it had gone undetected until the incident with the strep bacteria. A small opening in a blood vessel that should have closed itself shortly after birth, had failed to do so, allowing the strep bacteria access to my heart. I spent four weeks in the hospital where I was given massive doses of antibiotics to combat the infection. By then, the damage was done, and I underwent open-heart surgery to repair my heart valve and to close the artery that was the cause of all my problems in the first place.

"I know you're wondering what this has to do with steroid use, so bear with me another moment." He paused for a drink of water from the bottle provided for him. He cleared his throat again. "I was in the hospital for nearly two months. My brother came to see me every day after school. He brought my school work, kept me up to date on everything that went on in my absence, and told the worst jokes you've ever heard."

A low rumble of laughter filled the room. Jason glanced at his brother who smiled and shrugged his shoulders.

"We'd always been baseball fans. We played Little League the year before I became ill. Just two little boys having fun. But Jeff had another idea. Somehow, he got it in his head that we were good, and if we worked at it, we could play major league ball. He brought my glove to the hospital, and everyday he told me how he was going to learn to pitch, and I was going to be his catcher. It was his dream, but it became mine, too.

"I eventually got out of the hospital, and we returned to the baseball field. We were pretty awesome in high school, if I do say so myself." He grinned like the braggart he must have been back then, and the crowd erupted in laughter. He had them eating out of his hand, and he knew it.

"Every year we went for our physicals, and by then, it was pretty clear my heart was doing fine, but I still had to have special clearance from my cardiologist in order to play. When I was thirteen, he warned me about steroids. You see, there's evidence linking steroid use to the reopening of PDA. He was right to warn me. We both knew players who chose to use steroids in high school. For kids with major league, hell, even college aspirations, it was tempting. But my experience in the hospital, and the months of recovery following, convinced me I'd never do anything to risk a repeat performance.

"So, long story, folks, but that's it. I'd have to be insane to use steroids, and even though some people—" He nodded in Jeff's direction — "like my brother over there, might question my sanity, I assure you, I'm completely sane. Given my medical history and seeing what performance enhancing drugs have done to otherwise healthy and rational people, I would never use steroids or under any circumstances encourage anyone else to, and I certainly wouldn't provide them for anyone.

"I thank you for your patience today. If you'll hold your questions for a little longer, we have some information for you that explains more about PDA. Inside, you'll find an excellent article written by Carradine Taylor, the reporter who originally broke this story, outlining my commitment to local children who are going through similar experiences to mine."

Players handed out the prepared press release folders. Hands shot up. He called on reporters one at a time, patiently answering most questions and politely referring others to the more detailed report they'd been handed. She understood his reluctance to speak publicly about his private pain, and she'd been happy to help him translate his thoughts and emotions into words.

It seemed like they'd never run out of questions, but finally, Jeff joined his brother, followed by the team manager who took over while they stepped away from the microphone.

"That's all folks. Now, if you don't mind, we have a game tomorrow in Kansas City. I hate to break up the party," he said and motioned to Jeff, Jason, and the group still lining the walls, "but I gotta get these guys on a plane."

❧

"It's only three days," she said, nuzzling his neck.

"Three days too long." He caressed her breast, his tender massage coaxing her body to a slow simmer. Dipping his head, he teased her nipple with his tongue, and she moaned. "I like the way you taste."

Her arms felt useless, but she managed to lift one enough to run her fingers through his hair. "That feels good," she sighed. "So, so, good."

And wicked too, lazing around the house naked. She'd never dared before, but she'd dare just about anything to see Jason smile. She floated while he turned his attention to the other breast, giving it the same attentive care he had the other. His erection pressed against her hip. She wiggled her ass in hopes he'd take more of her. He released her breast, but before she could protest, his mouth came down on hers. His kiss spoke of good things to come — things they probably didn't have time for — but his lips were hot, his tongue insistent and thorough in communicating his desires. She gave herself up to his demands, opening for him, welcoming him between her legs. His cock nudged at her entrance, teasing. Her hips rose, inviting.

"Shh," he soothed. The weight of his body pressing hers into the sofa cushions felt like Heaven.

She groaned, and he placed feather light kisses on her temples, her cheekbones, her jaw line.

"I want to think about this while I'm gone. I want this image in my mind. You underneath me, offering yourself. This is what I want when I get home, to find you in my bed, all soft, warm, and willing. I want to make love to you all night then do it again in the morning for the rest of my life."

His hands stroked her hair, the lines of her face. He traced the shell of her ear with his tongue, and she shivered.

"Tell me you'll be here when I get home."

The head of his cock breached her. She groaned, and her hips lifted. "I'll be here."

"Uh-uh, angel." He rolled slightly to one side and pinched her nipple, sending a desperate message to her pussy. "None of that."

He tweaked her nipple again, and she arched her head back with another groan. Her pussy clenched, begging him to go deeper.

He scooted off her, and the sofa. Carrie cried out.

"Wait here," he said.

It was only a moment before he returned and swung her around, pulling her ass to the edge of the sofa. He grabbed throw pillows, wedging them behind her so she was in a half-upright position.

Kneeling between her knees, he guided his cock to her pussy and stopped. "I have something for you."

She sat up at the sight of the white velvet box he produced. It was too big to be a ring box, but still…he'd never given her anything in all the time they'd been together.

"I want to seal this deal. I want you, forever." He opened the box, revealing not only the most stunning diamond ring she'd ever seen, but a matching necklace and bracelet. "I bought the collar, but I wanted something you could wear all the time in public, so I got the bracelet, too."

She fumbled for words. Questions tumbled through her brain, so many she didn't know which one to ask first. She finally settled on one. "And the ring?"

"I want you to be my wife, and I want you to belong to me, too."

Her heart went out to him, the poor guy was as confused as she was.

"I think I understand," she said, running a finger over the beautiful, sleek lines of the collar. "The collar is a symbol of my submission, and you'd like me to wear it."

"Yes, that's what I want, andI realize you can't wear it all the time. But maybe you could wear the bracelet? I want you to wear the ring because that's something everyone will recognize. I mean…the collar and bracelet are for me, for us. Our private commitment. There's a wedding band, too, and one for me. Will you marry me, Carrie? Will you wear my collar and my ring?"

Tears sprang to her eyes. She dashed them away with trembling fingers. He wanted her! Forever! Oh God. She'd wear anything he asked if it meant being his for the rest of their lives.

"Yes, and yes! They're beautiful, Jason. I can't believe you did this."

He slipped the ring on her finger then placed the collar around her neck.

"Mine," he said, securing it with a *snap*.

"Yours," she said. "I don't want to take it off, ever, Master."

"I'll understand if you don't want to wear it in public, but promise you'll wear it for me."

"I promise."

She reached for him. He captured her wrists and guided her hands to her mound.

"Open for me. I need to be inside you."

She gently pulled her labia back, exposing herself to him. She blushed crimson. He'd seen her before, many times, but that had been in the Dungeon room where it didn't seem so...naughty. And then, she had been safe behind the blindfolds, only imagining the expression on the face of her unknown lover.

Now, she didn't have to imagine his face or the raw lustful expression on it. She could see his face with her own eyes. She'd never believed a man could look at her that way, like he'd been wandering in the desert for a week, and she was a fountain of fresh spring water. He licked his lips, and her pussy gushed.

"Christ almighty, Carrie."

He grabbed her ankles and brought them up to the edge of the sofa, spreading them wide, taking her knees along with them. He buried his face in her pussy. He fucked her with his tongue, made love to her with his lips, taking her to a place she'd never dreamed existed. If she thought she'd found Heaven before, she'd been wrong. This was it.

The moment his mouth closed over her, her fingers slipped into his hair. She clutched at his scalp, digging her nails in to keep him there. It was the most erotic display ever — his dark head rested between her legs, bobbing and thrusting while he held her ankles wide. Occasionally, he looked up at her, seeking her eyes in silent communication. *See. You're mine. This...this is mine.*

"Master...Jason!" she cried when the promised orgasm ripped through her.

He continued to torment her, teasing her clit with his tongue and teeth, drawing out her pleasure until the last ripple, the last twinge subsided. He placed a tender kiss on her inner thighs then one on her swollen mound.

He quickly sheathed himself, and fisted his cock. He

brought it to her pussy. "Watch, angel."

He pushed inside, just enough so the plump head of his cock disappeared. "Look. Isn't that fucking something?"

Seeing her pussy lips stretched to accommodate him was beyond erotic, but she needed more. "Please, Jason...."

"You want it all, don't you?"

"Yes, please."

"Do it again. Hold yourself open," he said.

She slid her fingers into her folds and spread them open.

"That's it. Now watch me fuck you."

He entered her slowly so she felt every increment. Watching her body take his inside was the most intimate thing she'd ever seen. He paused, and sliding his hands along her inner thighs, pressed her open even further. Her thigh muscles protested the stretching, but when he slid deeper she forgot everything but him.

"See that?" he asked with a scratchy voice.

"Yes, oh God, Jason...it's so...." Her heart flip-flopped. She searched for the words to tell him what she felt seeing him inside her.

"Beautiful," he said. "Fucking beautiful."

She nodded, unable to form words. He pulled out and stopped just before leaving her completely. She whimpered.

"See how wet you are?" he asked, swiping a finger along his glistening shaft. He lifted his eyes to hers. "You're mine, Carrie Taylor. All mine." He slid back in, his gaze never leaving hers. He wrapped his fingers around her wrist and moved her hand lower, splaying her fingers so his cock slipped between them. "This is us. You and me, Carrie." He held her hand there, slowly pulling out and filling her again, setting a deliberate, steady rhythm. "Watch."

She followed his gaze to where their bodies became one.

"I love you," he said.

She took him deep. "I love you, too."

ABOUT THE AUTHOR

Roz Lee has been married to her best friend, and high school sweetheart, for over three decades. These days she splits her time between their home in rural New Jersey, and Southern California, where her husband works. Even though she's lived on both coasts, her heart lies in between, in Texas. A Texan by birth, she can trace her family back to the Republic of Texas. With roots that deep, she says, "You can't ever really leave."

Roz and her husband have two grown daughters they couldn't be more proud of, and are currently raising a twelve-year-old Labrador Retriever, Betty Boop, who isn't aware of her canine heritage.

When Roz isn't writing, she's reading, or traipsing around the country on one adventure or another. No trip is too small, no tourist trap too cheesy, and no road unworthy of traveling.

Other Books by Roz Lee

Inside Heat (Mustangs Baseball #1)
Sweet Carolina
The Lust Boat
Show Me the Ropes
Love Me Twice
Four of Hearts
Under the Covers
Still Taking Chances
Making It on Broadway

Made in the USA
Charleston, SC
29 June 2014